Where
My Heart
Belongs

Where My Heart Belongs

TRACIE PETERSON

BETHANY HOUSE PUBLISHERS
Minneapolis, Minnesota

F PETERSON

Published by Bethany House Publishers
11400 Hampshire Avenue South
Bloomington, Minnesota 55438

Bethany House Publishers is a division of
Baker Publishing Group, Grand Rapids, Michigan.

Printed in the United States of America

Hardcover: ISBN-13: 978-0-7642-0396-1 ISBN-10: 0-7642-0396-7
Paperback: ISBN-13: 978-0-7642-0361-9 ISBN-10: 0-7642-0361-4

Library of Congress Cataloging-in-Publication Data

Peterson, Tracie.
   Where my heart belongs / Tracie Peterson.
      p. cm.
   ISBN 978-0-7642-0396-1 (alk. paper) —ISBN 978-07642-0361-9 (pbk.)
   I. Title.
   PS3566.E7717W54   2007
   813'.54—dc22   2007023747

In memory of Landon Ruth Meece
1994-2007
What precious joy you brought
to those who knew you.

And to Karen, Ed, and Edison Meece
May Jesus heal your wounded
hearts and hold you close
to Him.

Books by Tracie Peterson

www.traciepeterson.com

Where My Heart Belongs
A Slender Thread
What She Left for Me
*I Can't Do It All!***

ALASKAN QUEST
Summer of the Midnight Sun
Under the Northern Lights • *Whispers of Winter*

BELLS OF LOWELL*
Daughter of the Loom • *A Fragile Design*
These Tangled Threads

LIGHTS OF LOWELL*
A Tapestry of Hope • *A Love Woven True*
The Pattern of Her Heart

DESERT ROSES
Shadows of the Canyon • *Across the Years*
Beneath a Harvest Sky

HEIRS OF MONTANA
Land of My Heart • *The Coming Storm*
To Dream Anew • *The Hope Within*

WESTWARD CHRONICLES
A Shelter of Hope • *Hidden in a Whisper*
A Veiled Reflection

LADIES OF LIBERTY
A Lady of High Regard

SHANNON SAGA‡
City of Angels • *Angels Flight* • *Angel of Mercy*

YUKON QUEST
Treasures of the North • *Ashes and Ice*
Rivers of Gold

*with Judith Miller   ‡with James Scott Bell
**with Allison Bottke and Dianne O'Brian

TRACIE PETERSON is a popular speaker and bestselling author who has written over seventy books, both historical and contemporary fiction. Tracie and her family make their home in Montana.

Visit Tracie's Web site at: *www.traciepeterson.com*.

ONE

KATHY HALBERT OPENED THE front door to stare face-to-face at a ghost from the past. In a tone that wavered somewhere between shock and horror, she whispered the name of her nightmare.

"Sunshine."

A warm June breeze blew through the younger woman's bleached hair, ruffling the top layers to reveal darker roots. Her face was careworn, yet beautiful. The twelve years since Kathy had seen her sister—her only sibling—had altered Sunshine into a woman who scarcely resembled the eighteen-year-old who'd deserted her family.

"Hi, sis. Guess you're surprised to see me, huh?" She offered a smile, revealing perfect white teeth—maybe too white.

Kathy stiffened. *How dare she call me sis? How dare she show up here after twelve years without our knowing if she was dead or alive?*

"What do you want?" Kathy couldn't even bring herself to pretend polite indifference.

Sunshine seemed genuinely perplexed by Kathy's attitude. "What do you mean by that? I've come back . . . I've come home."

Kathy shook her head. "If you're here after all these years, there has to be a reason bigger than that. If you want money, forget it. There's none here for you. You've had your inheritance—twice, as I recall."

Sunshine's confusion seemed to grow. "Where's Mom and Dad?" She strained to look beyond the screen door and into the house where they'd both spent their childhood.

Kathy put her hands on her hips and squared her shoulders. "I asked what you wanted. I think my question deserves an answer first."

Sunshine folded her arms defensively. Kathy noted she was dressed stylishly in cream-colored linen slacks and a tan and cream short-sleeved sweeter. Small gold hoops graced each ear and a gold cross hung from a delicate chain that draped Sunshine's neck.

What hypocrisy! Since when does she care about God?

"Kathy, I don't expect you to necessarily be happy that I've come home, but I figured you'd at least be civil."

"This *is* me being civil. You can't demand your own way and turn your back on your family and not have some kind of repercussion for your actions."

"There have been plenty of repercussions, I assure you," Sunshine whispered.

Kathy felt herself harden even more. Every sad and painful moment from the past twelve years could be pinned to one source, and that source was her younger sister. Kathy didn't want to be uncaring; the entire family had dreamed of the day when Sunshine might once again return to the Kansas family farm. Kathy had practiced long tirades of things she would say, but every established thought fled from her now.

"I didn't expect to find you here," Sunshine finally said, shifting her purse from one shoulder to the other.

"I want to know why you're here." Kathy forced her mind to remain focused. The memories were pouring in from all sides, much like a dam that had sprung multiple leaks. Feelings, thoughts—even smells and sights—trickled in and began to puddle in Kathy's brain.

"Well, it's kind of a long story," Sunshine finally yielded. "I suppose you could say the bottom line is that I've turned my life around. I want to set things right with the people in my life, so I figured I should start at the beginning."

"You can't set the past right," Kathy said, shaking her head. "You have no idea what you're even asking."

Kathy's memory took hold of her like a raging lion about to feast on its prey. Twelve years faded away and in its place came a vibrant picture of the moment that started the demise of the entire Halbert household.

"I've changed my name," eighteen-year-old Amy Halbert declared rather pompously. She was dressed in very short cutoffs and a halter top—two pieces of clothing their mother had expressly forbid her daughters to wear.

Kathy looked up from the breakfast table in dumbfounded surprise. "You did what?" she finally asked. Only moments ago the focus had been on Kathy's own wonderful declaration. Kyle Dexter had asked her to marry him, and she had announced it to her parents at breakfast.

Amy had a way of dripping sarcasm without ever speaking a word. That expression was on her face just now, and Kathy detested it. When Amy looked like this, there was no reasoning with her and no getting her to listen to anything you had to say.

"Amy, why don't you sit down and tell us what you're talking about," their father said with a smile. "Your mama has fixed some mighty fine waffles."

"I don't eat waffles," Amy said with an emphasis on the apparently hated food.

Kathy didn't understand the harsh tone or the lie. Amy could have eaten them all under the table when it came to waffles.

Mom turned in surprise. She had just put a fresh waffle on a green glass plate and seemed at odds as to what she should do next.

"What are you talking about, sunshine?" Dad said, calling her by his pet name. "Of course you eat waffles."

"Not anymore," Amy declared. "I'm a new woman, and I'm starting a new life."

"What do you mean?" Mom asked.

"I mean I've legally changed my name, and I want my inheritance so that I can blow this stupid farm town. I went to the bank, but they wouldn't let me draw out the trust fund. They said until I was twenty-one, I would have to have your permission to take it out. So I want you to cut me a check for it or go with me to the bank so I can get my money."

Mom nearly dropped the plate as she put it back on the counter. "I don't think I understand."

Kathy recognized fear in her mother's tone. She looked up to study her mother's expression.

"I know I don't," Dad agreed. "What do you mean you changed your name?"

Amy leaned against the back of the chair that had always been hers at the Halbert table. "I saved up my money and went and got my name changed."

"Changed it to what?" Kathy questioned. The whole thing sounded like a big joke.

"Well, in a way Dad kind of helped me decide that," Amy said, dropping some of the sarcasm from her tone. "I changed my name to Sunshine."

"Sunshine?!" Dad looked at his younger daughter in disbelief.

"Don't you love it? It's such a great name—nothing like boring old Amy. In fact, it's like nobody else's name. That's why I did it. I'm an individual kind of person, and I needed an individual kind of name."

"You sound like a hippie," Kathy said, putting down her glass of orange juice. Amy scowled and probably would have stuck her tongue out, but Kathy guessed that was beneath her now that she was a "new woman."

"How did you arrange this?" Dad asked, still not seeming to accept the truth of it.

"I went to a lawyer in Hays and got it changed. I had to take my birth certificate and proof of who I was. Then I talked to a judge, but it wasn't a big deal."

Kathy could tell that her dad was upset. He had a way of narrowing his eyes and clenching his jaw any time someone crossed him or made him mad. "When did you go to Hays? You never told us about it."

"I'm eighteen. I'm an adult. I don't have to tell you everything I do."

"You do if you live under my roof."

"That's my point," Sunshine protested. "I don't want to live under your roof. Kathy may be content to go to college and live at home, but I don't want to. I want to do my own thing and live how I want to live."

Mom came to the table and sat down as if the shock was too great. Kathy reached over and gently patted her hand.

The joy of her own engagement was quickly forgotten in the wake of Amy . . . *Sunshine's* announcement.

"I want to leave Slocum. I want to leave Kansas. I hate it here and always have," Amy announced. "I want the trust fund money that Grandma and Grandpa left me."

"You know that isn't to come to you until you're twenty-one or when I deem you're ready for it," Dad said, putting down his fork. Apparently he had decided the matter was serious enough to stop eating and focus on the matter at hand.

"I'm ready for it now," Amy said in her persistent manner. "I plan to leave with or without it, but it's mine, and I think I deserve to have it now. It will make my life a whole lot easier and safer."

"That money was intended to help you with college or to buy a house of your own," Dad replied.

"Or even help with wedding expenses and things like that," Mom threw in.

Amy rolled her eyes. "I don't care about any of that. I'm not going to go to college and I'm not going to buy a house. I don't even have somebody to marry—at least not anymore. I broke up with Todd last week. He's such a waste of my time. He just wants to stay here and farm like his dad."

Kathy couldn't remain silent at this. "Todd's family has been farming in Kansas for five generations. You can't fault him for wanting to carry on a family tradition."

"I don't care what he wants. It doesn't match up with what I want, so I broke up with him." She turned to Dad. "I'm serious. I'll leave even if you don't give me the money, but I'll probably have to work my way to wherever I'm going and sleep on the streets. If that's what you want, then I guess

I'll deal with it." Amy had always been the queen of manip-
ulation, knowing exactly which buttons to push to get her
own way.

Kathy's gaze was fixed on her sister, but she heard their
mother begin to cry and thought the entire matter had gone
on long enough. "You're a spoiled brat. How can you just
come in here and threaten them like that?" Kathy had been
seeking to please her parents all of her twenty years of life,
while Amy always seemed to have their approval and did
nothing to earn it.

Amy pushed her long brown hair over one shoulder. "I
finished high school with a 3.9 GPA. I went to church every
time the doors were open. I learned to play piano until I was
good enough to outperform all the other pianists in the
state. I even worked at Myra's Café to learn financial
responsibility, as Dad called it. I've done everything that was
demanded of me. I want my freedom. I've served my time."

Mom sobbed into her hands. "Oh, Amy."

"My name is Sunshine," Amy insisted.

"Where is it you plan to go?" Dad asked.

Kathy could hardly believe he would give Amy's plan
credence. She pushed back her chair and jumped to her feet
before her sister could say a word. "Why do you have to ruin
everything? This should be my day. I just got engaged to
Kyle last night. I was happy until you had to come in here
and wreck everything."

"Well, that's your problem. If you aren't still happy to be
engaged, then I'd suggest you break it off."

Kathy wanted to throw something at her sister, but with
their mother still crying, she knew better.

"Kathy, sit back down and finish your breakfast. Amy, sit

down and talk to me reasonably if you expect me to give this any consideration whatsoever." Dad was brooking no nonsense, so Kathy quickly complied. Dad's patience had been exhausted. "Amy, sit down."

"My name is Sunshine!"

Remembering the way Amy had screeched at them that morning brought Kathy out of her reflection of the past. She stared at her sister, realizing she was talking. "What? What are you saying?" Kathy asked, feeling even more confused.

"I asked you where Mom and Dad are. I want to see them. I want to talk to them—ask them to forgive me."

Kathy tried to control her anger. That day so long ago had ended in a horrible scene. Sunshine had pushed her position until their father finally agreed to give her the money in the hopes that she would go have her fling and come back home to settle down. No one expected that it would be twelve years in the coming.

"You can't do this," Kathy said, forcing her voice to be steady. "You have no right to put us through this again."

Sunshine was back to looking stunned. "I don't know what you think I'm here to do, but I assure you, I only want to make peace. Now, are you going to let me in?"

"No," Kathy said matter-of-factly. "I'm not. You don't know anything about us. You didn't care enough about any of us to call or write a note to let us know you were alive and safe. Do you know the agony you put Mom and Dad through? Do you have any idea how they worried? Can you even begin to understand what it cost them—cost me?"

"I think I do now. I didn't then. I didn't think anyone

would really miss me or care," Sunshine said, sounding rather sad.

Her tone caused Kathy to lose all control. "You have no idea! Your selfish little antic took away everything I'd ever hoped for—everything I dreamed might be for my life. You took away the peace in this house. You took away the joy. Mom never laughed again—not to her dying day."

The color drained from Sunshine's face. "Mom's dead? No!" She clutched her purse to her chest.

Kathy folded her arms. "What do you care?"

Tears slid down her sister's face. Kathy tried not to be moved by the sight. Sunshine had hurt them all more than anyone could guess. It was apparent that her sister was deeply hurt by the news, but what about the hurt she had caused?

Sunshine bit her lower lip as her face grew red. It was clear she was trying not to cry, but it was a losing battle. "I didn't know. I didn't know."

Kathy drew a deep breath and realized she couldn't continue in such anger. She felt split right down the middle: A part of her hated her sister, while the other half was so happy to see her alive and safe. Sunshine looked absolutely miserable. Gone was any pretense of strength and sophistication. Her sister was obviously hurting—sorry for the truth of the moment. With a sigh, Kathy shook her head. "You would have known if you'd come home."

"What happened?" Sunshine's ragged breath caught in her throat. "When?"

"Amy?"

Kathy turned to find their father standing not ten feet behind. He clung to the banister of the stairs, weakened from the cancer that was ravaging his body.

"Is it really you?" he asked.

"It's really me!" Sunshine wiped at her tears and pushed past Kathy. "Dad, I've come back." She started to cry again. "Oh, Daddy, I've come to ask your forgiveness."

She fell into his arms and hugged him closely. Dad dropped his hold on the banister and held his daughter close. Tears welled in his eyes as he gazed upward murmuring two words over and over. "Thank you. Thank you. Thank you."

Kathy felt immediately convicted by the intense love that showed on his face. He didn't care that a dozen years had separated them. He didn't care that his child, long given up for dead, had given no consideration to her parents and their feelings. He probably didn't even remember that she had stolen money from him.

The lost had been found. The dead had come back to life.

Prodigal Sunshine was home.

Two

GARY HALBERT WAS A MERE SHADOW of the man he'd once
been. Born and raised on a Kansas farm, the man had never
wanted for more than to work the land. He loved farming,
and despite the market's ups and downs, weather problems,
and pests, farming was all he knew and all he wanted to
know. Of course, all that changed when he got sick.

Kathy hated the way the cancer had robbed him of his
life. The doctors said it was stage four now—spread from the
bladder to the liver, lungs, and bones. There was nothing
they could do but monitor the pain and control it with a
steady supply of narcotics. They told her it would be merely
weeks before he succumbed, and that had been five weeks
ago.

Dad had been quite stoic about the news. He had talked
through all the final preparations with Kathy as though he
were planning nothing more emotional than putting in a
new fence. Dad had told her what kind of funeral he wanted
and how she was to handle the sale of the farm and all its
personal property. He made calls to friends, giving them first
rights on the purchase of livestock and farm implements,
and seemed to adjust well to the fact that his life was at its
end. Still, Kathy wondered if he was holding on for something. Now watching him with Sunshine, she thought she
knew what he'd been waiting for.

After embracing his child for several minutes, Dad tear-
fully pulled back to look at her. "You're all grown up, Sunshine."

"I've got so much to tell you—to say. I'm so sorry, Dad. Sorry for all I put you through."

"Shhh, that's not important now."

Not important? Kathy's mind whirled. *How can he say it isn't important? How can he act as though nothing matters more than the fact that she's waltzed back into our lives? If he dares to tell her that it doesn't matter anymore, I swear I'll scream.*

He faltered on his feet and reached for the banister. Kathy took this as her cue to interrupt the reunion. "Dad, you need to be in bed." She took hold of his arm.

"Let me help," Sunshine whispered.

Kathy threw her a look that she hoped made it clear her help wasn't needed. Apparently it did the job because Sunshine took a step back.

"Why don't you go get your things," Dad suggested. "Kathy can show you how to make up the pullout sofa. I'm afraid with things as they are, your old room is full of boxes and such."

"That's not a problem, Dad. I don't even have to stay here if it makes you uncomfortable."

Kathy was trying to lead her father away from Sunshine, but he stopped. "This is your home too. You're always welcome here."

Kathy met Sunshine's gaze and realized her sister was waiting for some response. Kathy tightened her grip on the back of her father's pants in order to steady him. "I'll help you when I get Dad settled in." She tried, for the sake of her father, to sound civil.

When her father had taken ill, Kathy had converted what had once been the family's den into a bedroom. Dad wasn't able to make it up the stairs anymore, and the den was the perfect solution. It turned out to be a much better choice than Kathy could ever have imagined, in fact, because the large picture window and sliding glass door looked out over the vast wheat fields Dad had once farmed. It seemed to please him to at least have this small connection to the life he'd known.

Tony Anderson, long married to Kathy's best friend, Sylvia, had taken on the farming, and often stopped by to report all the details to Dad. That too brought him a great deal of pleasure. Especially now that he knew his days were numbered and that the farm would soon be sold.

"You mustn't wear yourself out," Kathy told him as she helped him swing his legs over the side of the bed.

"She's home," he said, shaking his head. "She's really come back."

"Yeah, she's come back, all right."

"You don't sound happy. What's wrong?"

She helped him to adjust the bed to a comfortable position. "I guess I'm surprised that she's come back after twelve years without a single word to any of us. That takes some nerve."

"Don't be angry, Kathleen. This is a good thing—it's a God-given answer to prayer."

"I know you feel that way, but I don't." Kathy helped him to get comfortable by tucking pillows under various parts of his body. There were about a dozen pillows of varying sizes, and they generally used them all. "I can't just act as if nothing's happened," she said as she pulled the sheet up. "I can't pretend twelve years haven't passed without a word."

"I love her, Kathy. I love her just as I love you." He

looked at her with such a pleading in his eyes that Kathy immediately felt ashamed of her outburst.

"Of course you do. I'm sorry." She offered him some water, but he turned it down. "Are you hungry?" She knew the answer even before her father opened his mouth.

"Not just yet. Maybe something later."

But Kathy knew later would be long in coming. Her father was eating very little these days. The doctor had already advised her that this pattern would continue until he ate and drank nothing at all. When that happened, it would probably be no more than a week before he died.

Dad reached out for her hand. "Kathy, I know you're angry, but I'm begging you to let it go. My prayers have been answered today. Seeing Amy again was the only thing I wanted before I died. The only thing I prayed for."

Kathy felt horribly selfish. Her own misery and pain over Sunshine's return were nothing compared to the peace she knew he'd be feeling. Their father would finally feel he could die. But maybe that only made her resent Sunshine's reappearance even more. Frankly, Kathy wasn't sure she was ready to say good-bye to Dad and all that she'd known on the farm.

Kathy drew a deep breath and studied her father's face. "I know. I don't know why it upsets me so. I guess I just keep thinking of how she cost me everything—how she completely altered my life with her selfish choices."

"Sit here with me for a minute." Dad pulled gently on her hand.

Kathy complied, but her heart wasn't in it. She knew he would tell her how forgiving Sunshine was the Christian thing to do. How they were really blessed because now they knew she was safe.

"I want you to know how much I appreciate your sacrifice for Mom and me," he began. "I always regretted that you didn't get a chance to finish college. I regretted too that you and Kyle never worked through the situation to marry."

"I couldn't have my focus divided," she told her father. "I couldn't give Mom the care she needed and also be a wife to Kyle. He made me see that when he walked away."

"But he came back and apologized. You hardened your heart to him."

"Never," Kathy said sadly. "I hid my heart from him. I never hardened it—not in the way you're suggesting. I knew I could never be the wife I should be. He needed to travel to get where he wanted to be in his career. I couldn't leave you and Mom to be taken care of by strangers. And even if we'd married and I'd stayed here, what kind of marriage would that have been? What if we'd had children? They would have suffered, because I could never have given them the attention they'd need. They would have lived in a home without their father in residence—at least he wouldn't have been there very often."

"I know you've said that many a time. I'm not convinced it would have had to be that way, but I think I understand your choice. I just want you to know that I appreciate what you did for us. That your sacrifice didn't go unnoticed."

"That was never what it was about. I loved you both—I love you still." Kathy glanced at the partially opened door. "I stayed because of that. She left because she didn't love any of us as much as she loved herself."

"It's true," her father agreed. "But now she's back. I want

you to forgive her, Kathy. I want you two to put the past behind you and start fresh."

"You don't know what you're asking me."

He smiled ever so slightly. "I think I do. But I know you're hurting right now and that doesn't allow you to think clearly. When I'm in a lot of pain from the cancer, I can't think clearly either." He gave a little chuckle. "And my mind is muddled when I'm on the pain medication too. Guess my thinking days are over."

"Dad . . . I'm afraid. Afraid that she's only come home to cause trouble. Afraid of what her expectations are for us."

He shook his head. "It doesn't matter what her expectations are. Expectations are dangerous things to have when they involve the reactions and actions of other people. I think your sister, however, has had a genuine change of heart. You need to respect that and give her a chance."

"A chance to do what? Change her name again and run off for another twelve years?" Kathy knew her father didn't deserve her anger and frustration, but she couldn't seem to rein in her emotions. "I don't see any reason to trust her."

"I didn't ask you to trust her. I asked you to forgive her."

"So she gets to just waltz in here like nothing happened, and we're supposed to be okay with it—pretend it never happened, pretend her choice was completely acceptable?"

"No," Dad said, shaking his head. His voice was ever weakening. "She knows her choice wasn't acceptable. She wouldn't have asked me to forgive her if she thought otherwise. She knows we can't forget or pretend that she hasn't been gone for twelve years. And she knows she's hurt us, and she'll go on knowing it—so long as we remind her." He looked at her and held her gaze. "Is that what you want—to make sure she hurts as much as we have?"

"She chose to hurt the people who loved her the most. She decided to run off and never tell anyone where she was or if she was all right. Now you want to celebrate her return. You want to act as though she did nothing worse than make a bad career choice."

"No . . . I want to remember that my choices are sometimes just as poorly made in the eyes of God. I want to remember that I haven't always pleased the people who loved me—that my choices were not always good ones and because of that, people suffered."

"You've never made poor choices like that," Kathy protested.

"That's not true. What about the fact that I wouldn't go to the doctor when my symptoms first started? That I didn't get the farm on the market sooner?"

Kathy felt as though the wind had been knocked from her. "That's . . . different."

"Is it? I don't think so. You suffered because of my poor choices." He paused and looked out across the fields. "She's my child, Kathy. I can't turn my back on her, even if she would turn her back on me."

Kathy knew he was right. Everyone made bad decisions. She'd made enough of those herself. She took a deep breath and patted her dad's hand. "I'll try for your sake to be kind, but I won't lie. If she asks me how I feel, I can't lie."

"I don't expect you to, Kathy." He sounded so sad, as though he knew there was an irreparable hole in her heart that had been put there by Sunshine. "I would hope, however, that you'd speak the truth in love, just as the Bible says. If you tear into her just for the sake of making her feel bad, how does that make it any better than what she did all those years ago?"

Kathy thought of the way her mother had suffered, the long hours spent crying and mourning the loss of her younger child. The questions and fears and her own imagination had been harder to deal with than had her mother just known where Amy was and what she was doing.

"At least my anger—my desire to put Amy in her place—isn't going to kill someone. She killed Mom as sure as if she'd put a gun to her head. Mom never would have suffered a heart attack and been left in such a weakened state had it not been for Sunshine's heartless disappearing act."

Kathy got up and paced beside the bed. "I'm glad for your sake that Sunshine has chosen to come home, but for me, I hate it. It opens up an entirely new set of problems to be dealt with, and frankly, I'm not sure I have the strength to face her antics again."

Sunshine stood in the hallway, listening to her sister's tirade. She had never expected to be welcomed with open arms after a twelve-year absence, but neither had she anticipated outright hatred. Kathy hated her—that much was clear. She hated her so much that she blamed Sunshine for the death of their mother.

Tears streamed down Sunshine's face. Why had she made the choices she'd made? Why had she done so many bad things?

If only I'd come home after I ran out of money. If only I'd realized the pain I was causing by my selfishness.

But Sunshine had learned that life could not be based

on "if onlys." Nothing could change the past. What was done was done, and there was no way to go back—no matter the depth of regret.

She heard Kathy say something about keeping the peace for the sake of their father and cringed. Something was desperately wrong with Dad. He was nothing but skin and bones, and he'd said something about not going to the doctor when his symptoms first started. She wanted to know what had happened and what the prognosis might be, but Sunshine was fearful of asking. She wasn't entirely sure she could handle the answer, for one thing. And for another, she wasn't sure she wanted to deal with Kathy's hostility.

Sunshine moved away from the den and into the kitchen. To her surprise it looked the same. The old farmhouse hadn't been remodeled or upgraded since she'd left. She touched the speckled countertop and thought of all the times she'd had to wipe it down. How she'd hated chores. Tall white cupboards beckoned her to explore. Sunshine remembered when she and Kathy had painted them white as a surprise for Mom. Dad had thought it the perfect way to brighten the kitchen, and Mom had loved it.

Sunshine found a startling reminder of her childhood in the Depression glass that still lined a few of the shelves. Her mother had inherited the dishes from her great-grandmother and had loved to use them. Sunshine remembered once asking if it was dangerous to use them for everyday, but her mother had laughed at this. She'd told Sunshine that they were only things and that things weren't much good if they couldn't be used.

Moving away from the cupboards, Sunshine went to the back door. There were still notches in the doorframe, where

Dad had measured her and Kathy as they'd grown. Sunshine touched the carved wood lovingly. It was a part of her history that actually seemed viable. Here was proof that she had once existed as a child in this house. Here was proof that she had once belonged.

Beyond the door was a small mud porch at the back of the house. The porch had been screened in the year Sunshine had turned twelve. She and some of her friends then promptly had a slumber party there, but it only lasted until around midnight, when all the girls had come inside after being scared by the noises of the night. Sunshine couldn't help but smile at the memory. Life had been so simple then. She had thought herself oppressed with rules and regulations, but if she'd only realized how protected and loved she was, things might have been different.

There it was again. If only. Oh, how she regretted the choices she'd made. Kathy no doubt thought her sister had enjoyed some magical life of prosperity and happiness, but Sunshine could set her straight on that count. There'd been streaks of both, but there had been nothing magical or overly good about the life she'd made for herself after leaving home.

Sunshine opened the porch's screen door and gazed across the backyard. Everything was just as she remembered it: her mother's clothesline, the chicken coop and yard, the barn and the storm cave. How she had hated that storm cave as a child. Most of her friends had basements in their houses, but not the Halbert home. This place had been built shortly before the First World War, and apparently basements hadn't been all that fashionable in Kansas prairie farmsteads. Nothing was ever so terrifying as having to leave the seeming safety of the house to venture into the storm itself in order to get to the cave.

She remembered crying in fear as a little girl. Storms had terrified her, but the cave was equally frightening. Nothing more than a hole dug into the ground and firmed up with a structure of corrugated tin and lumber, the cave was musty and dark, with a dirt floor. Bugs—especially spiders—had seemed to like to make their homes under the crude wooden benches where the family would sit out the weather. Sunshine always worried about what might crawl out from under the bench and would plead to sit on her father's lap. As the years went by their father made updates to the cave, but it was never a place Sunshine wanted to stay for long. Even now, the sight of the door peering out from the mounded ground gave her the shivers.

Turning back to the house, Sunshine made her way to the kitchen table. Twelve years ago this had been the scene of her departure. She remembered her arrogance . . . her lack of love . . . her bitter hatred.

My dreams had seemed so important then. I thought I knew best—thought I knew it all. But I hurt so many people with my selfishness.

She sighed and rubbed her hand atop the smooth, but dulled, wood. Sunshine sat back and looked around the room. Kathy had changed very little. Of course, Sunshine had no way of knowing when their mother had passed away, but she was glad Kathy had left things much as they had been. There was a palpable sense of her mother in the room, in the furnishings she had chosen, in the colors she'd painted the walls.

Mom, if I'd only known . . . She forced the thought away.

I cannot do this. Lana said it would serve no purpose. I cannot make up for my deeds or change the choices I made in the past. I can only work on the present.

Kathy stood in silence outside her father's room. She knew she needed to go find her sister and prepare the sofa bed, but in her heart she wrestled with the need to be kind for her father's sake and the need to guard her heart—for her own sake.

Her chest still ached from the emotion of seeing her sister standing there when she opened the door. The first year after Sunshine had gone, Kathy fully expected to open the door to just such an event. Then another year passed and then three and five and ten. Kathy had stopped believing Sunshine would ever return when the tenth year passed. That was the year she'd started using Sunshine's bedroom for storage.

It had started out innocently enough. Her father had wanted Kathy to locate some old photographs in the attic, and the heat of summer had made it impossible to work in the cramped, sweltering place. Her father had suggested they bring down everything in the attic and put it in Sunshine's room to make it easier and cooler for Kathy to process. The boxes of memories and old tidbits from the past were still taking up space in her sister's room. Kathy had meant to deal with them—especially since the farm was to be sold. Of course, so far, there'd been no buyers. At least none who were willing to take the farm as a complete package. Kathy pushed aside her concerns. She couldn't fret about the sale of the farm and deal with Sunshine at the same time.

"I suppose now I have to deal with her room," she murmured. After all, if Sunshine planned to stay very long, she'd need a proper bed and privacy.

Pushing off from the wall, Kathy decided it was time to deal with the situation at hand. She went upstairs to the linen closet and pulled down fresh bedding. As an afterthought, Kathy also grabbed an extra fan, remembering how Amy . . . Sunshine . . . had liked to have a fan running while she slept. The house had never been equipped with air-conditioning, and the nights were very warm during the long humid summers.

She thought of having to face her sister and momentarily panicked. A kind of war raged inside with a bitter, angry woman who seemed years beyond her age on one side, and a frightened—no, terrified—girl who had been forced to assume too much responsibility, too soon, on the other. Neither one offered Kathy much hope or comfort.

Her arms began to ache from holding all the stuff. There was no sense putting off the inevitable.

THREE

"SUNSHINE?" KATHY PEERED IN from the kitchen door.

"Call me Sunny. Everybody does these days."

"Doesn't surprise me," Kathy muttered. "I have the sofa made up for you."

"Can you sit with me for a minute, Kathy?"

Kathy looked at her sister and thought to reject the idea, but knowing how much it meant to their father, she nodded. "I guess so." Taking a seat opposite Sunny at the table, Kathy met her sister's gaze. It all seemed innocent enough, but something in Kathy screamed for protection. *Guard your heart. Guard your heart.* The words pulsated through her head.

Sunny folded her hands and leaned back against the wooden chair. "Look, I know this isn't comfortable for you, but I think we should talk. I mean I really want to talk. I want you to understand."

Kathy thought of a lot of flippant things she wanted to say, but she held her tongue. She kept thinking that she ought to pray about the matter—pray for peace of mind and ask God to give her a love for her sister. But the prayers went unsaid.

"So what's on your mind?"

Sunny shook her head. "Everything's on my mind. Twelve years of life here at the farm. Worry about Dad. Desperation to know the truth about Mom. I need to know, Kathy. I'm begging you to tell me so I don't have to question

Dad. Obviously he isn't feeling well."

"He has cancer," Kathy said without warning. "I don't want you upsetting him with a lot of questions. He deserves to spend his final days in peace."

Sunny leaned forward. She was surprisingly calm. "How long does he have?"

Kathy shrugged. "Days . . . perhaps weeks. The doctor told me it wouldn't be long. He eats and drinks less and less each day, and once he stops all together, it'll just be a matter of time."

"Shouldn't he be in a hospital?"

"He wanted to die at home. Hospice comes and checks up on him. He's surprised them all with his strength and endurance. The doctor said a weaker man would never have gotten this far."

"Dad always was a powerhouse," Sunny said, staring at her hands. "What kind of cancer is it?"

"The original culprit was bladder cancer. Dad waited too long to get help. He'd had blood in his urine for a long time and just didn't tell me. He thought it was an infection and tried to cure himself with lots of water and cranberry juice."

"Mom's remedy for bladder infections."

"Right. He started having other problems and finally told me about it. That was about seven years ago. The doctor told him he had a tumor in his bladder. They did an MRI and didn't see any other cancer, so they started radiation treatments. A year later the doctor gave him a clean bill of health, but it came back. In fact we've fought it off and on for the last few years. We thought for a while that he was getting better, then things just seemed to go downhill. In late April they did another MRI and found the cancer had spread to the liver, lungs, and bones. We knew then it would just be a matter of time."

"I'm sorry, Kathy."

"For what?" Kathy looked at her sister in confusion.

"For everything. I know it sounds lame, but I am. I hope as time goes by, you'll believe me."

Kathy looked away and said nothing. She wanted to just get up and walk away—forget that Sunny had ever come back into their lives.

"Please tell me what happened to Mom."

Kathy's focus snapped back to Sunny. "Why? What purpose would it serve?"

"I need to know. I need to know what happened."

"I needed a lot of things that I never got." Kathy clenched and unclenched her fists. "Mom needed things she never got. Why should you be the only one to get what you need?"

"Look, I know you hate me. I know you wish I'd never come back. I don't know what to say to you," Sunny admitted. "I would like to know what's happened in my absence."

"For what purpose?" Kathy refused to look away, despite the fact that she could see her close scrutiny made Sunny uncomfortable.

"I've changed, Kathy. I know I did wrong. I know I hurt you and Mom and Dad. I should have come back before now or at least let you know I was alive. I know I don't deserve answers, but I'm begging you to tell me what happened after I left. What happened to our mother?"

Kathy let her memory drift back across the years. "Fine, but don't expect me to sugarcoat it."

Kathy stood outside her sister's bedroom and heard her mother crying. She had cried nearly nonstop every day since Amy had gone. That had been three weeks ago.

"Mom?" Kathy knocked on the door. She balanced a tray in one hand while opening the door with the other.

"What?" Mom sniffed back tears. "Have you heard something?"

"No," Kathy replied quickly. "Dad wanted me to bring you some lunch. You need to eat. It's been too long since you've had something substantial. Do you want to eat in here or in your room?"

"I'm not hungry." Her mother got up from the rocking chair and went to the window.

"I know, but you'll make yourself sick if you don't eat."

"Do you suppose we could get the police to look for her?" Mom turned from the window, a look of hope flittering across her face.

"Mom," Kathy began as she put the tray atop the bed, "Amy—"

"She wants to be called Sunshine," Mom interrupted.

Kathy blew out an exasperated breath. "Sunshine is eighteen. She's an adult. She left of her own free will. The police already told Dad there isn't anything anyone can do."

"I just wish I knew if she were all right." She turned back to the window. "I just wish she'd call."

Kathy gazed at her mom, astonished by the recent physical changes in her. The one-time vivacious woman seemed completely altered: she'd visibly aged; her complexion was sallow and her eyes dull—almost lifeless. And she'd lost weight. Marg Halbert had never been a large woman by any means, but over the last few weeks she'd hardly eaten anything. Kathy guessed she'd probably lost at least twenty pounds, and that couldn't be healthy in such a short time.

"Mom, please try to eat something. I made a tuna salad sandwich. I know how much you like them."

Mom looked at her as though the words made no sense. "Do you think she'll come home—when the money's gone?"

"Probably. She has no job skills—not really. She can wait tables, but that isn't going to make her enough money to live comfortably. Not if I know Amy."

"Sunshine," her mother repeated.

"Sunshine," Kathy conceded. "Now please sit down and eat something."

Mom shook her head. She stepped back toward the rocking chair, then put her hand to her chest. "Oh," she gasped. Her face contorted as she gripped the back of the chair.

"What's wrong?" Kathy asked, coming beside her.

"My chest. It hurts so bad. Oh, Kathy, get Dad. I think . . . I think something's wrong. I feel so weak."

Kathy helped her mother to the bed. "Wait here. I'll go see if I can find him." She knew he'd been in the kitchen only minutes earlier. It was lunchtime and he'd come in from the fields to eat.

"Dad! Dad, come quick!"

There was no reply, and Kathy felt an overwhelming dread. If he'd gone back to the fields, there was no telling where he might be.

"Dad!" Kathy flew through the house and out the back door. "Dad, where are you?"

"I'm right here, Kathy. What's the problem?" Dad asked as he emerged from the barn.

"It's Mom. Something's wrong."

A month later Kathy sat with her mother and father as the doctor explained the state of Marg Halbert's health. Kathy had to bite her lower lip to keep from crying.

"Mrs. Halbert, the heart attack damaged seventy percent of your heart. You've probably always had a weak heart since your childhood bout with rheumatic fever. Still, you're a young and otherwise healthy woman, so I'm going to suggest a heart transplant."

"But why? If the attack is over and I'm on the road to recovery . . ." Mom seemed quite perplexed by the doctor's suggestion.

"Mrs. Halbert, you can't recover the damage. Your heart is barely functioning at a thirty percent capacity," he explained. "In fact, I'd go so far as to say it's less than that. Your body will begin to deteriorate, and without a transplant you'll be dead in just a few years."

Kathy's parents gasped in unison. Kathy was too shocked herself to say a word, but Dad had no trouble. "What do you mean? Are you saying this is going to kill my wife?"

The doctor nodded. "I'm sorry. Without the transplant, she cannot hope to live for long. You have to understand. The body is dependent on the heart for everything—oxygen, nutrients, cooling and heating. Your wife's heart is not able to pump at the rate or strength that it once did. Fluids will build up and drown the heart and lungs. We can give her medication to help eliminate the water, but eventually the heart's inability to work as well as it once did will lead to the body's demise."

Kathy finally found her voice. "How long will it be before she can have the transplant operation?"

The doctor seemed relieved that at least one of them was ready to press on with the matter. "We'll have to put her name on a list. She'll have priority status because the damage is so severe. Then we'll wait for a donor."

"Someone else will have to die first—right?" her mother spoke in a whisper.

"That's right. We can't just take a portion of heart—it takes the entire organ," he replied. "We have paper work for you to fill out, and I have a list of medications I want you to start taking immediately." He picked up a piece of paper. "It's important also that you follow a strict low-sodium diet. I'll have my nurse go over all the details with you."

"What else will she need?" Dad asked. Kathy could see that all of this had taken its toll on him.

"She needs a great deal of rest." The doctor looked at Mom, and Kathy could see he knew it would be a struggle to convince her. "You cannot go about your usual duties. You'll need to turn the running of the house over to your daughter." He turned to Kathy. "You do still live at home, correct?"

She nodded. "I'll help her in any way I can." In the back of her mind Kathy realized it was already the first of August. She was supposed to be heading back to college in two weeks. The realization of what was happening hit her at that moment. *There's no way I can return to school. I can't leave her alone during the day, and Dad can't stay with her. He'll need to work.*

"You'll need to allow your daughter to help you," the doctor said, turning to Marg. "I want you to rest and only get up to take yourself to the bathroom or to wash up. In fact, I'd like your daughter to be there to watch over you even when you do that. You may find a recliner comfortable."

"But I feel so much better," Mom began. "I'm still a little weak, but it's nothing like it has been."

"I'm glad you feel better," the doctor replied. "I'm glad you feel stronger. But honestly, Mrs. Halbert, you aren't better. You're merely stable at this point. You have to follow my instructions or you won't even make it to the point of getting a new heart."

Kathy hated him for his harsh reminder of death. She wanted to say something, but he obviously knew what she was thinking. "Look," he began, "I know I sound very caustic and unfeeling. Believe me, that isn't my intention. But I do need you to take this seriously. So many times patients won't listen. They have another attack and their bodies can't recover. I don't want you to compromise your health before you have a chance to have the transplant. Do you understand, Mrs. Halbert?"

Mom nodded. "I just don't want to put that kind of burden on my family."

"Nonsense, Mom. I can put off finishing college, but you can't put off taking care of your health." Kathy knew in that moment the decision had been made. She wouldn't go back to school. In fact, she would have to somehow find the courage to tell Kyle that she couldn't marry him. At least not yet.

Two days later, Kathy stood on the porch, telling Kyle the news. "I can't marry you." She handed him his engagement ring. "Mom needs me to take over the house while we wait for a heart. Even then, she'll be a long time recovering from the transplant."

Kathy didn't cry. The truth was, she was cried out. She had spent so many nights in tears, sobbing into her pillow so that no one could hear.

"But, Kath, I love you. You love me. This doesn't matter. We can work it out," Kyle said, reaching for her.

Kathy pulled back. If he touched her, she honestly didn't know what she'd do. "I can't be what Mom needs me to be if I don't focus all of my attention on her and the things I have to do. She's going to need me twenty-four hours a day—there's no one else. Dad needs to work and then rest. He won't be able to keep the farm going and pay the bills if he can't keep to his routine."

"So you're putting your mom and dad ahead of me?"

Kathy frowned. "What a selfish thing to say."

"Me? You're the one who sounds selfish." Kyle looked at her as if she'd just plunged a knife into his gut. "You're not giving me any say in this."

"No one gave me any say in it either."

"That's not true," he said, his voice rising. "You've made all these decisions and never once thought to consult me on how I felt—what I needed."

"You aren't sick. You aren't watching your mom die unless she gets a new heart."

"I am watching my dreams of the future die. I'm watching you turn your back on our love."

"That's not fair. I don't feel that way at all."

Kyle stormed off the porch. "I'm not sure you feel at all. I thought people who loved each other were supposed to help each other bear their problems."

Kathy felt her mind whirl. Everything she'd thought and planned had seemed so well organized when it was just in her head. She hadn't expected Kyle to respond this way, but now he was acting as if she'd just told him there was someone else in her life. The thought of that hit her hard. She supposed there was someone else.

"Well, fine. If that's the way you want it—if that's all the more our love meant to you, then forget about it." Kyle stormed off to his car. Without another word he started the car and floored it.

Kathy ran from the porch and circled the house. Forgetting about everything else, she ran long and hard into the empty fields where once her father's finest wheat crop had grown. Tripping on the stubbled ground, Kathy continued to run until her sides ached and she could scarcely draw a breath. When she finally stopped, she raised her tearstained face to the sky.

"Why, God? Why is this happening? Why do we have to suffer this misery?" She felt alone . . . deserted. It was then that her heart started to harden.

Kathy opened her eyes to realize that she was safely back in the farmhouse with Sunshine hanging on her every word. For several minutes Kathy could say nothing more. The pain of those memories had drained her of all energy.

"What happened after that?" Sunshine asked. "What happened to Mom and the transplant surgery?"

"There never was any surgery. Mom's condition deteriorated much faster than the doctor had expected, and by the time a heart was available, it was too late. Everything else had started to shut down and her condition was far too compromised. They gave the heart to someone else. Some-one more healthy."

"I'm so sorry, Kathy," Sunshine said hesitantly.

Kathy looked at her sister as if she'd lost her mind. "Sorry? You should be, but it doesn't change anything. Sorry won't bring our mother back to life. She died because of your selfishness. The pain of losing you was too much for her to endure."

Kathy couldn't ignore the anger that hung on her every word. She moved to the door. "I hope you were happy with the choices you made, Sunshine," she said, barely able to keep the sarcasm from her tone, "because none of the rest of us ever were."

FOUR

SUNNY WAS ABOUT TO STEP INTO the kitchen when the telephone rang and Kathy answered it. "Still nothing?" she heard her sister say. Then, "Yes, I know it's a lot of money. Yes, I can appreciate the situation, but surely you can appreciate my circumstances."

Intrigued by the comments, Sunny continued to listen. She knew she probably shouldn't, but she feared Kathy wouldn't volunteer more information.

"It's really the only hope I have. I've depleted all of my savings."

What in the world was she talking about? Sunny heard the desperation in Kathy's voice. Something was wrong.

"All right, then. Well, call me if you have any other news."

She hung up the phone and Sunny heard Kathy heave a heavy sigh. Rather than confront her about the situation, Sunny decided instead to visit her father. She backed down the hall and nearly jumped a foot when Kathy said her name.

"Can you stay with Dad for a few minutes? I need to go out."

Sunny smiled. "Of course. I want to be useful."

"He shouldn't be alone," Kathy stressed. "If you can't do it, say so now."

"I'll do it. Don't worry." Sunny knew her reputation was in shreds where Kathy was concerned, but here was a chance to prove herself. "Just go for as long as you need."

Kathy said nothing more. She brushed past her sister in the narrow hall and headed out the front door. "I shouldn't be gone more than an hour."

There was no other explanation. No comment about the phone call. Sunny watched her sister leave and felt the heaviness of the moment. Something wasn't right.

❧ ❧ ❧

Kathy knocked on Sylvia's back door and waited. After everything that had happened at home, Kathy longed only for some refuge—some semblance of normalcy. This familiar Kansas farmhouse would do the job. Kathy had been seeking help and encouragement from Sylvia for as long as she could remember.

"Kathy, what a surprise," Sylvia said, pushing back strands of blond hair. "I was just canning green beans. Come on in."

"I knew you'd most likely be busy, but something has happened and I needed to talk to someone."

Sylvia frowned. "Has your dad passed?"

"No, but it won't be long. He's eating so very little, I know he can't last." Kathy followed Sylvia into the large kitchen. "The reason I came is going to come as a shock, so prepare yourself."

Sylvia shook her head. "I don't like the sound of this."

"Neither did I. Amy . . . I mean Sunshine . . . has come home."

"Your sister?"

Kathy nodded. "None other."

"She's alive!" Sylvia continued to shake her head. "She's actually alive."

Kathy couldn't even begin to work up enthusiasm for that truth. "Yes. She's alive all right. Alive and full of questions."

"Goodness, but it's been over . . . eleven . . . twelve years. Where has she been all this time? How is she?" Sylvia seemed quite pleased. "It's an answer to prayer. Your dad must be so happy."

Kathy felt an instant sense of frustration. If her best friend in the world couldn't understand the pain this reunion had caused, no one would. "Dad is happy, but I'm not."

Sylvia pointed to the table. "Sit. I'll get the coffee. The beans will wait." Sylvia swung into action. She energetically maneuvered through the kitchen, first turning the heat down on the stove, then pulling down two mugs from the cupboard.

Kathy took a seat at the rectangular table. Twenty clean quart jars were lined up and ready to receive the beans, but there was still plenty of room for the mug of coffee Sylvia placed in front of Kathy.

Wiping her hands on her apron, Sylvia took a seat opposite Kathy. "I want to hear everything. Start at the beginning."

"I opened the door yesterday and there she was. She acted as though she hadn't been gone any longer than to run to the store for milk. I didn't want to let her in—something in me just rose up in protest. All I could think of was her barging back into our lives and hurting Dad worse than he was already hurting."

"What does she look like? Has she changed?"

Kathy sipped the coffee and considered the question for a moment. "She's all grown up. She's filled out and doesn't have that gangly teenage girl look to her anymore. Her face seems . . . well, it's more like Mom's, but not exactly." Kathy frowned. "Actually, she looks a lot like Mom. Anyway, she seemed no worse for the wear. She dresses better than I would have expected and more conservatively too. She bleached her hair, but it seems to suit her. She's got dark roots though." Kathy added the latter as if it somehow lessened Sunshine's appeal.

"Wow, I can't believe this. It just doesn't seem real."

"Tell me about it. That's why I came here. I don't know what to do."

Sylvia leaned forward with a puzzled look. "What do you mean?"

Kathy put down the cup. "I don't want her here. I don't know what she wants or why she suddenly chose to come back. Dad acts like it's something to celebrate, and for him I'm sure it is."

"But we used to pray for her to come back. Don't you remember?" Sylvia toyed with her cup. "I remember all those times we cried over what happened and begged God to bring her home."

Kathy hated Sylvia's accusatory tone. "That was then. I stopped praying for her to come back a long time ago."

"But why?"

Kathy hated the way she felt. "I know I sound absolutely awful, and I really don't want to feel this way. I know I should be happy about Sunshine coming home—Dad was. Goodness, but you should have seen his face. He couldn't have been happier if Mom herself had walked through the door."

"Well, in a sense, a part of her did. I can't imagine what I'd think or feel if one of my children disappeared for twelve years and then suddenly reappeared."

Kathy felt such a sense of guilt. "I know. I thought about that." She looked at her friend and buried her feelings of longing. For so many years Sylvia had lived the life Kathy had wanted. A good husband, three beautiful children, a farm and peaceful life. Sylvia had it all.

Sylvia reached out and touched Kathy's hand. "I can see you're in pain, Kathy. I hate that you're hurting, and I want to help . . . if I can."

Kathy sighed. "I'm a terrible person. I know that now. I should be happy to see Sunshine come home. But, Sylvia . . . I'm not. I'm terrified of being hurt. I'm frustrated by her intent to come back to make everything right, when it will never be right again. A part of me says she's just here to ease her conscience so that she can get on with her real life, while another part says to give her a chance."

"I think you should listen to the latter part."

"I know what I should do," Kathy said, shaking her head, "but I don't want to do it. I keep trying to pray about it, but I just end up straying from talking to God, and I start thinking of all the horrible things I want to say to Sunshine."

"Like what? Maybe if you say them to me, it will somehow diffuse the power they have over you."

Kathy considered the idea for a moment. It had merit. "Well, I guess I'd say she has no right to come back—not after all this time without a single word to let us know whether she was dead or alive. Not after having caused our mother a heart attack. Not after leaving our father so full of sorrow that he stopped being the man he once was—all vibrant and happy. She has no right to assume she could go off on her own terms and come back on them as well."

"So you think she should be here on your terms?"

"I don't think she should be here. Period."

"Do you wish she'd never let you know she was alive?"

Kathy looked away. "Yes," she whispered. "I think I would."

"But why?" Sylvia's tone caused Kathy to meet her friend's gaze.

"I know it may sound strange," Kathy said, drawing a deep breath, "but if she hadn't come home, I could always pretend that she had tried years earlier and failed because she died or met with some tragedy."

"Would you really rather that have been the case? Would you prefer she had died?"

Kathy folded her fingers together and then unfolded them. "Please don't hate me, but I think I might. I could have pretended that she actually loved us. That she realized how stupid her choices had been, and that in repentance she had headed for home just days after leaving. But then something happened and she died. I know it doesn't sound right, but it's the only way I could have it all make sense. I used to lie awake at night and imagine that she'd been in some car accident and died while driving back home."

"And that made it better?"

Kathy thought back to those memories. She had been convinced in her heart that if something along those lines had taken place, it would have somehow redeemed her sister.

If Sunshine had died while trying to make her way home, Kathy could forgive her lapse of judgment and selfish demands. Of course, now it was very clear that nothing even remotely similar had happened.

"It made it bearable," Kathy finally managed.

"I guess I never knew that," Sylvia said, lifting her mug.

Kathy wanted to crawl into a hole. She knew how stupid and heartless she sounded. "Sylvia, would you be able to forgive your children no matter what they did to you?"

"Sure."

"Just like that?" Kathy looked at her intently. "There would be no thought to withhold that forgiveness—to make them pay for what they'd done?"

"No. I suppose I would imagine all sorts of hideous ways in which they'd already had to pay. Kathy, a home should be a sanctuary or refuge. It should be that one place that, no matter how much time has passed, would always be open to you to offer hope and restoration."

"No matter the price to those you hurt? No matter the loss?"

"I don't think this is really about Sunshine at all. I think you're terrified of losing your father and leaving the farm. I think you feel displaced and you're wondering how in the world you can make the pieces fit together when someone keeps knocking the puzzle on the floor."

"It's about people making selfish decisions without considering other people's feelings."

"And you've never made a selfish decision?"

"Not like Sunshine made. Her choices hurt people."

Sylvia got to her feet and went to refill her coffee cup. "So deciding to leave Slocum and all your friends wasn't a selfish decision that hurt people?"

Kathy heard the pain in her friend's voice. She'd never once considered that Sylvia would be upset by Kathy's choice to move to Colorado Springs. "I suppose I never thought about it that way. I didn't realize it bothered you so much. I mean, you have Tony and the kids. How much could you possibly miss me?"

Sylvia came back to the table with a look of disbelief. "We've been best friends since forever and you can ask a question like that? Won't you miss me—miss our talks?"

"Of course. But we're lucky if we see each other once a week, and usually it's more like once every few weeks, especially during the summer. I know we talk on the phone more than that, but it's usually not for very long—and more times than not it's related to our farms."

"Still, I always knew you were there—just down the road. I knew I could call and you'd be here. That's not going to happen once you're gone. You're going to be looking for a job and a place to live. You're even going to try to rekindle the romance that you put off. That was a selfish choice as well."

Kathy squared her shoulders, almost feeling as if she were preparing for a fight. "How can you say that? I put Mom first. I even put Kyle first—not myself."

"Don't be so sure. You did what you had to do to get by—to deal with the mess at hand. You gave Kyle no say in the matter."

Kathy set down her mug with more force than she intended. "I did. When he came back and apologized for getting so angry with me, I heard him out. I listened to what he had to say. You don't understand how it was, Sylvia.

Kyle's career would require him to travel. He needed that in order to advance. We knew then that it could even require international travel. He knew that eventually it would mean we'd have to leave Kansas. I couldn't go, so I set him free. What's selfish about that?"

"You chose how things would be and then dictated those choices to him. You did the same with me. I can still remember that phone call telling me that we couldn't get together anymore on Saturday mornings. That I probably shouldn't even call unless it was some sort of emergency. Do you have any idea how that felt?"

Kathy rubbed her temples and tried to think. "It was only until Mom was better. I felt too incapable of handling the situation unless I put up boundaries. I knew Mom would need a lot of care. I knew I couldn't give her the quality attention she needed and keep up with fifteen other things. If that's selfish, then all right—I was selfish."

"But why should your selfishness be any more forgivable than Sunshine's?"

"Because my choices weren't made for me. They were made for my mother."

"Think about that for a minute, Kathy. Your mother would have loved to have you marry Kyle. She was delighted that you two were planning to marry. Kyle would have been on the road working for the pharmaceutical company, and you would have been free to live at home and care for your mom. When he came home from his trips, he could have comforted you—encouraged you—loved you. Those would have been positive things—not negative. Your mother might have even found his presence a comfort. Instead, she may very well have died believing that it was her fault for having separated the two of you."

"That's not true. She knew better. I told her I sent Kyle away because . . . well, because I needed the space. I needed the . . ." Kathy stopped. She hadn't thought about the way she'd handled things as being anything other than selfless. Now her best friend was telling her that the choice had been selfish, and unfortunately, it all made too much sense.

"I'm sorry," Kathy finally said after several moments of silence. "I never meant to hurt anyone. I felt like I was coming apart at the seams. I took the only way out that I knew would work."

"I don't want you to regret the past and your choices, Kathy. I just wanted you to see how easy it is to misjudge motives. Sunshine made selfish choices based on what she felt she had to do. She probably felt like she was coming apart at the seams. Leaving was no doubt the only way out that she thought would work."

"But leave for twelve years and say nothing to anyone? Never send a letter? Never call?"

"At first she probably didn't care to do either, and then, as the years went by, maybe she thought that no one would receive it even if she tried."

"Why are you on her side?"

Sylvia shook her head. "I'm not. She was wrong—cruel to leave you all guessing. But I'm a mother, and I'm trying to help you understand why I would open my arms to a child who hurt me so deeply. The deeper you love someone, the more painfully they can hurt you. Your father is dying. Seeing the child he'd given up for dead or thought lost to him forever has got to be the biggest blessing in his life. He probably feels like dancing a jig. He probably feels better than he has in months. Would you take that away from him?"

"Of course not." Tears came to Kathy's eyes. "I guess I never thought of it that way."

"When you love someone, you only want the best for them. Just like I want the best for you. If that best is in Colorado Springs, then I can bear the pain of my loss."

Kathy wiped her eyes and gave a little laugh. "You make it sound like I'll be gone forever—like I'll never come back."

"What do you have to come back here for? Be honest, Kathy. Your father and mother will be gone—the farm sold. Short of a few friends, Slocum, Kansas, will have nothing of interest for you."

"It's only a five-hour drive. I'll come back often—I promise."

"Please, Kathy. Don't promise me something like that. It's not fair. I'll always love you and be your friend, but don't pretend that things won't change. We'll both do what we have to do to get by. I'll invest myself even more in my family, and you'll turn to Kyle and your aunt and uncle. We might even make other friends."

"But none of them will ever take the place of what we have," Kathy protested.

"Of course not. We will always be close, but it will be different. Kathy, you have to find a way to leave the past behind you. You have to find a way to forgive Sunshine or you'll never be any good to Kyle or anyone else. No matter how many miles separate you and your sister, you'll steep in an anger that will eat away at your heart."

Her words slapped Kathy in the face. And later, as she drove home, Sylvia's warning continued to echo in her mind, the sharp sting of their truth undeniable.

FIVE

SUNNY SPENT HER SECOND NIGHT on the farm in a restless state that wouldn't let her sleep. The first night she'd been so exhausted emotionally and physically that she'd fallen asleep almost as soon as her head hit the pillow. But not so tonight. Tonight the demons of the past tormented her.

She rolled over and punched down the pillow. The sheets were rather scratchy, definitely nothing like the Pratesi sheets she used to have on her bed. She'd been introduced to Pratesi linens in Beverly Hills, and she'd never used anything else after that. She rubbed her hand over the material near her face. These were no doubt inexpensive sheets picked up on sale for thirty dollars instead of three thousand. In frustration Sunny cast off the offensive piece and let out an exasperated breath.

She glanced at the lighted alarm clock Kathy had put beside the couch. It was just after one in the morning. There had been a time when this would have been Sunny's favorite time of the night. She and her friends would have just been starting to party. Pushing back the covers, she sat up and looked around the darkened room. There was a hint of illumination from the hall light Kathy had left on, but otherwise the room was nothing but shadows and shapes.

Getting up, Sunny stumbled to the living room window and pulled back the shade. The night was quiet and the farm seemed to rest comfortably.

"So why can't I?" she asked.

Why wouldn't sleep come? There was no good reason. Sure, she was troubled by the way Kathy acted. "She hates me. That much is clear," Sunny muttered. But Dad was happy to see her again. That should count for something. And of course, it did. Sunny knew such a great peace in his pleasure. He had told her that nothing had mattered more to him than seeing her again and knowing she was safe. Apparently Kathy didn't share their father's desires.

Sunny let the shade fall back into place and switched on the lamp. A photograph of her mother hung on the wall near the living room entrance, and Sunny couldn't help but go to it. She gazed at the picture, struck by the youthful spirit and excitement in her mother's expression. This was her graduation picture. She no doubt was excited about starting her new life and leaving childhood behind. Mother must not have been afraid of growing up and taking on new responsibilities—at least not like Sunny had been.

"If she'd been afraid, she would never have married so young." Sunny touched the glass that covered the photo. She knew from stories told that her mother and father had married two days after Marg Clarey had graduated high school. There had been no plans for college or trips abroad. There had been no thought of going off to live on her own and make a career for herself. Mother had always and only wanted to be a wife and mom. She had told her daughters that very thing on so many occasions that Sunny never doubted the truth of it.

Sunny frowned. "We might look something alike, but that must be where the similarities stop. Kathy acts much more like you than I did."

"Amy, is that you?"

Sunny looked down the hall to find her father standing just outside his room. "It's me," she answered.

"What are you doing up so late?"

She came to where he stood slouched against the door-jamb. His dark red plaid pajamas hung on him—obviously created for a much larger man. "I was just going to ask you the same thing. Come on, let me help you."

He gave no protest and leaned heavily on Sunny as they walked the few feet back to his bed. "I heard noises. I thought maybe something was wrong."

Sunny guided him to the edge of his mattress and stead-ied him as he sat down. "I'm sorry I woke you. I couldn't sleep. I feel like I've hurt you all more by coming home than by staying away."

"Never say that. I couldn't bear it. Not knowing whether you were dead or alive—that hurt more."

Sunny's eyes filled with tears. "I'm so sorry, Dad. I never meant for that to happen. Really, I didn't. I just needed so much more than what I could find here—at least I thought I couldn't find it here."

"And now?"

"Now ... I don't know." Sunny looked at her father, longing to cry. He was just a ghost of the man he'd once been. "Kathy told me about Mom. She blames me for Mom getting sick, and she's probably right. I think Kathy hates me."

"I can't see Kathy hating anybody. She's always giving of herself, and hateful people don't do that."

"She's been through so much, Dad. So much that she shouldn't have had to endure by herself. I should have been here to help."

"Yes. I suppose you should have been here, but you weren't," he said, sounding stronger than he had just moments ago. "Recognizing the truth is always important, but you can't undo the past that way."

"I can't undo the past no matter what I recognize, but I'd just be happy if my actions could at least stop the pain from passing on to other people."

"Your sister has given a good portion of her life to see to my needs," her father said, as if changing the subject. "I wasn't much good to Kathy after Mom died. I walked around in a stupor for months. I don't even remember a whole lot about what I did or said. I just remember the emptiness."

"Why don't you tell me about it?" Sunny urged. "It might help me to better understand."

Dad shrugged. "Not a whole lot to tell. With your mother gone, I felt I'd lost a part of myself. I didn't know how to go on without her. For so much of my life we'd been together. I remember Kathy promising to take care of me— to keep the house and gardens—and all I could think was how it was a good thing she knew what she was doing, because I sure didn't."

Sunny sat down beside Dad and took hold of his hand. "Kathy's always been strong."

"You're right. She has. By the time I started feeling like I could function again, we found out about the cancer. Kathy was faithful to see me to the doctor for treatments and checkups. She tried to keep me cheered up and encouraged. I could see it was taking its toll on her, but I was selfish and I couldn't suggest we do things any differently."

He tried to move back on the bed a bit and Sunny saw him grimace in pain. "Why don't you lie back down, Dad?

You can talk to me while you rest."

He didn't argue with her as Sunny helped him under the sheet and arranged the pillows. When he was settled, he began again. "I should have sold the farm a long time ago, but I just couldn't bring myself to leave. Now I've put this burden on Kathy." He moaned and tried to shift his weight. Sunny attempted to help, but he was still just as miserable.

"This was the place Mom and I had lived since our wedding. It was the place we raised you girls. If I'd had to leave, it would have been like losing everyone I loved."

"But you didn't lose Kathy. She was here all along."

"She was here, but in a sense I lost her too. She was never the same after you left. She missed you and worried about you just like the rest of us. Kathy tried never to talk about it, but I knew it was there. I knew the anger and fear, regret and sorrow were eating away at her once easygoing nature, but I couldn't do anything to stop it."

Sunny found the comments shocking. She would never have expected Kathy to give her departure more than a cursory consideration. She had fully expected her mother to be sad, but she hadn't even figured Dad would be all that upset.

"I have to tell you, Dad," she began softly, "I never thought things would turn out the way they did. I never intended to stay away for so long. I always meant to write or call. In my mind, my very immature and selfish mind, I didn't figure anyone would really care all that much. You would have the farm, Mom would have Kathy and the wedding to focus on, and Kathy would have Kyle. I didn't see how my leaving could possibly matter."

"Oh, sweetheart, it mattered a lot. You were a part of our family. We weren't complete after you went away."

"But I would have gone eventually, even if not then," Sunny said. "I would have found someone to marry and leave home for."

"Yes, but that would have been different. We would have still been a part of your life. We would have known you were safe and taken care of. You don't have any idea of what it's like to have a child somewhere, but you don't know where or if they're safe."

Sunny looked away and tried to keep back the tears. There was so much she wanted to tell her father. So much she wanted to say . . . to apologize for.

"What happened? Where did you go after you left here?"

Sunny closed her eyes. She had worked so hard to forget the past and push aside the memories that threatened to smother her.

"I went to hell. At least it felt that way. There was nothing good or noble or pure—nothing of God in the places I went. You know that psalm that speaks of how even if you made your bed in hell, God would still find you? Well, that's where He found me, only I didn't want to be found." Sunny remembered a morning twelve years earlier.

"Hi. I'm Mitch Haas."

Sunny looked up from where she tanned beside the pool. She put her hand to her eyes to better see the handsome mustached stranger. "I'm Sunny."

"I know. I asked about you. You're new here, aren't you?" He took a seat on the lounger beside her.

"Yeah. I just moved here last week." Sunny had chosen this particular complex because it had furnished one-bedroom apartments for rent. She wasn't sure when she signed the six-month lease if she really wanted to live in Las Vegas for six months, but she was willing to give it a try.

"Where are you from?" he asked, giving her a grin that made her stomach do a flip.

"Nowhere important." She sat up and suddenly felt very self-conscious about the tiny bikini she wore. Taking up her towel in a casual manner, she pretended to blot her skin in an effort to cover up.

"I know it well."

"Know what well?" Sunny asked.

"Nowhere important," he replied. "I lived there for years myself."

Sunny laughed. "We probably just missed each other in passing."

"You wanna have lunch with me? I know a great little place within walking distance."

Sunny felt completely under his spell. "I'd like that. Let me go change. I can be ready in ten minutes."

"I kind of like what you're not wearing right now."

Sunny got up and wrapped the towel around her body. "I thought the way you were staring perhaps implied disapproval. I'll be right back." She batted her eyelashes and threw him an impish grin as she looked back over her shoulder. She knew this look to be quite effective on the boys at school.

The look he gave her in return was almost smoldering. It left Sunny weak in the knees and almost breathless. By the time she reached her apartment, Sunny felt all reasonable thought flee her mind.

Two months later, as she agreed to be Mitch Haas's wife, her ability to reason was still strangely absent. She could hardly believe this was happening. Marriage was the last thing she had on her mind when she'd left Kansas, but Mitch made it all seem so very necessary.

"We're going to have the best time, Sunny," he whispered just before kissing her soundly.

The justice of the peace completed their paper work and congratulated them. Mitch paid the man with money Sunny had given him on the way to the chapel. He'd forgotten his wallet back at the apartment, but Sunny didn't care. She loved him. He was strong and capable, and he made her feel like a princess.

For the first six months things seemed ideal. Sunny had never been happier, in fact. She thought about calling home and letting her family know where she was and what she'd done, but one thing after another conspired to keep her from such action.

Then one night when Mitch came home from work late, Sunny forgot all about her family. Mitch was angry, but he wouldn't say why for the longest time. Then he finally threw a bank statement at Sunny.

"Why didn't you tell me you had a separate bank account? We've been married for months now—that money should be in a joint account."

Sunny looked at the open envelope. "You opened my mail?" She would never have tolerated that kind of thing at home.

"You want to make something of it?" he asked sarcastically. "I'm your husband. I'll do whatever I please."

"I just thought we respected each other," Sunny said, trying not to let her anger overrun her mouth.

"Me respect you? You're barely nineteen. I'm twenty-seven. I know a lot more about the world than you could imagine. I'll start respecting you when you know as much as I do. Tomorrow, you go to the bank and transfer that money to our joint account. I mean it."

"I have a right to keep my own account," Sunny said, feeling rather defiant. "My father gave me that money. I have a job, and I put the money I earn there in our joint account. That ought to be enough."

He delivered a slap across her face so quickly that Sunny didn't even have time to defend herself. "I didn't ask for your lip. I gave you an order. Do you understand?"

Sunny could hardly see through her tears. "Why are you doing this, Mitch? I thought you loved me."

"I thought you loved *me*. Love doesn't keep secrets or hoard money. If you loved me the way you claim to love me, you wouldn't have any problem with sharing what you have."

But she did have a problem with it. She supposed there was something in the back of her mind that cautioned her to keep the money separate just in case. Just in case the marriage didn't work out and she needed to move on. Just in case she needed something that Mitch wouldn't get her.

Without warning, he pulled her up out of her chair and threw her against the wall. "I'm not taking this anymore." He grabbed her and threw her back against the wall again. "I mean it. You're going to do things my way or suffer the consequences."

Sunny's head hit the wall with such force she momentarily saw stars. She tried to fight back, but it was no use. She was five-four and weighed all of a hundred pounds. Mitch was six-two and had at least eighty pounds on her.

When he'd finished beating her, Mitch stared down at her in indifference. He almost seemed surprised to see her there in a heap on the dining room floor. "Get that money transferred tomorrow."

He left the apartment, slamming the door hard behind him. Unable to move without hurting, Sunny curled up in a ball and fell asleep—confident that this must be some kind of nightmare that she would awaken from in the morning.

Sunny looked up to see tears in her father's eyes. "Don't cry, Daddy. It's behind me now—behind us both. I'm sorry. I should have never told you about Mitch or the problems we had. It's an ugly truth that's best forgotten."

"Don't apologize, Sunshine. The things I used to imagine—the things I thought might be happening to you are so much worse. I figure the truth will set us free."

Sunny said nothing. She knew the truth was much worse. Worse than anything she would ever confide to her father. She could never tell him about the endless hours of physical and sexual abuse she'd suffered at the hands of her husband. The truth of her life with Mitch Haas would never set anyone free.

"Try to get some sleep," she told her father. "We can talk more in the morning." But she knew she wouldn't. She couldn't bear to put him through that kind of misery.

She went to the kitchen and poured herself a glass of milk. Sitting at the table, Sunny shuddered. She hadn't allowed herself to remember Mitch in such a long time. In fact, there was a great deal she hadn't allowed herself to remember. Her friend Lana had said that sometimes allowing the memories to come was a good thing. When a person could look at the past—remember the events and people who had changed their lives forever—it sometimes unlocked the door to better things. Much like freeing yourself from a prison.

Sunny's hand shook violently as she raised the glass to her lips. There was nothing freeing about the memories she'd just shared. Mitch had hurt her far more than she cared to remember. Maybe because he'd been the first person she'd really given her heart to. She'd honestly fallen head over heels in love with the man . . . and he'd nearly killed her.

"But it was a love built on lies," she reminded herself. He'd only wanted her for her money. Someone had told him that Sunny was wealthy and that sent him crashing into her destiny.

"I was such a fool," Sunny murmured. "Such a fool to leave home. Such a fool to believe in love."

Six

KATHY TURNED THE HEAT DOWN on the bacon, then went to make coffee. She had no idea if Sunny would want breakfast, but it seemed a reasonable thing to expect. Funny, she really didn't know much at all about her sister. She didn't know what Sunny liked or disliked. She didn't even know if her sister ate breakfast. She obviously watched her weight, because her figure was perfect—maybe too perfect. Kathy was suspicious that her sister had probably had breast augmentation. None of the women in their family filled out a blouse in quite the way Sunny did. Of course, that could just be happenstance.

The phone rang, distracting her coffee count. "Did I put in four scoops or three?" she questioned aloud as she stared at the basket. With a sigh she decided it was four and closed the maker.

"Hello?" she answered on the fifth ring.

"Hello, sweetie. It's Aunt Glynnis."

Kathy glanced at the clock. Glynnis lived in Colorado Springs and the time was an hour behind. "Goodness, but you're up early. It's only six-thirty your time."

"I didn't think. Did I wake you?"

"No." Kathy laughed. "Even when I sleep late, I don't think it's ever much past eight o'clock. It's that early-to-bed, early-to-rise mentality of the Kansas farmer, don't you know."

Glynnis laughed. "Well, for me it's forty-plus years married to a man who has to be to work at six in the morning. I've been getting up at four-thirty most of my adult life. Look, I got the message about your sister. Has she really come back? Is she all right?"

"Yeah, she's here all right. Showed up without warning and she seems to be fine."

"What a wonder. An answer to prayer, even if it took twelve years in coming. Where has she been all this time?"

Kathy frowned at the prayer reference. She still hadn't been able to bring herself to see Sunny's return as an answer to prayer. "I really can't say. We haven't talked much. I've been afraid of what I might say, and she's been pretty consumed with Dad's dying."

"I can well imagine. No doubt she took the news about your mom hard too."

"I suppose. I guess I don't actually care. I mean, I don't want to sound callous, but I figure when you don't bother to keep in touch with your family, you can't expect anything more."

"You don't sound callous at all, sweetie. You sound enraged."

Kathy sighed. "I am. I don't know how to be anything else. I guess I'm happy for Dad, because it means so much to him. Otherwise, I'm just frustrated and angry. Oh, Aunt Glynnis, none of this makes sense."

"It makes more sense than you'd imagine. There are a lot of years of pain and sorrow built up inside you. You probably even thought Amy . . . I mean Sunshine had died."

"I did. It sounds crazy, but like I was telling my friend Sylvia, I comforted myself with that thought. I guess I figured it made her seem less heartless. After all, if she were dead, she couldn't come home. Then it was no longer her being mean and selfish, but rather she had no choice."

"We comfort ourselves the best we can, with whatever seems reasonable. Still, you don't want to let that keep eating at you. Letting your mind dwell on the bad things will give the devil an opportunity for mischief."

"I think he's had enough of that in this family already."

"Well, he's not likely to stop until he destroys as much as he can lay hands to. Anyway, I hope I get to see Sunny. Does she plan to stick around?"

"I'm not sure. Like I said, we haven't talked much."

"If you find out, let me know. Oh, I also called because the Realtor told me about a couple of places you might want to consider. He said you could go on the Internet if you wanted to. I have the Web site address for them."

Kathy considered this for a moment. "I can look, but it seems kind of silly. I don't know how much longer Dad's going to last, and if he lingers for a long time, I'll have to figure that into my plans."

"The agent knows all of that. I think the places he has in mind for you are ones that won't be available until fall anyway. Have you had any offers on the farm?"

"No. A couple of people have called, but they only wanted parcels of land. One wanted twenty acres and another wanted ten. Oh, and I guess there was some land developer who was snooping around, but apparently the location wasn't right for him."

"I'm sorry to hear that."

"Not as sorry as I am. I honestly don't know what I'll do if someone doesn't make an offer soon. The agent had us drop the price once already. If we drop it much more, it won't cover everything."

"We'll just be praying that God sends the right person along. Someone who needs a Kansas farm."

Kathy pulled a pencil from the drawer and grabbed a notepad. "And has plenty of money. Okay, give me the Web site address. When I go into Hays next time, I'll go to the library and check it out on their computers."

Her aunt rattled off the information and ended the conversation by asking more about her brother. "You know I want to be there. I want to see him one more time on this side of heaven. I've been trying to get Will to bring me over. He's retired from Jackson Pharmaceuticals, but you'd never know it."

"I wouldn't wait too long, Aunt Glynnis. Dad is still coherent, but his pain is increasing all the time. The doctor feels it'll just be a short time before he's going to have to put him on morphine. So far Dad's refused, but the pain is really increasing. Once they start morphine, his ability to talk and make sense may change considerably."

"I understand. I'll try to get there soon. You tell that stubborn old coot that I said to mind his manners and have the decency not to die until I can come for a visit."

Kathy laughed. Her aunt was always joking with her brother about doing things her way—telling him not to get any sicker or die before she said it was all right to do so. Dad always found it amusing. He usually told her to stop being such a bossy older sister, but Kathy knew he loved Glynnis's attention.

"I'll tell him, Auntie. Look, I'm cooking breakfast so I'd

better go. Tell the Realtor I'll check that information out as soon as possible."

"I'll do that." Her aunt paused as if struggling to find the right words. "You know I love you, Kathy. You're doing a good job. Please know that we see what you're doing—what you've done. You have made the end of Gary's life something special. God sees it too."

"Thank you." She sighed and felt a little emotional over the praise. Sometimes she thought nobody knew what sacrifices she'd made. Sometimes it seemed she had given up her whole life and no one knew what it had cost her. "I love you too."

Kathy hung up the phone and turned around to find Sunny watching her. Sunny seemed to realize she'd been caught eavesdropping and startled. "I'm sorry," she said, shaking her head. "I meant to let you know I was here, but . . . well, I'm sorry."

For a moment, Kathy was angry about the intrusion. She opened her mouth to criticize her sister's action, then realized it wasn't all that important. "Do you want some breakfast?" she asked instead.

"That'd be great. I feel starved." Sunny took another step into the kitchen. "Is there anything I can do to help?"

"No. I have the coffee brewing and the bacon is done. I need to put the toast down and fry up some eggs. How do you want yours?"

"Hmm, over medium, I guess." Sunny came to the basket where Kathy kept the bread. "I can at least take care of the toast."

Kathy knew she was genuinely trying to be helpful. "All right. I just want one slice of the multigrain."

Sunny nodded and went to work, while Kathy got the eggs from the refrigerator. "How many eggs do you want?"

"Two. Hey, are those from our chickens?" Sunny asked, her expression lighting up. "I've tried for years to tell my friends how different—better—farm eggs are from store-bought ones. They never believe me. They couldn't see how you could alter the taste of an egg."

"City folks," Kathy said as if in explanation. "And to answer your question, yes, they're from our chickens. But not for long. I've given the batch to Sylvia. She'll take them in a few weeks."

"Sylvia Tanner?"

"The one and only. She married Tony Anderson and lives just down the road. Tony has actually been farming the land for Dad. He's helped for the last few years, but this year he did it all himself."

"And you've been friends all these years. That's incredible. I've never stayed friends with anyone that long."

"Maybe because you've never stayed around long enough," Kathy replied without thinking. She wanted to bite her tongue for the quip, but instead turned to fry up the eggs.

"I didn't mean to listen in on your conversation, but I gather it was Aunt Glynnis. How is she? Is Uncle Will still alive?"

"They're both fine. They plan to come see Dad before he dies, so you can see for yourself—if you're here."

"Is there really nothing the doctor can do for Dad?"

Kathy cracked the last egg and let it drop into the bacon grease. "They've been doing all sorts of things for Dad."

"What kinds of things?"

Kathy turned to find Sunny watching her. She'd dressed in jeans and a white gauzy blouse with a white tank top beneath. She looked so much like their mother that Kathy wanted to cross the room and touch her sister's face. She resisted the urge.

"When a person is diagnosed with cancer, they have to have a lot of doctor's exams. They run all kinds of tests and have all kinds of consultations. We had to go to Hays for everything, because Slocum isn't equipped to handle his diagnosis and treatment. We even went to the medical center in Kansas City.

"Dad had surgery and more tests. Radiation treatments and round after round of medications and diet changes." Kathy tried to remain unemotional as she delivered the information, but she felt herself growing angry.

"But that hasn't been the worst of it. I didn't mind the long drives, following the doctors' orders for treatments and medications, altering how we ate. The endless nights helping Dad through the pain were far worse. The horror of watching him decline before my very eyes, even as we fought to keep him alive. Like I told you earlier, he wanted to die at home, so hospice comes out every few days and the doctor and I stay in close contact."

"Dad was always such a strong, vibrant man," Sunny said. "It just doesn't seem fair."

"It isn't fair." She turned and flipped the eggs, then turned off the burner. Reaching for plates, Kathy tried to steady her nerves. There was no sense in fighting.

"So tell me about Kyle. You said something earlier about ending your engagement so you could take care of Mom. I guess I'm confused by that. Why did you do that?"

This stripped Kathy of any pretense of control. "What do you mean, why did I do that? I did what was required. You weren't around to help. Mom probably wouldn't have been sick had you stayed. I would have been planning a wedding instead of her heart transplant." She put bacon on the plates, then added the eggs.

"Did Mom ask you to break your engagement?"

Kathy brought the food to the table just as Sunny brought the toast. "What do you think? Mom would never ask that of me."

"Then it was your choice."

Kathy gripped the back of her chair. "I never had a choice. My choices were made for me. Your choices decided my fate."

For the first time Sunny took a stance that looked something other than passive. "That's not true, Kathy, and you know it. Everyone makes their own choices. I admit my choices were bad ones, but I've been through enough counseling to know they were my choices, and even when I thought someone else was imposing them on me, I still made the final decision."

"Oh sure, and what was I supposed to do? Walk away like you did?"

Sunny shrugged. "You could have. Who would have stopped you? You could have married Kyle and moved away. You didn't have to stay. When Mom got sick you could have let Dad hire a nurse. There was money for it."

"She was my mother. Yours too. How could I allow a stranger to care for her? What would people have thought of me?"

"People let other people care for their loved ones all the

time. In fact, most people don't have the time or ability to care for their parents the way you have. Besides, who cares what someone else might have thought?"

Kathy shook her head. "I cared."

"Which is exactly my point. You made choices based on what mattered to you. You didn't want people to think badly of you. I didn't care what people thought of me. I just saw my life slipping away into the boredom and routine of country Kansas, and I couldn't bear it. I didn't leave here to purposefully hurt you or Mom or Dad. I left here because I knew that if I stayed it would kill me. Unfortunately, the choices I made nearly killed me as well."

Kathy had no reply. She didn't want to give Sunny any ammunition to use against her. Sunny, however, seemed not to realize how deeply she'd driven the point.

"Kathy, it's important that you recognize that you did what you did of your own free will. You'll never convince anyone that you didn't have a choice, and here's why: You assessed the situation and chose the high ground. You chose, for whatever reason, to do what the majority of people would say was the 'right thing.' You deserve credit for what you did, Kathy. Don't say you didn't have a choice in caring for Mom, because you did—and your choice makes it that much more special. You chose to give up your own plans and ambitions to care for your mother—our mother. I for one will be eternally grateful you did. It comforts me to know she didn't die in the care of strangers."

Kathy considered her words but said nothing.

"You chose to stay here with Dad, and when he got sick, you chose to care for him. You could have walked away. No one held you hostage here. No one forced you to remain.

You could have taken your inheritance and left, just as I did. It was your right, but you took the high ground once again. You sacrificed on his behalf. You deserve praise and credit for that as well."

Kathy hated the truth that rang clear in her sister's explanation. All her life she had found some degree of re-assurance in telling herself everything bad that had happened was Sunny's fault. That if Sunny hadn't done the things she'd done, Kathy would have had a chance to live her life the way she wanted. Now Sunny was daring to say that Kathy had made her own choices—that the life she'd lived these last twelve years was at her own hand—her own decision.

Kathy sat down and tried to force all the pieces of confusion back into place. Her mind felt overloaded with thoughts and images. "I've had to plan two funerals without you," she finally murmured. "You have no idea how hard that is."

"Oh, but I do," Sunny said in voice barely audible. "I know what it is to plan a funeral." She looked down at her plate. "I had to bury my stillborn son. His father was no help. In fact, he was the reason my son was dead."

The shock from that statement assaulted Kathy from her head to the tips of her toes. "Good grief . . . what happened?"

Sunny didn't look up. "I was twenty and nine months pregnant. I'd married a very abusive man who had a drinking and gambling problem. None of which I knew before I foolishly married him. The first time he beat me was when he found out I'd kept a separate bank account after we were married."

"Why didn't you leave?"

"I made a bad choice," she said, finally looking Kathy in the eye. "I'd chosen to marry an abusive man, and frankly I figured it was my punishment for having left home in such a bad manner. Every time he hit me, I told myself I deserved it." Sunny frowned and looked down at her plate again. "But I knew my unborn child didn't deserve anything of the sort."

Kathy didn't know what to say. It was difficult to imagine that her sister was married and had a child. "Where's your husband now?"

"We divorced. Mitch was a gambler, like I said. He went through money as if it were his personal duty to deplete our bank account. He wouldn't let me have any money. I guess he was afraid it would make me independent of him. I wanted to call home during that time, but he wouldn't allow it, and frankly, after a time, I was too ashamed to call. I was just days away from my due date when things fell completely apart."

Sunny traced a pattern on the tablecloth. "I had managed to sneak money out of Mitch's wallet over the months of my pregnancy. I knew I'd need things for the baby, and whenever he was passed out drunk, I'd take a little here and there. Never enough to make it noticeable, you know?"

Kathy nodded, imagining her sister sneaking around, fearing for her life should her husband wake up and figure out what was happening.

"I would hide the stash in different places. Mitch always tore through my things when he was desperate for money. I don't know why he presumed I would have any, since he never gave me any. I suppose he figured friends might share some good fortune with me.

"Anyway, one day he found the money I'd managed to save. I'd never seen him so mad. He accused me of everything from selling myself on the streets to getting money from home. I told him I was just saving it up for the baby's needs. I reminded him the baby was due in just a few days and we had nothing for him. If welfare hadn't been picking up the bill for the doctor and hospital, I wouldn't have even had that much going for us."

"Couldn't he understand that?" Kathy asked, her tone softened in compassion for the terror her sister had endured.

"Mitch didn't understand anything but blackjack and liquor. He was glad for the money but wasn't about to let me get away with what I'd done." Sunny gave a shudder. "The details aren't important. He beat me—it seemed to go on for hours, although I was told afterward it was only a half hour or so. Neighbors heard and called the police. Mitch was still beating me when they arrived. He was in such a rage he didn't even hear them knock. He didn't realize they were there until they bashed in the door and pulled him off of me." Sunny fell silent and slowly shook her head.

Kathy couldn't keep from asking, "What happened then?"

"They called an ambulance. I was in pretty bad shape. Mitch had kicked me so hard he'd busted several ribs as well as my arm. I'd tried to protect the baby by blocking the blows, but it didn't do any good. At the hospital they told me the baby had died. They gave me something to start my labor, and I delivered my son about ten hours later. They let me hold him."

Tears were streaming down Sunny's face, and Kathy's own eyes welled with emotion. To lose a parent was difficult, but to lose a baby . . . that was unthinkable. Without even considering what she was doing, Kathy reached out and took hold of Sunny's hand.

"He was perfect," Sunny said. "He didn't look dead—he just looked asleep. I sat there and rocked him for a long time."

"What did you name him?"

Sunny smiled. "Gary. After Dad. He's buried in Las Vegas. I visited the grave on my way here."

"What happened to your husband? Did he go to jail?"

"Yeah. He was sentenced to ten years and got out in six. I have no idea where he went or what he's doing. And I don't care. My choice cost me the life of my son. It's not something I can ever forget, but it is something I have to live with. Just like you have to live with your choices."

SEVEN

SUNSHINE REGRETTED HER LAST few words the minute they were out of her mouth. She'd never intended to bring it back to Kathy and her attitude. She had honestly thought that if Kathy knew that Sunny could own her poor choices, then maybe Kathy could recognize her own choices and feel less the victim. Instead, Sunny had clearly crossed a line.

Kathy nearly knocked the kitchen chair over as she got to her feet. "I'm not hungry."

"Please don't go. I didn't mean to make you mad."

"I'm not mad. I have to take Dad his medicine," Kathy said very coolly.

"Look, why don't you let me do it?" Sunny got to her feet. "I want to lighten your load."

"My load is just fine. I don't need your help." Kathy began pulling medicine from the cupboard.

"Kathy, please try to understand," Sunny began.

Kathy turned around. "What I understand is that you have caused this family more than a little pain." She seemed to struggle with her words. "I'm sorry about your baby. What happened . . . well . . . it's awful. But this is something completely different." Kathy whirled back around and gripped the counter. "I wish you'd never come back."

Sunny knew it would do little good to try and argue her point. She looked back for a moment at the table. Why should her sister's rejection be any different from all the other times she'd been cast off?

"I guess I'll go to town." Sunny picked up a piece of toast and a few slices of bacon and made a sandwich. "I'll be back by afternoon."

Kathy said nothing, but Sunny hadn't expected her to. Kathy's anger caused Sunny a moment of frustration. Wasn't this why she'd left in the first place?

Nobody here ever understood me. Nobody ever saw anything outside of their own needs—their own interests.

Sunny slid into her car and took a deep breath. She hadn't intended to tell about her baby son. She supposed a part of her had told the story hoping Kathy would be shocked enough to stop taking her anger out on Sunny. Another part of her just wanted Kathy to understand that her choice to run away hadn't given Sunny a life of beauty and luxury as her sister might think.

She thinks I somehow missed out on the pain.

The car roared to life and classical music filled the interior. Beethoven's "Ode to Joy" blared out as if to cheer her up. Sunny shut off the CD and threw the car into gear. There was no joy in her life right now and no sense in pretending there was. She took a bite of the toast sandwich and headed down the gravel road.

The drive into downtown Slocum took less than ten minutes. The drive through town took less than two. Built as a support to area farmers, the town had once boasted a spur line on the Union Pacific, as well as the promise of a major highway system. When the highway failed to materialize and the railroad line was eventually shut down, the town of Slocum slowly settled into obscurity.

Sunny noticed several empty businesses on Main Street. Where a bakery and café had once served as a gathering

WHERE MY HEART BELONGS ঙ 87

place for high school students, there were only boarded up
windows and a sign that read *Out of Business*. The same was
true of the old appliance store, veterinary clinic, and quilt
shop.

Parking in front of the small grocery store, Sunny
decided to get something cold to drink. She felt as though
the toast and bacon were still stuck in her throat and fervently wished she'd not gulped it down on the drive over.

A bell rang on the door of the tiny store called Somner's.
When Sunny had been a girl, this store had been handy for
those immediate needs, but they didn't buy bulk purchases
there. Her mother always drove to Hays for their monthly
supplies. Somner's was much as she remembered it. The pro-
duce section was just to the left, and to the right were two
checkout lanes. Friday nights were always busy, Sunny
remembered, and usually Mr. Somner had both lanes open.
Today, though, the place was nearly empty, as usual.

"Can I help you?" a man questioned.

Sunny didn't recognize the man, nor did he show any
idea of knowing her. "I'm after something cold to drink."

The man nodded and pointed. "Back of the store.
There's a selection of soda in the refrigerated section."

Sunny smiled and made her way through the aisles.
There was something comforting in the familiar store. She
had just rounded the corner when someone let out a gasp.
She looked up to see a tired-looking woman. The face was
familiar, although aged.

"Mrs. Stover?" Sunny knew it had to be her mother's
best friend. Mrs. Stover had taught grade school and Sunny
had been in her third-grade class.

"So you're alive. I can't believe you have the nerve to

show your face in this town again, Amy Halbert." She said the name in a tone of near disgust.

Sunny was immediately taken aback. "I beg your pardon?"

Mrs. Stover was a short woman. Sunny had at least a couple of inches on her, but at this moment Sunny had the distinct sensation that the woman was looking down at her. "I didn't think you could be so heartless as to show up now. I suppose you heard that your father is dying and came back to offer him your attention. It would have been nice if you could have done that for your mother. Poor woman. Her heart broke in two the day you left. Worried herself to death over you—and for what?"

Speechless, Sunny could only stand and stare at the woman. Renea Stover wanted—probably needed—to condemn Sunny in the way she might have done years earlier if she'd had the chance.

"Your parents never did anything but spoil you and give you whatever you asked for. I told Marg it would be the ruin of you. I told her you weren't a bit grateful. If you hadn't been so selfish, she'd be alive today."

"I'm sorry I've caused you pain, Mrs. Stover. You may not believe it, but I miss my mother very much. I wish I could have been here with her."

"Don't bother to tell me lies. You're good for nothing, Amy. This town and your family were better off without you."

Sunny still didn't know what to say. She thought perhaps it would be best to move on and leave the woman to her misery. "I need to go now," she murmured.

"No doubt. Probably going to run off again."

"Amy, is that you?"

Sunny turned to find her old friend Debbie Williams. A little boy clung to her leg while another one carried a loaf of bread and package of cookies. "Debbie?"

"I can't believe it's you. It's been forever. Do you have time to join us? We're going to the park. I'd love to talk to you."

Mrs. Stover turned up her nose. "Deborah," she murmured with the slightest nod of her head. With that she spun and hurried to the front of the store. No doubt she would spread the news of Sunny's return.

"I came here to grab something to drink," Sunny explained.

"Good. I'm getting us something too." Debbie pointed the way. "They don't have much to choose from, but at least it's cold."

Sunny picked the closest cola and waited for Debbie to make her selections. The boys watched Sunny with a rather suspicious curiosity. The younger of the two was acting shy, while the older one clearly wanted information but seemed to know better than to ask.

"Ready to go to the park?" Debbie asked the older boy.

"Mom, can we get some candy too?"

Debbie shook her head. "There's enough sugar in the cookies. We'll have plenty of sweets without candy." She looked up and met Sunny's gaze. "These are my boys. Isaac is four and Josiah is six. Boys, this is my friend Amy."

"I don't answer to that name anymore," Sunny said, trying to forget Mrs. Stover's attack.

"As I recall you didn't much answer anyone, by any name," Debbie teased. "What shall I call you?"

Sunny tried not to be further upset by Debbie's comment, but the fact of the matter was everyone in this town knew who she was and what she'd done. "I changed my name to Sunshine, but my friends call me Sunny."

Debbie grinned. "I remember when we used to talk about changing our names. We hated them so much. I'm still not that fond of Deborah, but Debbie doesn't bother me like it once did."

Sunny nodded and they made their way up to the front of the store. Mrs. Stover was nowhere in sight. They paid for their selections and walked outside. Debbie pointed across the street.

"They put in a little park just behind the post office. Our house is three blocks that way so we just walked over."

Sunny pointed to the burgundy car. "That's mine. I can give everyone a lift. I doubt it would be right to leave it here. Someone might need to park close to the store."

"We'll just walk and wait for you there. The boys need to expend their energy." She gave a bottle of pop to her youngest, while Josiah held the sack rather possessively. "See you there, Sunny."

Sunny watched for a few minutes as Debbie walked away with her sons. Her life seemed good—a far cry from the life Sunny had known. With a sigh, Sunny got in her car. She thought of the strange encounter with Renea Stover, and of the stiff manner in which the man at the store handled Sunny after Renea had no doubt informed him of who she was. People in Slocum weren't going to be all that forgiving, Sunny knew. Her parents were much beloved, and people would no doubt have little tolerance for the returned rebel.

The park was a cute little affair. There were swings and

large concrete tunnels half buried in the earth. A complex of platforms, slides, and cargo nets constituted the main attraction, and it was here that Debbie's boys immediately headed.

"This is great," Sunny said, joining Debbie on a bench. "I'm sure the boys love it."

"They do. There isn't much else for them to enjoy. The school doesn't have much of anything anymore. In fact, they're going to shut it down all together. Marty and I have decided to homeschool rather than see the boys bused too far away."

"So you married Marty Dunmire then?"

"Did you ever doubt it? Goodness, but I couldn't possibly have loved anyone else. He's a great husband and an even better father. The boys adore him."

"What does he do for a living?" Sunny asked, not really caring but desperate to keep the conversation on Debbie.

"He owns a couple of mechanic's shops. Fixes cars mostly but also gets the occasional tractor or lawnmower. There isn't a lot of work for him here, but he co-owns a shop in Hays with his dad, so it's just enough to help us get through. He drives over there three days a week and works here three. His folks sold us their house when they moved to Hays, so we got a really good deal. It's paid for, in fact, so we don't need a lot of money."

Sunny found her comments rather strange. Who didn't want more money? Yet Debbie seemed perfectly content.

"So where have you been all these years? Did you marry anybody?"

Sunny took a deep breath. "I lived in Las Vegas and LA, mostly. I did marry, but . . . well, it isn't important." She looked at her watch. "Is there a pay phone around here? My cell phone doesn't get reception out here. I need to make a call, and if I don't do it soon, I'll miss the person I'm trying to reach."

"Sure. The gas station has a phone. It's down at the east end. Marty's garage is just next door. Can you come back and talk some more after your call?"

Sunny shook her head. "Dad's condition isn't all that good. I don't imagine I should be away from home for long."

"I understand. Do they know how much more time your dad has?"

Sunny got to her feet. "No. It's just a matter of weeks, maybe even days, they keep telling me."

"I'll bet you're really glad you came home—you know, so you could see him."

"I am glad for that," Sunny admitted. But in all honesty she wasn't glad for much else. "Maybe I'll see you later."

"I'd like that. You know where the old place is, don't you?"

Sunny nodded. "I remember."

She left Debbie and drove to the gas station. The pay phone was on the side of the building, so Sunny parked right in front of it. She left her purse in the car but took her calling card. Times like this she wished fervently that her cell phone would pick up a signal.

"Hello?" Lana Hersh answered from the other end of the line.

"Hi, Lana. It's Sunny." Lana was a registered nurse in Anaheim, California. She had been instrumental in helping Sunny find God's truth and the peace that she so desperately needed. Without Lana's help, Sunny knew she'd never have survived the last few months.

"Sunny! How are you? I was beginning to worry. Are you okay?"

"I guess I'm as well as can be expected. I'm here in Kansas."

"Have you seen your mom and dad, and your sister—what was her name?"

"Kathy. I've seen her. I've seen Dad too, but my mom . . . well . . . she passed away a long time ago. It was my fault."

"Excuse me?"

"Mom had a heart attack shortly after I left home. They said she . . . They said her heart broke after I left. She wouldn't eat or do much of anything. She had a massive attack. Kathy gave up everything to stay here and take care of her and Dad. She's still here, in fact."

"Did your mother die from the heart attack?"

"Not right away. It destroyed a good portion of her heart. She was supposed to have a transplant but never made it that far."

"Well, that is hardly your fault. You can own a lot of responsibility for various things in your life, but I hardly think your mother's faulty heart is one of them."

"But I broke her heart. She would never have gotten sick to begin with if I hadn't run away. Kathy said she didn't eat or sleep. She was just devastated and it killed her. Kathy blames me."

"Look, you no doubt hurt her in leaving. You did wrong. I won't lie and say that your choices didn't hurt people. They hurt you too. But you've repented. You've asked God to forgive you and He has."

"But they haven't. Oh, I think my dad forgave me long ago, but Kathy hasn't and neither have the people of this town. I ran into my mom's best friend and the woman was vicious. I think she would have pulled my hair out by the roots if she'd thought she could get away with it."

"They need time, Sunny. Having you show up after twelve years of silence is going to be hard. You have to give them time. They'll come around."

"But we don't have a lot of time. My father is dying from cancer. It's spread everywhere."

"Oh, I am sorry. How long does he have?"

"Days, maybe weeks. Not long. Kathy says he's in the final stages."

"Sounds like God took you home just in time."

"I know, but it's so hard. I want to make things right. I want them all to know how I've changed, but no one wants to know that. They just want to rant and rave at me—blame me for everything. I think they'd like to just pick up where we left off twelve years ago—as if I were the same person I was then."

"People in pain tend to act that way. They only know the old you, Sunny. You'll have to prove to them that you're different—that you truly have changed for the better."

"I know, but sometimes I think I should never have come back. Kathy says she wishes I wouldn't have come."

"And what of your father?"

Sunny thought for a moment. "He says I'm answered prayer."

"And you are. You really need to understand that. God has a plan in all of this, Sunny. He's known where you were all these years. He loves you and won't leave you. Just remember that."

"I'm trying to, Lana. It's just very hard."

"Like I said, you need to give them time. Especially your sister."

"I'd give her all the time she asked for—even forever— but we don't have that much time. Dad wants to see things set right before he dies, and I don't think Kathy is ready for that. No, I'm sure she's not ready."

"Trust the Lord, Sunny. He's bigger than this. He knows what it's going to take to reach your sister. Trust Him and not the circumstances."

EIGHT

"DAD WANTS TO SEE YOU," Kathy said as Sunny stepped out of her car, her mood apparently unchanged. Sunny noted her sister's waist-length honey brown hair had been braided down her back—a sure sign she was about to get to work on some project.

"How's he doing?"

Kathy's eyes narrowed as she frowned. "He's in a lot of pain. I've called hospice and the doctor. I'm hoping they'll put him on a morphine drip."

Sunny nodded. "Look, I'm really sorry about earlier. I wasn't trying to give you grief. I can see that it's been incredibly hard on you."

Without answering, Kathy turned to walk away, then stopped as if she'd thought of something to say. She didn't look around or turn to face Sunny; she just stood there as if trying to regain her composure. Sunny wanted to say something, but the words felt stuck in her throat.

What can I possibly say to make her feel better? To make things right?

"I've thought about what you said," Kathy finally said. "You're right. I did make my choices. I felt like they were made for me though." She looked at Sunny. "It doesn't invalidate my feelings just because the situation was something other than what I thought. It still hurt. I still felt trapped. I still figured there was no other answer."

"I know. I'm sorry, Kath. I can see that it wasn't easy, but you have to know I'm not the same woman I was twelve years ago. I'm not asking you to pretend the past doesn't exist, but rather I'd like for us to build a new relationship for the present—maybe even for the future."

A pickup truck pulling a horse trailer rumbled down the long gravel road that ran past the farm. "That will be the Meyers," Kathy noted. "They're coming to buy the horses. I'll be in the back if you need me."

"Okay." Sunny walked to the house, grabbed a glass of water, and went to her father's room. She knocked against the open door. "Dad, Kathy said you wanted to see me." She went to his bedside and pulled up a chair.

Dad opened his eyes and smiled. "It's still hard to believe you're really here. I figured we should talk. Kathy's got a plan to get me on some strong pain medication, and after that I don't know how well I'll be able to communicate."

"I'm sure you needed the medication a long time ago," Sunny said, shaking her head. "You deserve not to hurt."

"That will come soon enough." He drew a deep breath and grimaced. "Soon enough."

"What did you want to see me about?" She sipped the water and held up the glass. "Are you thirsty? I can get you something to drink."

"I'm fine. I just wanted to have some time with you. To have you tell me what you've been up to—where you've been. Maybe answer any questions you had. Especially if you needed to talk about Mom. You look so much like her. Sometimes just seeing you makes me feel as if she's still here."

"I'm sure it was hard for you to lose her. I can't imagine any two people more in love than you and Mom."

"She was the light of my life." He smiled and closed his eyes. "I never knew anyone with more patience or understanding for my needs. She always seemed to know what I needed before I did." He opened his eyes again and Sunny thought they looked a bit clearer. "Do you want to talk about her death?"

Sunny was taken aback by his abrupt question. "Kathy told me about some of it. Probably most of it. I know she blames me, and I feel that's only right. I mean, Mom stopped eating and taking care of herself because of my running away."

"That's true enough." Dad reached out and took her hand. "Sweetheart, I won't pretend that you had no part in it. It wouldn't help anything. You already blame yourself, and nothing I say will change that. And too, there are consequences for our choices. Mom had consequences. You have consequences."

"The worst of it is, Dad, I can't even tell you for sure that back then I would have done things any differently had I known what would have happened to Mom." Sunny bit her lower lip and took a deep breath. "I feel horrible for saying that. It makes me sound so ruthless—selfish. But I was. I was horribly focused on my own needs. I hate who I was back then."

"I think it shows a huge mark of maturity for you to say that you don't know for sure that it would have changed things. Most folks would say, 'Oh, if I'd only known I would have done things this way or that way.' When in truth, they probably wouldn't have changed things at all. The fact that you realize that is a credit to your sincerity."

"Yet it doesn't change the past." Sunny looked beyond

him to the fields outside. "There's so much I wish I could go back and change. So many poor choices—bad decisions. Times when I felt clearly I should have done one thing, but instead did something else. I often wondered how things were here for you all—if things were running smoothly in my absence. I liked to believe that everyone realized just how right I'd been about everything. I imagined you all gathering for dinner, commenting on how you'd only wished you'd seen the truth sooner." Sunny smiled. "Does that shock you?"

Dad shook his head and gave her a hint of a smile. "Not really. Sounds like the old Amy."

"I just wish now that I could have known the truth then. I hurt so many people. Today I ran into Mrs. Stover at the grocery store. She spoke her mind and made it clear that she blames me for Mom's passing. I was so shocked that she would just come right out and say it—but at the same time I was almost relieved that she had. Kind of like with Kathy. She's made no pretense of being glad to see me, and I really can't blame her—but it hurts so much."

"It's the consequences of your actions," her father said. "I wish I could spare you the pain of them, but we each have to deal with the decisions we make."

Sunny nodded. "I know. Kathy and I were talking about that earlier. Still, I don't understand why you would spare me the pain, after all the pain I caused you."

He frowned. "Because you're my daughter. If I could take the pain for you—if the pain of this disease could somehow ease your own misery, I would gladly bear it."

Blinded by her own tears, Sunny squeezed her father's hand. "I know you would. Dad, I'm so sorry for all I did."

"I'm partly to blame," he said. "I should never have given you the money to begin with."

Sunny thought for a moment. She knew in her heart it wouldn't have made a difference. Oh, she might never have met Mitch and been lured into his control had she not been well set financially, but then again, there were plenty of men like Mitch who would have used her for other gain.

"It wouldn't have made a difference, Dad. I would have gone with or without the money. I was desperate and selfish. Nothing else drove me."

"I guess I've always known that." He moved to the right and let out a groan. "Sorry."

"Don't apologize for your pain, Dad. I think people spend entirely too much time doing that. I'm determined to apologize for the things that I actually had something to do with. Like Mom. I'm sorry I caused Mom's death."

"Her weak heart caused her death. You couldn't know that she had a heart condition. None of us did. When she was young she had rheumatic fever. It damaged her heart severely, yet no one ever picked up on that. That condition was aggravated by her depression—not eating, throwing up when she did eat, crying for hours on end after you left. But there's something else you need to know."

"What?" Sunny asked, dropping her hold on Dad to wipe her tears. She could hardly speak for the lump in her throat.

"Mom was responsible for her sickness too. She knew she was hurting herself, but she let the sorrow overcome her. She didn't turn to me or even to God for a time. She knew better. Sometimes we know better about something . . . then do what we want to do anyway."

"Like me."

He nodded. "Yes. But there's something more."

"What?"

"Mom forgave you, just as I did. You are no longer held responsible, even for whatever part you played. The problem was dealt with long ago. You didn't even know it, but shortly before she died, Mom and I knelt together and prayed. We asked God to forgive you—to forgive us. We asked God to ease your sorrows when you learned the truth, and we pleaded with Him to bring you home."

"Oh, Daddy." Sunny eased against his chest and sobbed. "I love you so much. I loved you both, and only after leaving did I realize just how much you meant to me. Nothing was ever right again. Even when it seemed to be good, it was always tainted by the past. I just wish I could have talked to Mom. I wish I could have heard her say I was forgiven for leaving—for the way I treated you all."

Dad held her close. His embrace was weak yet reassuring to Sunny. He patted her gently. "I have a way for you to hear from her," he said softly.

Sunny leaned up. "What are you saying?"

He pointed to the dresser. "Top drawer. There's an envelope there for you."

Sunny straightened and went to the dresser. She pulled open the drawer and looked inside. Sure enough, there among her father's socks was an envelope. She picked it up and realized it contained more than a letter.

"Your mother made a tape and wrote you a letter as well. I think it comforted her to know that someday you would have these and be able to hear her voice—see her writing."

"Oh!" Sunny held the envelope close. It was more than

she could have ever hoped for or even imagined. She could not speak as her tears once again spilled over. All she could do was hug the letter to her breast. It was almost like hugging her mother.

❧ ❧ ❧

"They look real good," Jim Meyers said as he considered the horses Kathy brought into the pen. "That sorrel has long been a favorite of mine. Too bad your dad had him gelded. I think he would have made a good sire."

"He was just too spirited," Kathy said, giving the horse a pat as he came up to the edge of the pen. He seemed to understand they were talking about him.

"Your father was always a good judge of horseflesh and men," Denton Meyers declared. Jim's father was probably some twenty years older than Kathy's father, while Jim was at least ten years Gary Halbert's junior. Both men admired her father, however, and had maintained a friendship with him over the years as they ran the town's ranch and farm supply store.

"They're great to ride. I had Phoebe out just the other day." Actually it seemed to Kathy as though it had been a million years ago. Since Sunny had come, everything including time felt skewed.

"Well, you know they're going to a good home. We'll see they get the best of care." He handed her a check.

"I know you will, Jim." Kathy pushed away from the pen and tucked the check in her jeans. "I'll help you get them loaded."

She tried not to think of how she was losing yet another piece of her childhood and life on the farm. Soon enough it would all be gone, but losing it bit by bit seemed almost cruel. That was something else she resented Sunny for. Sunny had no attachment to anything here on the farm. She could easily walk away and never think twice about the things Kathy loved so much. Sunny would have it easy compared to what Kathy was enduring.

If I could have afforded it, I would have just stayed here. But of course that was out of the question. The farm and sale thereof was going to be used to pay her father's debts, with the remainder being her inheritance, especially given the fact she'd used most of her trust fund just to keep things up and pay the farm's mortgage and utilities. There was no job in Slocum that would enable her to make a living—much less one that would pay well enough to keep up this property.

Besides, she told herself, Kyle was in Colorado Springs. If there was any hope of rekindling what they had once had, she would have to go there. Of course, it was unlikely he would even want to have her back in his life. Her Aunt Glynnis said Kyle had never married. He always asked about her—always wanted to know the details of her life and how she was doing—but that didn't mean he wanted her back. Kathy had made him promise when she'd sent him away that he wouldn't call her or write to her. She had known the pain would be impossible to bear if he were in her life, but only from the fringes.

During the short time after her mother's death and before her father's illness, Kathy had worked up the nerve to call him but had learned from her aunt that Jackson Pharmaceuticals, where Uncle Will had helped Kyle land a lucrative job, had sent Kyle abroad for some kind of specialized training. By the time he returned, Kathy's father was ill. She assumed God had intervened to keep Kathy from having to send Kyle away twice. Obviously it was her lot in life to care for her dying family members.

Still, Kyle had told her that he'd wait for her. Wait forever, if that's what it took. Kathy liked to imagine him waiting for her, loving her from afar . . . but at the same time she hated the thought. She did not want him to put his life on hold for her—not when she knew how painful it could be to have everything on perpetual pause.

"Well, that does it," Jim said as his father headed for the truck. "Any offers on the place yet?"

"No, I'm afraid not. The Realtor is going to advertise in some other papers. He thought we might spread out and send some ads to Kansas City, Oklahoma City, and even the Denver area."

"It's such a great place. I'd hate to see it torn up into parcels," Jim said, looking beyond Kathy at the house. "I've seen folks sell out like that, and it always makes me sad to see another farm destroyed."

"I know, but farming isn't what it used to be. Most of the time you're lucky to break even," Kathy said. "It's just not a good time for sellers, or so my agent tells me."

"Keep your chin up, missy. An offer will probably come soon. Summer's on us and schools are out. Folks will be looking to relocate before school commences again." He gave her a brief wave and headed back to the truck.

Kathy watched Jim and his father pull out of the drive,

106 🌺 Tracie Peterson

taking the four horses with them. She tried not to get emotional about the situation.

"I'm doing the right thing," she told herself aloud. "It
has to be this way." But a part of her couldn't help but wonder how different things might have been. It hurt so much
to watch the things she loved slip away. How could she hope
to make Sunny understand her pain? There was a part of
Kathy deep down inside that wanted more than anything to
embrace her sister and create a new bond. After all, once
Dad died, Sunny would be all that was left of their immediate family—of the security Kathy had once known in childhood.

"We'll always be best friends," Kathy had promised Amy
when they'd been all of ten and eight. "Nobody will ever
come between us."

The words haunted Kathy now. The pledge had obviously had no value to her sister when she'd made the choice
to leave. She'd broken the trust, and Kathy was unconvin-
ced that it was worth mending.

🌿 🌿 🌿

Sunny made a frantic search through the house for a
tape player. She grimaced at the thought of having to ask
Kathy. She didn't even know if her sister was aware that
their mother had left the tape for Sunny. What if she wasn't
and it proved to be just one more thing that separated them
and caused ill will?

The letter had been brief and had only whetted Sunny's
need for more. Her mother had expressed her worry about

where Sunny had gone and whether she'd ever see her daughter again. She talked about how she prayed Sunny would come home before she died but knew her time was short. She promised she had said more in the tape, and perhaps that's why Sunny felt a growing need to hear it.

"Maybe I should just drive over to Hays and get a player," she whispered to the air. If she did that, Kathy wouldn't need to know. She sighed. Hadn't this family suffered enough from secrets and unspoken thoughts?

She heard Kathy come in from the back porch. The screen door always made a distinctive sound when it opened or closed. Sunny smiled at the familiarity. It was nice that some things had not changed in her absence.

Sunny deliberated for a moment, wondering if Kathy would linger there in the kitchen or seek out Dad. Surely she would want to check up on him. But as she strained to listen, Sunny was convinced by the scraping of the chair against the kitchen floor that Kathy had decided to remain where she was.

She marched with a determined step to the kitchen, but slowed down with the last few steps. "Do you mind the intrusion?" Sunny asked.

Kathy looked up from the table. She had a stack of mail in front of her. "I figured you'd still be with Dad."

"He was tired. I didn't want to overtax him."

Kathy nodded and went back to sorting. "I have some sandwich fixings in the fridge if you're hungry. I suppose I should really start planning better for our meals. I've let the supplies get way down since I knew I'd soon be leaving."

"Who bought the farm?"

Kathy grimaced. "No one, yet."

"Oh. I figured the way you were packing and . . ."

"I'd rather not talk about it."

Sunny could see that Kathy was upset and decided to change the subject back to their meal planning.

"I can always buy food for us," Sunny offered. "I was thinking about going to Hays for a couple of other things anyway. Maybe if you made a list, I could just get it all while I'm there."

"I suppose I could."

Kathy's response surprised Sunny. "Good. I'd like to help."

Her sister straightened and met Sunny's gaze. "Did he give you the letter and tape?"

Sunny felt almost as if she'd been punched in the stomach. She could only nod. She felt helpless to ask about the tape player situation, but Kathy seemed to have the matter under control.

"There's a radio cassette player upstairs in your old bedroom. I put it there to listen to music when I'm sorting out junk."

"Thanks. I did look around a bit to see if there was one down here," Sunny admitted. "It was one of the things I thought I might need to buy in Hays."

"No sense in it unless you need one otherwise."

Sunny fidgeted with the hem of her blouse as an awkward silence fell between them. Kathy went back to work looking through the mail. She seemed grateful for something to do.

Finally Sunny blurted out the one question she could not seem to force from her mind. "How did you know about the tape?"

Kathy shrugged. "I helped her make it."

The statement made Sunny feel even more uncomfortable. "You helped her make it?"

"She was too weak to do it alone. She couldn't remember how to make the thing work, so she asked for my help. She worked on it a little each day for about two weeks."

Sunny didn't know what else to say. She put her hand into her pocket and felt the tape for reassurance. "I guess I'll go listen to it."

"I'll make us some lunch."

Sunny went upstairs without further comment. She wanted desperately to hear her mother's voice—to know whatever Mom wanted to share with her, yet she was also worried about Kathy. Apparently the sale of the farm, or lack thereof, was a real concern. Sunny made a mental note to ask about it again later.

Pushing open the door to her old bedroom, Sunny felt the past come rushing at her. The faded pink print curtains still hung at the single window. Her mother had made those curtains and Sunny—no, Amy—had despised them. She had shown her mother some curtains she liked in a catalog, but rather than buy them her mother had tried to make them. They were a poor substitute, and Amy had made certain her mother knew it.

I was so cruel. So inhumane. Mom had given her best, and it wasn't good enough. *And haven't I suffered at the hands of others for that same reason? Always giving what I think is my best, only to have it pointed out to me that I'm a sorry second best?*

Sunny put her hand over her mouth, as if to keep any of the miserable thoughts from being vocalized. Then she spotted the tape player and made her way through the stacks of boxes, many open and awaiting attention. It was a sad collection of the wreckage that had been their lives.

Sunny popped the tape into the player and sat down on an overturned metal milk crate. She remembered her mother saying she had saved it from her childhood days, when the milk was delivered to her home in town. Her mother had boasted about learning to iron clothes at the age of five by standing on this very crate. The memory made Sunny smile.

Drawing a deep breath and praying for strength, Sunny pressed the play button. For several seconds there was nothing but silence, and then she heard the voice of her sister.

"Okay, Mom, it's recording. Just talk normal—as if you were talking to me."

Another pause, and then the sound of her mother filled the room. "Sunshine, I don't know when you'll get this tape, but I probably won't be here. I'm very sick. My heart has been damaged beyond repair, and I've deteriorated faster than they thought I would. My heart broke when you went away, so it didn't surprise me when the doctor told me I'd suffered a heart attack.

"Oh, Amy—I mean Sunshine—how I wish you were here. I want so much to know you're safe and happy. I look at the moon at night and wonder if you're seeing it too. Sometimes it makes me feel closer to you, but other times it just makes me feel very alone."

Tears streamed down Sunny's face. She hugged herself and rocked back and forth on the crate. How wonderful to hear her mother's voice. Weak, but recognizable, it comforted Sunny in a way nothing else could. To her surprise, however, she thought her mother sounded a lot like Kathy.

"I wanted to make you this tape for several reasons," her mother went on. "I wanted you to know how very much I love you. Nothing will change that. My love for you is something that will never end. If you ever have children, you'll know what I mean. There's nothing you could do that would make me stop loving you."

There was a pause for several seconds. Empty air that settled down around Sunny like a smothering blanket. Surely that wasn't all there was to the tape. Kathy had said she'd made it over two weeks. Sunny was about to reach for the player when her mother spoke again.

"Sunshine, no matter what anyone says—no matter what they do—I want you to know that I forgive you for everything. You aren't totally to blame. I failed you in so many ways."

"No!" Sunny interjected before realizing no one could hear her.

"There were things I should have done better—choices I should have made and didn't, and some I made and shouldn't have. If you're still the tenderhearted girl I knew you to be, you'll probably try to blame yourself for what happened to me—but you can't. My choices put me here. I let the situation destroy me. I could have been strong like Dad and Kathy, but it took too much energy. I should have trusted God more. I see that now. I should have left it in His hands, knowing that He knew where you were and what you were doing. I should have put my sorrows and pain at His feet, because I knew He was bigger—more powerful than anything that could happen or had happened. And besides . . . we all have to die sometime. The doctor says I probably always had problems with my heart and just didn't know it. I had a bout of rheumatic fever when I was very young and it no doubt weakened my heart forever.

"My sweet girl, I love you so much. I have a peace now about you. I know you'll be back. Maybe not right away, but someday. Because I know that tender heart will always be there somewhere inside you. Someday you'll come face-to-face with the need to make peace with your family, and when you do, this tape will be here waiting for you. I forgive you, Amy. I can only hope—pray—that you forgive me as well."

The rest of the tape was more of the same interlaced with a few stories—reminders of the past. By the time the tape concluded, Sunny realized a half hour had passed. In her heart, however, it seemed the tape had spanned twelve years.

NINE

SUNNY HAD JUST COME OUT onto the porch when a blue Suburban drove up and stopped near the house. A woman
stepped out. She was tall and slender, dressed in jeans and a
sleeveless pink blouse. Her blond hair had been cut in a styl-
ish manner to frame her face—a face that wore very little
makeup but seemed radiant.

"I came to see Kathy," the woman announced, "but I'm
glad to see you as well. Do you remember me?"

She smiled broadly and Sunny saw something familiar in
her expression. "Sylvia?"

"The one and only. How are you doing?"

Sunny shrugged. "As well as can be expected, I guess."
She wasn't sure if Sylvia's comments would take a negative
turn, so she remained guarded. "It's hard to see Dad like
this, but I'm glad I have the chance to say good-bye."

Sylvia nodded. "And what about Kathy? Are you two
able to talk and work through the past?"

Sunny came down the porch stairs. "Not really."

"This is a shock to her. You have to keep that in mind."

Sunny sighed, glad to have someone to talk to even if
things might take a bad turn. "I wish I could wave some
kind of magic wand and have her understand my heart and
my desire to make things right. I wish she could just see the
truth of the situation and stop being so . . . so . . . defensive."

"Yes, well . . . you really don't have a right to expect

that, now do you?" Sylvia's words weren't harsh or angry; they were simply stated in a matter-of-fact manner that gave Sunny pause.

"I'm not sure what you mean."

Sylvia tilted her head as if sizing up Sunny's sincerity. "When we do something that hurts people, we always wish they would come to a quick understanding and immediate healing. That way we can feel better about ourselves as well." She gave a slight chuckle. "Believe me, I know. I've done enough things that hurt others and I always want them to get over it as quick as possible, so that I can forget that I ever had a hand in it."

Sunny like Sylvia's frankness. She was truthful without trying to wound. "I know it would be so much easier to be here if Kathy's response had been like Dad's. The thing is, maybe I crave Kathy's approval or forgiveness even more than I did his."

"Why?"

Sunny frowned. "Because we were always so close. Even when I was going through my stupid phases, I always talked things out with Kathy. She knew I wasn't happy in Kansas— Slocum. She knew I longed to go elsewhere, but I never told her about my plans to change my name and leave."

"I'm sure that must have hurt her."

"In all the time I was gone, it was Kathy I missed the most. There were so many times just after I left that I would reach for the phone to call her."

"So why didn't you?"

"I guess I was afraid. I knew she'd probably have the power to convince me to come home—and I just couldn't do that, Sylvia. I was dying there—here. I knew if I stayed I would marry one of the guys I hung around with and we'd probably drink a lot and fight a lot." Sunny shook her head and smiled at the irony. "I guess it wouldn't have been any worse than what I put myself through."

"Sometimes that's how it is. But in all honesty, I think Kathy is just trying to process everything and deal with the shock. We gave you up for dead, Sunny."

"I was dead. Completely dead until I came back to God. Funny how I always took my church upbringing for granted. I didn't think I needed God. But as for Kathy, I know she blames me for a great deal, and rightfully so on some of it. I shouldn't have left the way I did. I had no right to treat my family that way. Yesterday I listened to a tape my mother left for me. It was wonderful to hear her voice and forgiveness, but difficult because my mother blamed herself for so much, and I couldn't be there to help her change her mind."

"We all have to work on our own minds. People can offer convincing arguments that help us, but ultimately we have control over what we think and feel."

Sunny hesitated a moment, then decided Sylvia would be the best one to ask about the farm. "Say, I was wondering . . . do you know what's going on with the farm?"

"What do you mean?" Sylvia seemed genuinely puzzled.

"I mean, is there a problem with it selling?"

Sylvia nodded, her expression immediately registering understanding. "Kathy hasn't told you?"

"No. I mentioned it, but she didn't want to talk about it."

"It's a sore subject. One that is really starting to worry her. I suppose I shouldn't be the one to talk about it. I wouldn't want Kathy to think I was betraying her trust."

"I swear I won't say a word to her about it. I just wanted to know what was going on."

"The farm has been on the market since earlier this spring. Kathy had tried to convince your dad to sell a long time ago and to move with her to Colorado Springs. But he didn't want to go. He was convinced he'd get better and be able to continue farming. Of course, that didn't happen, and by the time he started feeling poorly again, the market had changed and it's been harder to sell farms in this area."

"But it hasn't been on the market all that long. Surely no one is too worried at this point."

"You need to understand something." Sylvia looked around, as if to see if anyone might overhear. "There are problems financially."

"I saw the car," Kathy said as she came around the corner of the house.

Sylvia smiled and dropped the subject of the farm. "Sunny was just coming outside when I arrived. I thought it'd be a great chance to get to know her again."

Sunny could see that Kathy felt uncomfortable and decided to give her some space. She wanted to know more about the financial problems, but she supposed she wasn't going to get any answers at this point. "Well, I need to run into town. That's where I was headed when Sylvia arrived. Kathy, I saw we were out of milk. Do you know if we need anything else?"

"There's the stuff we planned to get in Hays."

"I could go ahead and drive over today. Dad's asleep, so it seems a good time. I'll just do that."

Kathy nodded and Sylvia held up her hand. "Could you pick up a couple of things for me too?"

Sunny smiled. She remembered that in the old days whenever someone was heading to the bigger city, there was always a request from someone to pick up things for them as well. "I'd be happy to. Do you have a list?"

"Nope, but it'll just take a jiffy." She hurried to the Suburban and climbed inside.

"You sure you feel like doing this?" Kathy asked.

Sunny nodded and grinned. "It'll give me a chance to be in air-conditioning."

Sylvia returned with the list and handed it over with a twenty-dollar bill. "I think this should cover everything, but if not, just keep the receipt and I'll make it right with you."

"No problem." For the kindness Sylvia had shown her, Sunny would have happily bought every item on the list at her own expense. "I'll be back by supper."

Sunny got in the car and looked at Sylvia's list. Several items were listed that Sunny knew would be hard to find in Slocum. And at the bottom a hastily jotted note said, *We can talk about it later.*

Sunny tucked the note into her pocket. Apparently there was a whole lot more to this situation than she knew about.

With Sunny gone for the day, Kathy felt that she could relax a bit. There was no need to carry any pretenses with Sylvia. The woman could read her like a book anyway.

"So what does Sunny think about you selling the farm?" Sylvia asked as they walked toward the chicken coop.

Kathy tensed at the question. "I have no idea. I haven't talked to her much about it."

"Does she know about the finances?"

"Why should she? She hasn't been here to worry about it."

"How's your dad?"

Kathy was grateful to change the subject. "In a lot of pain. Well, I hope it's less now. The doctor doubled his pain-killers. He doesn't want to put him on morphine just yet—mainly because Dad doesn't want it."

"Why not?"

"Says he wants to be as coherent as possible for as long as he can. He wants to be able to talk to me and Sunny . . . and anyone else who visits. He says once he's in heaven, he won't hurt anymore and it seems a small price to pay. It seems huge to me."

"How are things going with Sunny and your dad?"

Kathy stopped walking at this question. "He's definitely happy. I guess I can be glad about that. I'm still awfully confused by her. She's changed a lot, but I guess I don't know if that's good or bad."

"Seems like it's good," Sylvia offered. "I mean she cared enough to come back and try to make amends."

"How do you make amends for something like what she did? She left our parents to believe she was dead."

"I suppose you could say that."

"I have to. It's the truth. She could have called or dropped a postcard at any time. She didn't need to remain silent all those years. It really hurt them . . . and me."

Sylvia put her arm around Kathy's shoulders. "I know it did."

Kathy felt her tears come unbidden. "I thought she was dead. Remember, we even had our own little memorial service when I decided I had to let Amy go and stop waiting for her to call—to come home."

"I do remember—it's only been a couple of years. But, Kathy, she's not dead. She's here and she's probably hurting as much as you are. She told me that the separation of her family was hard on her, but probably worst of all was losing you."

"Me?" Kathy couldn't imagine that was true.

"I probably shouldn't say this, but that's what she told me. Kathy, I really think you have a chance here to fix something that should never have been broken. But it's up to you."

Kathy stiffened. "Why? Why is it always up to me? Why can't it be somebody else's responsibility for once?"

"It's going to take both of you being responsible," Sylvia said softly. "You know it works that way, even if you don't want to face up to it just yet. And after all, Sunny has taken the first step. She's exposed herself to the ridicule and retribution that she knows she deserves. She's made herself very vulnerable to everyone."

Kathy walked to the chicken yard and opened the gate. Sylvia passed quickly into the yard and waited for Kathy to secure the latch. In her heart, Kathy knew that Sylvia was making a good point. What was most frustrating was that even Sunny had been making good points. Dad wanted his daughters to make peace and to lean on each other, but Kathy was the one holding out. She knew that now, but she still felt incapable of doing anything about it.

Kathy looked at her friend and frowned. "She could have let us know that she was all right. Even if she didn't want to talk to us or be a part of our family—she could have sent even the shortest note to say 'I'm alive and well.' It would have taken very little time and very little money."

"True," Sylvia agreed but offered nothing more.

"If she would have at least called collect, Dad would have accepted the charges in a heartbeat. If she'd called soon enough, we could have told her about Mom." Kathy measured out feed for the hens and fought to regain control of her emotions.

"Kathy, all of this is true, but it's in the past. Do you plan to punish her for it for the rest of her life?"

Dabbing her eyes with the tail of her work shirt, Kathy considered the question. Was that what this was all about—punishing Sunny for what she'd done?

"Look," Sylvia said, "I think you and Sunny need to sit down and talk. Really talk. You need to be honest, even if it makes you more vulnerable than you're comfortable with. If you don't do this, Kathy, I have a feeling you will always regret it. It's your choice."

"Everybody keeps saying that. Sunny said I made choices that kept me here—that it wasn't her fault that I chose to give up Kyle and marriage. You said something similar yourself once." Kathy felt her anger return and tighten around her like a warrior's belt. "But I never felt like I had any say over the matter. I wasn't like Sunny. I couldn't just walk away, no matter how many times I considered it."

"But you could have, and that's where you aren't being honest with yourself. You had the same choice, but you took a different path. What people thought of you mattered. What you thought of yourself mattered too. You knew if you walked away you couldn't live with the consequences. Sunny didn't have the same feeling."

"Obviously not." She turned and started toward the

gate, but Sylvia reached out to take hold of her arm.

"Please hear me. I'm not trying to hurt you or cause you more pain, but Sunny's choices don't make her completely wrong, just like your choices don't make you completely right. Sunny went about things in the wrong way—but she was of age and your father gave her the money she had coming to her."

"She took it twice. Don't forget she took the advance he gave her on her trust fund, and when she was twenty-one, she arranged to steal the money that was still in the bank under hers and Dad's names. Only then, because she was of age, she could have it without question. She stole money that wasn't hers to take."

"Be that as it may, as I said, Sunny didn't do everything wrong or right. She lived her life the way she thought she could deal with it. You did the same thing, Kathy. Don't think there weren't people who questioned your judgment just as they did Sunny's."

Kathy shook off Sylvia's hold. "But why would they? I did what I could. I stayed here where I knew I could be useful. I remained in my father's house to care for my mother and now for him."

"Which are admirable choices, but you're ruining your deeds by allowing bitterness to take over. Instead of rejoicing that you got to be here—to share time with your mother up until the end, you're angry because Sunny wasn't here. You have something she can never have. You had those last few years—those tender quiet moments—those shared times of sorrow. Sunny has none of that. She probably never even imagined it possible that her mother was dead, much less that she'd find her father ill as well."

"But that's what she gets for not keeping in touch," Kathy said, folding her arms. "It's the consequence of turning her back on us."

"I agree. I'm not your enemy in this. I only want you to see reason. You stayed here where you were safe and protected. You had plenty to eat and no one to cause you physical harm. You had your mother's company, and yes, you had to watch her die, but at least you were her comfort in those final days. You'll always know how much that meant to her.

"You had your father's love and company. I doubt Sunny even had a fraction of the peace you had. I don't know what her story is or what all she's been through, but there's a look in her eyes that suggests a great many hideous things. I won't try to guess them, but maybe it would help you both to share your miseries and try to help the other one see what happened over the years."

Kathy thought back to Sunny talking about the baby she'd buried and the man who'd beat her badly enough to take that child's life. Kathy had never had that kind of fear. But on the other hand, Kathy would have never put herself in that position. All Sunny would have had to do was pick up the phone and call for help.

But pride wouldn't let her. Just like it won't let me leave the past behind.

The thought startled Kathy. Was that what this was all about—pride? She let the idea linger for a moment. She could see that there was merit to the thought, but admitting it was so hard.

"I've blamed Amy for so long," Kathy finally admitted. "And I've hurt over her desertion and betrayal. Sylvia, I don't know that I can trust her again. I don't know that the journey is even worth the bother."

Sylvia shook her head. "I have three children and each is precious to me. Each can be a burden as well. But I can tell you without a doubt that if any of them ran away, I would welcome them back with open arms whether they came home the next day, the next year, or decades later. My love for them is unconditional. No matter their behavior, I will go on loving them. It sounds to me that your love for Amy was conditioned upon her doing things your way—or at least in a manner that met your approval."

Her assertion was like a slap in the face. Kathy wanted to scream at Sylvia to get out, but she couldn't even speak. It was almost as if the truth of the matter were strangling the words in her throat.

"Look, I didn't come here to hurt you," Sylvia began. "We've been friends too long to lie to each other. I know you love your sister. That's why this hurts so much. That's why you can't just show her the door and forget she ever came home. It isn't because of your father being alive. It isn't because you think you have no choice in the matter. It's because you made a choice a long time ago to love her unconditionally."

Kathy felt her defenses drop. "It just hurts so much," she finally whispered.

Sylvia hugged her close. "Sometimes that's how it is with love."

Kathy held on to Sylvia for several minutes. She felt as though she were a lifeline, and if she didn't grab it now, she would drown in a sea of bitterness and sorrow. Her father would die in a short while, and she and Sunny would go their separate ways—maybe forever if she didn't at least try to bridge the past to the future.

"I want to make this better," she cried as Sylvia patted her back.

"I know. I wouldn't have said anything otherwise."

Kathy pulled back. "Just tell me it's worth the effort. Tell me it will be what I need it to be."

Sylvia gave a little laugh. "Only if you tell me that my children will all grow up to be successfully employed, they'll be madly loved by a wonderful Christian mate, and they'll always love the Lord."

Kathy couldn't help smiling as she wiped at her tears. "No guarantees, eh?"

"Not a one."

TEN

KATHY TOSSED AND TURNED IN BED until she decided it was foolish to even try to sleep. The humidity and heat of the night was overpowering any relief the little window fan had to offer. Clad in lightweight sleeping shorts and a tank top, she grabbed her pillow and went out to the porch hammock. Maybe the air would somehow be cooler there. Plus, the hammock wasn't that far from her father's window and sliding glass door. If he needed something, she'd probably hear him call.

She settled into the hammock and closed her eyes to the gentle sway. Kyle had bought this hammock for her father as a birthday gift. He had shown up at the farm with the huge box wrapped in comic strip paper. Her father had praised Kyle for not wasting money on wrapping paper and had loved the gift. Just a few short weeks later, Kyle was out of her life. The memories came unbidden.

"I was wrong to get so angry," Kyle had said in a husky whisper. "Please forgive me. I love you, Kathy. I'll wait for you." He had tried to hold her, but Kathy had pushed him away.

"Don't. I don't want you to wait. I can forgive you for your anger, but not for your lack of understanding." Kathy knew she had to stand her ground. Kyle wasn't able to deal with her mother's illness. The fact that he'd stormed off once before was proof enough.

"I'm sorry for the way I acted, Kathy. I was in shock. I

wish you'd understand that and know that I'm strong enough to help you through this. I do need to consider my career and how to make it all work, but I want to marry you now and help take care of your family."

"It's not your responsibility. In time you would only come to resent us."

"That's a terrible thing to say." He stepped back, the hurt evident in his eyes. "Before your mom took sick, we were about to become a family. . . . Of course they're as much my responsibility as yours."

"But we aren't getting married. I can't. I told you that."

He shook his head. "I don't see why you're doing this. Just tell me to my face that you don't love me. You owe me that much."

"I don't owe you anything. You walked away—remember?"

He narrowed his eyes. "Only after you demanded I get out of your life. Look, I don't understand why you can't marry me and still help your mother. I know you're hurting and afraid, but you don't have to take it out on me—on us."

Without warning Kyle took her in his arms, and Kathy found herself unable to resist. "I don't care how long it takes," he told her. "I don't care what you say. I'll wait for you. You're the only woman I've ever loved. The only woman I will ever love." He kissed her passionately, and Kathy very nearly gave up her resolve to send him away.

A noise—something creaking—wormed its way into her memory. The damp heavy air seemed to pin her in place. "Who's there?" she called.

"It's just me. Sunny."

WHERE MY HEART BELONGS 127

Kathy yawned and forced herself to sit up. "Is something wrong? Is it Dad?"

"No. I couldn't sleep. It was just too hot."

Kathy nodded. The backyard light gave enough illumination to allow them to make out each other's form. Sunny was dressed nearly identically to Kathy and shared the same miserable expression.

"It's not much better out here. I'm drenched—whether by sweat or humidity, I can't say."

"I know. Me too." Sunny slid down the wall and sat on the porch. "I had hoped there'd at least be a breeze out here. California summers never made me so miserable as the ones here."

"You lived in California?" Kathy asked. "When?"

Sunny drew a deep breath. "It was after the trial and my divorce from Mitch. I went there hoping to get together with some friends."

"And did you?" Kathy hoped her tone wouldn't offend. She wanted to better understand her sister.

"Yeah, for all the good it did."

"Can you talk about it? I'd like to know, if you feel like telling the story."

"I needed money. There was the money I had saved for the baby, but it wasn't enough for a lawyer, and I knew I had to divorce Mitch no matter how the trial turned out. Since there were no children involved, it wasn't that difficult to get some pro bono help. Still, I needed funds in order to make my move to California. That's when I remembered the trust fund. I was desperate, Kathy. It was wrong of me to take it, but I wasn't thinking right at all. I needed money to bury Gary, and I needed money to survive. I didn't want to take the money. I knew I wasn't entitled to it."

Kathy felt compassion for her sister. The idea of being alone and having to bury a child, divorce your baby's killer, and endure a court trial was too much for anyone to have to go through.

"I got my divorce while Mitch was waiting to go to trial. He asked to see me, and because I've always been a glutton for punishment, I went. I felt nothing for him. Well, that's not true. I felt a great deal of hatred. I told him it was a good thing he was behind bars, because if he were out on the street I'd kill him for what he did to our baby—to me. It was the only time I ever felt like he was afraid. He told me how sorry he was—that he never meant to lose his temper. I walked away. I couldn't stand his apologies. I knew they weren't sincere." She paused. "You know how that is. You can generally tell when someone is seriously sorry for what he did."

Kathy wondered if her sister was trying to make a point with her about the past, but she said nothing. And in truth she didn't need to, because Sunny was already talking again.

"With my divorce final, I went to my bank and told them I had a trust fund in another state. I gave them the information as best I could and they handled the rest of it. A few days later, I had the money in hand. The thing that always amazed me was the paper work that came with that money."

"What do you mean?"

"The bank here in Hays contacted Dad. He signed the papers for the money to be transferred and the account to be closed."

"What?" Kathy leaned forward. "What are you saying?"

"I'm saying Dad knew I was taking the money, but he didn't protest it. He didn't have to sign the papers. I was twenty-one. But his friend at the bank let him know where I was, because he knew Dad was worried about me. I always figured Dad did what he did as a way of showing me that he was freely giving me the money once again. It almost made me come home."

"I don't believe this. All these years, he's never said anything. How could he do that? He didn't tell me you were alive—he didn't say a word about the money until later when he needed a new tractor and I suggested he use your trust fund money. He told me he couldn't because you had it." Kathy put her hand up to rub her eyes. "I just don't know why he didn't tell me."

"I don't either."

Kathy barely heard her sister. "Every time I've commented on your stealing that money, he's always told me no—that you had the money with his blessing, but I thought it was just figurative. Like he knew you had taken it but wasn't going to prosecute you. Therefore he was giving it to you with his blessing." She sighed and shook her head. "I suppose it doesn't matter now."

"I'm sorry. I thought you knew."

"It's all right. Go on with your story. What did you do after you got the money?" Kathy knew the only way to get past the shock was to hear the rest of Sunny's tale.

"I bought a cheap car and moved to California. From the frying pan into the fire."

"What do you mean?"

Sunny pulled her knees up to her chest and encircled them with her arms. "I hit the floor running when I arrived in LA. I found my friends and easily fell into their lifestyle. They were into partying, and I was into forgetting. I made friends with a guy who had his own band. When he heard I could do keyboards, he asked me to join them. We started playing a few gigs and got to be fairly popular. Somewhere along the way someone got the bright idea to sex up my appearance. I got a whole makeover, including a breast job."

"I wondered about that," Kathy said without thinking.

Sunny laughed. "I figured it was pretty obvious. Randy loved the change—said people would come just to see me if nothing else."

"Randy?"

"My second husband and the leader of the band," Sunny said matter-of-factly. "Randy made me feel special—loved. With Randy I finally felt important."

"You were important and loved here too," Kathy said rather snidely. "You were Mom and Dad's darling sunshine, who could do no wrong."

"Well, I never felt like I could measure up to you."

"Oh, come on now. You had everyone wrapped around your little finger. You even got our piano teacher to change the day of the recital because it interfered with your cheer-leader tryouts. Everyone gave you everything you asked for and more."

"You know, Kathy, I don't know whose childhood you're describing. It wasn't mine. At least not the way I remember it. I thought you had it pretty good."

"I didn't have it all that bad. There were times I was jealous of your abilities. You seemed to make good grades without trying and you were popular. Cheerleader, class president, honor roll student, and never without a boy-friend. You know very well I didn't have any of that."

"But did you even want any of that? You were so focused on going into business with Dad that you put off anything else. Well, except for Kyle. Kyle was always there for you."

"Yes. Yes, he was." Kathy sighed. She really didn't want to regret the way she'd dealt with him, but in light of the present she couldn't help it.

"You never cared about cheerleading—you told me that was nonsense," Sunny added. "So why blame me for enjoy-ing it and wanting it as a part of my life? Actually, you really hurt my feelings back then. I wanted to be a cheerleader for the longest time and you always put me down for it."

Kathy tried to remember such an attitude. "I know I made comments about how the cheerleaders just seemed to be using sexuality to stir things up. You always said, 'If you got it, flaunt it.' Frankly, I just saw that attitude get you into trouble. And I guess I was probably jealous of the attention you got."

"Like I said, I think we're talking about two different people." Sunny paused for a moment. "Don't you see, Kathy? We each have our memories from the past. We saw things through different eyes. It doesn't mean we're wrong in how we felt or what we thought—it just means things were altered by our own views. I'm sorry you were jealous, because in my mind you had nothing to be jealous of. I was miserable."

Kathy needed to move on to something else in order to keep from saying something hurtful. "Tell me more about Randy. You have a ring on your hand—are you still married to him?"

"No. We lived hard and partied harder. We did drugs as if it were our job. We were both hooked on cocaine. At first it was just a little here and there at parties and after gigs. Then it gradually became something we couldn't live without. We used a lot of our money for coke. I lost an amazing amount of weight and thought I looked fantastic. Later, after getting clean, I saw a picture of myself and was shocked. I looked like an old hag. My eyes were sunken, my skin sallow. I was skin and bones, yet my face was puffy."

"Do you still use drugs?"

"No. Like I said, I got clean."

"What made you do that? I mean, it doesn't seem like a very easy thing to quit."

"It wasn't, but I quit because of Randy."

Sunny woke up with the worst headache of her life. She'd forgotten to draw the drapes the night before when she and Randy had tumbled into bed, and now an intense morning light threatened to blind her.

She snuggled down deeper into the covers and Randy's arms, but something wasn't right. Somewhere in the back of her mind she knew something was very, very wrong. Forcing her eyes open once again, she listened for sounds coming from outside the bedroom. She was extremely paranoid that someone had broken into the house. Worse yet—that the cops were raiding the place.

"Randy. Randy, wake up." She shook him while leaning forward to listen. She couldn't hear anything, but that didn't mean they weren't out there. Especially since she and Randy had just bought a large amount of cocaine. No doubt someone had told someone else and the word was out.

"Randy. Wake up." She shook him again but realized he wasn't responding. In fact, he seemed almost stiff to the touch.

Reality wasn't registering in any large dose. "How can you sleep at a time like this?" She looked at the alarm clock at the side of the bed. It read four o'clock.

"Four o'clock?" No way. That meant it was the afternoon. They couldn't have slept away the entire day. She pushed back her long blond hair and tried to remember what day it was. Saturday, wasn't it? Yeah. It was Saturday. They'd celebrated their most successful gig ever last night— just the two of them. Things were looking up and they were going places. An agent had taken note of them and wanted to talk next week.

"Next week," Sunny said and fell back against the pillows. Her paranoia was fading. There was no sense in getting too uptight. She rolled closer to Randy and snuggled up against him. He didn't move.

"Hey, sweetie, wake up. Talk to me," she murmured against his ear. He was face down on the bed with his nose half buried in the sheets.

With a start, Sunny realized his eyes were open, but they didn't seem to see anything. "Randy?" She reached over to touch his face. It was strangely cool. Realization dawned in a terrifying way.

Pushing away from him, Sunny began to scream. "Randy! Randy!" She leaped out of bed and went around to the other side. She shook him hard, but there was no response. Picking up the phone, she dialed 9-1-1 and began to scream at the operator to send an ambulance.

She couldn't stop screaming and was still doing exactly

that when the police and paramedics arrived. She had to be put in restraints by the time they loaded her into a second ambulance.

Randy was dead. They told her later it was a combination of cocaine and alcohol. Worse still, they figured he'd died, probably of a massive heart attack, shortly after collapsing in bed. Sunny couldn't get the image of Randy out of her mind, nor the idea that she'd slept in the arms of a dead man all night and most of the day.

Kathy looked at her sister in disbelief. "What did you do?"

Sunny pressed her hands to her temples. "There wasn't much I was fit to do. I was so hysterical they hospitalized me and kept me sedated for forty-eight hours. I woke up in a violent state of mind when they finally took me off their drugs. I wanted someone to tell me it had all been nothing more than a bad dream. I pleaded with them to get Randy, but they told me he was dead."

"Oh, Sunny, I can't even imagine."

"Nor would I ever want you to," she said sadly. "The nightmares were more than I could bear. I kept feeling Randy's lifeless arms around me. I kept seeing his open-eyed stare. I went into rehab. The doctor told me that getting clean would help me overcome those hideous memories."

"And did it?"

"To a point. It was almost more than I could stand. It was bad enough trying to quit cocaine, but there were other things. The police, the media, our friends. I can still hear them all asking their questions, demanding their answers. Answers that I couldn't give because I had been too high to know what had happened. All I knew then was that some-how a bag of coke that should have lasted us several days was gone. I suppose we'd used it up that night. I really can't be sure."

"Do you ever miss it? I mean, do the urges to use it come back?"

Sunny shook her head. "No. I was lucky . . . blessed, as my friend Lana would say. Rehab was the hardest thing I ever went through, but every time I thought of giving up and quitting, I saw Randy's dead body and knew I couldn't let him down." She straightened her legs and leaned back against the porch wall. "He was such a sweet man. He had the kindest nature and such a gentle spirit. He would listen to me for hours and share ideas and thoughts. I really saw us growing old together. I guess because of the drugs, we did just that."

ELEVEN

THE NEXT DAY KATHY SAT BESIDE her Dad's bed. "Why didn't you tell me that you let her have the money? That you knew where Sunny was and that she was alive?" They had been discussing Sunny's confession for several minutes.

Dad shook his head. "I didn't see how it would matter. She wasn't coming home. She hadn't tried to contact us, and I figured it best to let the past remain in the past and not stir up false hopes. I signed the papers because I wanted her to know that I knew what she was doing—that I knew where she was. I wanted her to know, because I'd hoped it would tell her I still loved her and wanted her to come home."

"Why didn't you at least tell me she was alive? It would have helped to know just that much."

Dad eyed her with an intensity she hadn't seen in months. "Be truthful, Kathy. Would it have helped? You told me around the time Mom died that you figured Mom and Amy were together, because surely Amy wouldn't have been so cruel as to not contact the family after all that time. You said other things as well, but when I learned about Amy being alive and taking the money, I knew it would serve no useful purpose to tell you."

Kathy was hurt by her father's long-ago decision but said nothing. "But all the times I've said something about her stealing that money right from under your nose, you always said—"

"I always said that she didn't steal it, didn't I?" he interjected. "I told you that she had it with my blessing."

Kathy thought back and nodded. "I suppose you did."

"I know I did. I could have prevented her getting the money by taking it out of the account before she turned twenty-one. I knew there was a possibility she would one day try to take that money out. I told my friends at the bank and asked them to let me know if she did. When that happened, I signed the paper work to send a message to Amy . . . Sunshine, that she wasn't fooling anybody."

His weak voice reminded Kathy that she should let him rest. She got to her feet and picked up his breakfast tray. He'd eaten very little. "Do you want the television on? It's Sunday morning and there might be some good preaching to listen to."

"No. Say, have you heard anything from the real-estate agent?"

Kathy didn't want to lie to her father, but neither did she want him fretting about waiting so long to put the farm on the market. "Things are moving along well. We're sure to have a buyer any day."

He smiled and closed his eyes. "That's good. Glad to hear it. I don't want you having to spend much more of your own money to keep up with the expenses. Be sure you keep a good record. I want you paid back first."

"I'll take care of it," Kathy said, knowing at least that much wasn't a lie. She was nearly out of money and wasn't sure what else could be done once her money was gone. It wasn't like she could go and borrow more. There was no telling how much more she'd have to come down on the price of the farm before it finally attracted a buyer. She had to make sure she had enough to pay all the debts once the sale was complete. If she borrowed any more, there definitely wouldn't be much profit.

"I think I'll rest now. Why don't you go to church and let me sleep? I know it's been a long time since you felt you could go. Why not leave Sunny with me and head out?"

The offer was tempting. "I suppose I could." The idea became more appealing to Kathy with every passing moment. "Yes, I think that would be great."

"Good. Just tell her I'm going to sleep for a bit. She can come check on me later." He pulled his covers up despite the growing heat of the day.

Kathy went in search of Sunny and explained. She found Sunny quite content to stay at home. In fact, she told Kathy she'd like to do this for her. Kathy thought about that even as she listened to a visiting missionary give a sermon on extending your love to people who did not love you in return.

I haven't wanted to be in debt to Sunny, so I haven't let her do much with Dad or the house. Sunny had offered several times to help Kathy with packing or gardening, but Kathy had been too prideful to accept that help.

She does seem different, but what if it's all some kind of a game? What if she's just playing us so she can get more money? She might have learned that Dad was dying and figured to come here and get in on the inheritance.

The church service soon concluded and Kathy found several people approaching her.

"We haven't seen you in ages. How's your dad?" Gayle Murphy, an old friend of Kathy's mom, questioned.

"He's very weak. The doctor is amazed he's still here," Kathy admitted.

"Is it true your sister came home? I heard from my cousin that Amy is back in town."

"That's what I was going to ask you about," Donna Meyers said. "My Jim came home saying that Amy was back."

"She changed her name to Sunshine," Renea Stover said as she joined the group. "And it's all true. I ran into her in the store. She was uppity as ever. She always thought herself better than the rest of us."

Kathy frowned. She couldn't imagine Sunny acting uppity with anyone. She had changed—just as she'd pointed out to Kathy. Whether it was a permanent change or whether it was put on for the purpose of impressing remained to be seen.

"What has your dad had to say about it?" Donna asked, ignoring her teenage son, who waited impatiently to go.

"Dad said it was answered prayer," Kathy finally replied. "He feels he can die in peace now."

"Too bad your mother couldn't have done the same thing," Mrs. Stover snapped.

"We did our best for Mom," Kathy said defensively.

Renea's hard expression softened just a bit. "Of course you did. Poor thing. You did everything a good daughter should. You sacrificed your life to care for your folks—that's a mighty selfless act. Don't think we don't know what your choice cost. Your sister's choices were completely based on her own needs—she didn't think of anyone else."

The word choice struck Kathy, but she couldn't comment because Mrs. Stover was already continuing with her tirade. "Marg was my dearest friend and we talked long hours about you girls. She knew her youngest was trouble. She told me that nearly every time we got together." Renea patted Kathy's arm, no doubt intending to show support, but Kathy only wanted to jerk her arm away and be left alone.

"Your sister was cruel to leave. She was even more heartless to let no one know she was safe and alive. People with a conscience just don't do things like that. How hard would it have been to drop a postcard to the family? She killed Marg as sure as her heart did."

No one, including Kathy, seemed to want to contradict the statement. *How can I?* Kathy asked herself. *I've said the same thing many times.* The only thing was, hearing it from Renea Stover made it sound so hardhearted and unforgiving. The situation made Kathy feel rather awkward.

"Where was she all these years?" Gayle questioned. Gayle had fared better in Mom's absence. Kathy knew the loss had hit her mother's friends hard, but where Renea had become bitter and hostile, Gayle had seemed to accept it as a part of life.

"Various places," Kathy admitted. "I don't know a whole lot, but she had a pretty hard time of it."

"Serves her right. God's punishment for her wickedness," Renea quickly put in.

"I suppose some might see it that way," Kathy said.

"If they're smart they do," Renea said. "God won't be mocked. He doesn't put up with nonsense like that. He let your sister suffer so that she could understand the wrong she'd done."

"Suffer the consequences of her actions," Donna agreed.

Kathy couldn't agree more, but on the other hand, was God really into letting people suffer the death of children and husbands as a means of putting them in their place? Was that God's idea of justice? She didn't find it very comforting to see God as someone who would take a child from his mother to punish her. Besides, Mitch had killed baby Gary. God wouldn't have condoned Mitch's actions. Yet He had allowed it. Kathy rubbed her temple.

". . . and that's why I wouldn't let her stay," Renea Stover concluded, drawing a deep breath.

Kathy realized she'd heard little of what the woman had said. "I'm sorry. I have a headache. I should probably head home."

"It's no wonder you have a headache," Gayle said sympathetically. "I'm not sure how you do all that you do. You have such a sweet nature and pure heart. Your motives are evident. Your father and mother would be very proud of you. You've suffered in silence and now have to deal with your sister's unfeeling actions. I agree with Renea. I'd tell her to leave."

"It's really not up to me," Kathy said, feeling less and less like discussing the matter. She knew her heart wasn't as sweet and pure as the others were suggesting. "It's Dad's place and he's delighted to have her back."

"Poor thing." Renea again patted her arm. "To think after all you've given up, you would have to endure this as well. Sometimes it seems there is no justice."

"Really I'm fine, but thanks for your concern." Kathy shifted her purse from one arm to the other. "I need to go now."

They bid her good-bye, following her outside.

"If you need to talk, Kathy, you have my number," Renea called. "You don't owe your sister anything. She took what didn't belong to her and did irreparable damage to your family. She doesn't deserve your kindness."

Kathy got into her car with those words echoing in her head. "Irreparable damage?" she murmured as she put the air-conditioning on high. Was the situation irreparable? Was this matter too big, even for God to make right?

"But do I want it made right?" Kathy wondered as she drove home. She knew the Bible called for her to forgive her sister, but so far Kathy couldn't find the way to do that. She still had so much anger and hurt—twelve years' worth built up inside and firmed in place with an equal amount of bitterness and regret.

"She's had a bad life," Kathy reasoned aloud. "I've had sorrow with Mom's death and Dad's condition, but I haven't had to live the life Sunny's had to endure. I should forgive, but it's so hard. I loved Amy so much and it was like she threw that love back in my face."

Something the missionary said came to mind: "*Often-times we reach out to people who would rather not be reached. We love people who reject our love and would just as soon spit in our face, but Jesus asks us to go on loving—go on reaching. It's easy to love someone when they love us, but so much harder to love when we are treated poorly by that person.*"

Sylvia had said it was as if Kathy's love for Sunny was conditional upon doing things Kathy's way. Was that true? Kathy wrestled with her thoughts all the way home.

She was surprised to spy Dad and Sunny sitting on the front porch together. Dad would no doubt be exhausted. Sunny should have known better than to encourage such a thing. Of course, maybe the full extent of Dad's illness wasn't yet real to Sunny.

Kathy hated to leave the crisp coolness of her car for the heat of the day. The wind whipped at her long broomstick skirt as she made her way to the porch, but it was a hot, heavy air that offered little comfort.

"What are you doing out here? Dad, you'll wear yourself out."

"Not for long," he replied, sounding surprisingly clear-headed.

"Sunny, it really wasn't wise to do this."

"Sunny only helped me do what I asked her to," Dad countered. "She had no say in this. I told her I intended to sit on my porch, and if she wanted to come along she could."

Kathy could see that Sunny was uncomfortably caught in the middle. "I understand how that goes. You can be a real pill sometimes." She smiled and made her way to the door. "I'm going to change my clothes and then I'll start lunch."

"Why don't you wait? Sit here with us for a little while," Dad encouraged.

Kathy drew a deep breath and held it for a moment. She wanted to be considerate of Dad and even of Sunny, but she feared where this threesome conversation might lead. If Dad tried to force the issue of forgiveness, Kathy wasn't sure what she'd do or say. She knew he wanted her and Sunny to set things right, but Kathy didn't feel like she could do that just yet. Still, she saw the hopefulness in his eyes.

"All right," she said against her better judgment. She pulled up one of the metal chairs and took a seat.

"I've been explaining some things to Sunny," Dad began. "I thought some of it you should hear as well."

"Like what?" Kathy asked. Suspicion mounted as she thought of all sorts of changes he might be contemplating. Changes to plans long made and put into motion.

"Well, for instance, I told her how you and I had taken care of arranging for the farm and the funeral. I wanted Sunny to understand some of the decisions I've made over the last few years."

"Such as?" Kathy was afraid to make any comment, and it seemed less risky to ask questions instead.

"Such as the fact that I put you in charge of my will and that I left everything to you."

Kathy looked at Sunny as if to determine her thoughts on the matter. She didn't have to wonder long.

"Which I think is only fair," Sunny threw in. "With all things considered."

"Did you tell her that a good portion of the farm sale will go to cover the loan you took out to cover medical bills—Mom's and yours?"

"I did. I also told her that I felt you deserved whatever was left and then some, especially because you've exhausted your trust fund keeping this place running."

"I would have rather neither one of you knew about that," Kathy said.

"You can't hide things like that, Kathy," Dad said, shaking his head. "I'm sorry it's come to that, but I mean to see it made up to you, and Sunny agrees."

Sunny nodded. Kathy could feel her sister's tension. She seemed very concerned that Kathy understand her position. "Well, so long as we're all in agreement," Kathy finally said.

"Look, I'm still happy to help you in any way I can," Sunny stated. "I didn't come back here for money. I came back to try to make a new start with my family. I want to help if I can."

"I think you ought to be a great help to your sister," Dad said in a tired voice. "There's still a lot to be done—even though we worked out all the details." He turned to Kathy. "I've been talking to Sunny about the auction we planned. But I do have a small request. I want you two to go through things and keep what you want. Even keep it all. Kathy, I'd like you to share the things in the house with Sunny."

Kathy hadn't really thought about it until now. A part of her rejected the idea as unfair, but another part thought it more than appropriate. Many of the things here were mementoes from their childhood. They would mean just as much to Sunny, no doubt, as they did to Kathy. "Sure. No problem," she replied.

"And there's one other thing," her father said.

Kathy stiffened as she waited for him to continue. *Please don't ask me to forgive her. I'm already battling myself over this. God knows I'm trying to understand the past and let it go, but it hurts so much.* She sat looking at the table in order to avoid her father's and sister's eyes. Had they been plotting all morning how to approach her? Had Sunny conspired to press for this premature reconciliation?

"I'd like Sunny to stay here until the sale of the farm is complete."

Kathy looked up at this. She turned to her sister, ready to question her on the matter, but Sunny was looking at Dad with an expression that betrayed her lack of knowledge on this latest development.

Dad quickly continued. "This is my idea, Kathy. Sunny knew nothing about this. I don't know if Sunny has to be someplace. I don't know if she has a job or family that needs her to return, but I think it would be good for all of us—especially you two—if she stayed here until you move. You said things were going well and that the farm sale won't be long in concluding. You two can use that time to get to know each other again and help each other deal with my passing."

"I suppose so," Kathy said, but her heart wasn't really in it. She hadn't considered how long Sunny might stay but figured it wouldn't be much past Dad's death. Her real fear was that the farm wouldn't sell. If that happened, she'd be in Colorado having to earn money enough to meet the mortgage and utilities or face losing the place. There was always the possibility she could rent the house out and have Tony keep farming the land, but she doubted that would be too successful. No one in this area could afford the kind of rent she'd need to make to cover her payments.

"I don't have long, girls. I know that. I feel it more every day. There's nothing more for me here. Sunny's come home. Kathy's provided for, and I feel I've done all I ever needed to do. I'm not afraid to die, and I don't want you girls being afraid to let me go. I don't want you to be all mournful and sad."

"But I'll miss you," Kathy told him. "We've been together so much these last few years."

"And we shouldn't have been," he countered, his voice ever weakening. "You should have been with Kyle or at least someone who could comfort you after I'm gone."

"I'll be here for her," Sunny promised.

Kathy found it hard to put any stock in her sister's words.

She had said something similar long ago. Pledging her undying love—her promise to always be there. That had clearly meant nothing to her, so why should this time be any different?

"Look, Dad, you need to get to bed. I can see for myself that you aren't feeling well. Please let me help you back and get your medicine."

He nodded. "So long as you promise Sunny can stay. You two can work together to get her room set up so she can be comfortable. Just put all the stuff in my old room and sort it there."

"I'll take care of everything," Kathy promised. "Sunny can stay as long as she wants." She forced a smile as she glanced Sunny's way.

Kathy couldn't identify the feelings that coursed through her as she helped her father back into the house. Sunny had gone to the kitchen for the medicine, and Kathy was actually glad for this. She needed time to think on all that had just happened. Sunshine seemed so sincere about everything Dad had presented. She didn't seem to mind about the inheritance, but that didn't mean she wasn't putting on an act for Dad.

But it doesn't seem like an act, Kathy thought. *Maybe she honestly means everything she's saying. Maybe her heart really has changed.*

"Thank you, Kathy," Dad murmured as she lifted his legs up on the bed. He was so weak he couldn't manage it himself.

"It's not a problem, but you shouldn't have stayed out there so long," she said as she arranged all the pillows.

"I meant . . . for Sunny. Thank you for agreeing that she could stay."

"Dad, it's your house."

"But I want it to be more than that. I want you to let her stay because you want to work things out."

Kathy frowned. "I honestly don't know what I want, Dad. I'm trying to figure that out, but it hasn't been easy. Having Sunny come back has been a big shock. I doubt it would have been more shocking had I opened the door to find Mom on the other side."

Her father gave a weak laugh. "It would have been more shocking to me."

Kathy adjusted the last pillow as Sunny came into the room. "Here we go. I have the medicine and the apple juice. A feast to be sure."

"There are enough pills there to make a guy feel full up," Dad said, closing his eyes. "I'll be glad when it's all behind me."

Kathy exchanged a look with her sister. Sunny's eyes instantly dampened with tears. Perhaps seeing Dad this way was harder on her sister than Kathy had given credit for. After all, Kathy had had a long time to prepare for their father's death, but it was all new to Sunny.

TWELVE

LATER SUNDAY AFTERNOON Kathy began clearing out the mess in Sunny's old room. She hadn't gotten far, so the next morning she headed back up before it got too hot. The sky promised rain, which Kathy prayed would cool things down, but knew it could only serve to make the air stickier.

Most of the stuff from Sunny's old room was in boxes. After Mom had died, Kathy had boxed up the junk left behind by Sunny. Mom had left it like a shrine to her younger daughter, but Kathy found the entire matter too difficult to face on a daily basis. Packing Sunny's childhood memorabilia had given Kathy a measure of closure.

The remaining boxes and furniture were from the attic. She'd meant to deal with most of it long before now, but time had gotten away from her.

"Some of this stuff isn't even good enough to give away," she said, holding up an old worn blouse her mother had probably owned for over thirty years. She decided in that moment Dad had a good idea. Just clear the stuff out—put it in his and Mom's old room, then sort it there. Not only was there more room in the master bedroom, but it would take less time to get Sunny installed in her old room that way.

Kathy spent the next half hour moving box after box to her parents' old room. She was down to a few mismatched pieces of furniture when she realized she had no idea where Sunny was. It would have been nice to have had her help.

The house seemed so quiet that Kathy felt certain her sister must have slipped out. Kathy glanced at her watch and knew Dad would probably be sound asleep.

The furniture wasn't that hard to move—it was mostly small stuff, awkward to carry but not heavy. When it was all completed Kathy stood in the doorway to the room she'd always thought of as off limits, especially as a child, and felt a little nostalgic. Her parents' room had always been a very private place, but at the same time Kathy knew it to be a refuge when they'd been young. Many a bad dream had been dissolved by going to her mother's bedside.

The old wallpaper had seen better days. Kathy remembered when her mother had put it up. She and Amy had gone off to elementary school and when they returned, Mom was finishing up the last strip. She was so proud of the job she'd done, pointing out how she'd carefully aligned the roses in the floral design.

Their furniture, now hidden by boxes, was mostly mismatched pieces passed down through the family. They'd inherited the bed when Kathy's great-grandmother had passed away, and Aunt Glynnis had left the large dresser with her brother when she'd moved from Kansas to Colorado.

There were other items—just as nondescript and unfashionable as the bed and dresser—but they were soon to be sold at auction. Before she knew it, the entire house would be nothing more than empty rooms and memories.

Kathy tried not to be sad about the changes. She fervently believed that God had a plan in all things, though it had been hard to remember that since Sunny's arrival. Closing the door behind her, Kathy decided it was time to go find Sunny and share the news. Her room was nearly ready for occupancy.

Kathy wondered if Sunny would like being in her old room again. Kathy knew it would have to be cleaned, but she figured Sunny could help with that. She had, after all, been offering to help since she'd arrived at the farm.

Downstairs was completely silent. Kathy checked on Dad before beginning her search for Sunny. Peeking in so as not to disturb her father, Kathy could see he appeared to be resting comfortably.

Searching through the living room and kitchen proved futile, but catching movement through the kitchen window, Kathy decided to check out in the yard. Perhaps Sunny had gone there to enjoy the morning.

Kathy went out the back door and looked around. She frowned, realizing the yard was deserted. The barn door was open, however. Maybe Sunny was inside. Kathy went to check, but again found the area deserted. It was then she heard voices. Had someone come to the farm?

The conversation sounded one-sided, however. As Kathy retraced her steps and went to the far side of the barn, she realized her sister was the only one present. Her words were intended for the purpose of petitioning God and no one else.

"I need help, Lord. I cannot do this without you. Sometimes it's so lonely and so difficult. I want to be patient, but I also want to see this made right. I know I don't really have a right to expect things to work out—nothing else short of coming to know you has gotten me much of anyplace, but please hear me. Please stop sending me problems and give me some solutions instead."

Kathy bit her lower lip. She was a part of the problems Sunny talked about—not one of the solutions. That thought really bothered her. All of her life she'd wanted to be helpful to people—offer answers and fix problems. But she certainly wasn't in that position in her sister's life.

Clearing her throat, Kathy advanced around the barn, hoping her sister would hear her coming and not realize she'd been eavesdropping. "Oh, hello." Kathy noted that Sunny had a small trowel and was on her knees before one of Mom's prized rosebushes.

"I hope you don't mind," Sunny said, looking up like a child caught sneaking out of bed.

"Not at all. I've been meaning to get out here for ages."

"The roses are so pretty. Do you ever cut some for the table?"

Kathy noted the abundance of yellow tea roses. "I think that would be a wonderful idea. There are some scissors for that in the kitchen drawer."

"I'll get them in a minute. I can't believe they've grown so full. You've done a good job of keeping them. I always figured they'd only grow for Mom."

"That's what I thought the first couple of years after she was gone. They really seemed to suffer. I read up on rose care—even talked to several of her friends. Finally they pulled through."

"What will you do with them now? I mean with the sale and everything."

"I had thought to take at least one or two with me to Colorado. I'm hoping to buy a place of my own where I can plant them. Of course, I should probably find a job first. Uncle Will says he can get me on at the pharmaceutical company, but I don't know." She let her voice trail off. The last thing she needed was to get in a conversation with Sunny about Kyle. But in truth, Kyle would probably determine whether Kathy wanted to go to work for Jackson Pharmaceuticals.

"I think transplanting them sounds like a good idea," Sunny said rather wistfully.

"I could dig up a couple for you too. If you have a place for them." Sunny quickly looked away, and Kathy couldn't help but wonder about it. For all the stories Sunny had shared, she still hadn't said too much about her current circumstance.

"I keep meaning to ask you about where you live now," Kathy said, watching Sunny grow increasingly uncomfortable. "Do you have someone waiting for you? Did you remarry and have a family? We just haven't talked much about what you left behind."

"I'd rather not talk about it."

Kathy couldn't imagine, after all the other things Sunny had shared, that this could possibly be a problem. "Why not? Don't I have a right to know?" Even as she said it Kathy knew it was a stupid thing to say.

"Don't I have a right to know what's going on with the sale of the farm?"

"That's different," Kathy said. "You have no reason to distrust me."

Sunny got to her feet. "So that's what it's about? Trust? Fine. Maybe you think I should trust you, but I don't. Not with my heart." She stomped off without another word, leaving Kathy stunned by her actions.

Sunny hadn't meant to run away from Kathy's questions, but at the moment they were just too hard. Kathy needed to understand that she couldn't simply demand answers and get them. Sunny felt her heart pounding a beat that seemed to accelerate with every step she took.

She drove into Slocum, realizing she would have to answer to Kathy when she got home. It had been rude and selfish to act the way she had, but honestly she was running out of patience and time. There was something waiting for her back in California, but for now she just wanted to forget about it.

Without really meaning to, Sunny ended up at Debbie's house. The old Victorian three-story had been restored to its original charm and seemed to outshine all the other houses in the neighborhood.

Sunny sat for a minute in the car and thought about how her life might have been different had she stayed here in Slocum. She and Debbie might have been neighbors. They might have planned get-togethers with each other's families and celebrated birthdays and anniversaries together. A sadness washed over her and she let out a sigh.

"Why did I think it would be so much easier—so much better out there away from home? Why couldn't I see the truth of things for myself—even then?"

She supposed a part of her had known there was no ideal place or person, but in her heart Sunny knew that the old Amy had been convinced that while she might not find "ideal," she was bound to find "pretty good"—but not in Slocum.

The idea of having wasted her life was something that haunted Sunny. She'd been married and pregnant, abused and neglected. She'd seen a taste of fame and fortune, as well as real love.

"But here I sit, back in Slocum," she murmured and shook her head. It just seemed there was something God wanted to teach her that wasn't getting through.

She got out of the car and walked up the steps of the beautiful whitewashed porch. Several chairs surrounded a couple of small tables on the porch, and toys were scattered around the floor. Obviously this was a gathering place for the family. Sunny smiled at the thought and imagined them all seated there enjoying the end of a day.

"I thought I heard someone pull up," Debbie said, opening the screen door. "I'm so glad you came by for a visit."

"I feel bad just barging in," Sunny admitted. She liked the carefree way Debbie had styled her hair by pulling it back into a ponytail. But to give it a bit of extra attention she had put a rhinestone barrette on either side of her head. She didn't have any makeup on, yet the natural glow of her complexion was perfect.

"Nobody worries about calling ahead around here. Everybody just kind of owns everybody. You remember how it was."

Sunny nodded. "Part of the reason I left."

Debbie smiled. "I remember your list of grievances against Slocum, Kansas. Hey, do you want to come in or sit out here? We spend a lot of time out here."

"I figured as much. It looks like a comfortable place."

"It is. Why don't we start here and then I can give you a tour."

"Where are your boys?"

"In Hays with Marty's folks. It's kind of nice to have the

time to myself. I just finished painting one of the upstairs rooms."

Sunny took a seat on one of the chairs, settling into the comfortable thick cushions. Debbie pulled her chair a little closer and sat. Down the street a man Sunny didn't recognize was watering his lawn, but otherwise the neighborhood was pretty quiet.

"Is it always like this?" she asked. "So still and relaxing?"

"For the most part. Several of the neighborhood ladies are at the church for one of their regular meetings. They're probably finalizing plans for the Fourth of July celebration. There's usually a big potluck picnic at the church and then fireworks. It's always a lot of fun. I hope you can make it."

"It's hard to believe the Fourth is coming right up. Seems like just yesterday we were celebrating the new year."

"I've noticed time goes a lot faster now," Debbie agreed.

"So you mentioned how things went for you and Marty. Where did everyone else end up?" There had been only twelve kids in their rural graduating class and most of them had been pretty close. Sunny had a feeling the others had remained that way.

"Well, let's see. Ruddy ended up in the army, and I lost track of him. His folks moved back East after the railroad pulled out. The Gruber twins went off to college and never came back." Debbie bit her lower lip and gazed to the ceiling. "Hmm." She seemed momentarily stumped. "I know that Kate and Jean moved to Topeka. They always were inseparable friends. They're both married now and have families, but I don't really remember how many or what sex." She laughed. "I haven't tried to think of where every-body went for a long time."

"I figured most would have stuck around here," Sunny said. The tally had already accounted for over half their class and only Debbie and Marty were still here.

"Well, Christopher did. He lives here with his wife and kids. He married Cara Lewis. She was two years behind us—remember?"

"I do. They were an item from grade school. I can't imagine having a romance like that."

Debbie picked at the lint on a cushion. "They still seem very much in love. They've got six kids and own a nice farm on the north side. The old Carlson place."

Sunny found all the references familiar. Funny how the childhood memories and information were firmly etched in her mind. "I always liked that farm. It was so well man-aged."

"I did too." Debbie rocked for a moment in her chair. "Oh, did you know that Linda Marshall died? It was a car-train accident up near Lindsborg."

"No, I didn't know about that." Sunny thought of the terminally happy Linda. "That's so sad."

"It really was. She'd just gotten a teaching job at the college there. I saw her a couple of days before she was killed. She told me she had never been happier. Felt her whole life was just about to start in earnest. Instead, it was ending. It really made me think about how frail life is."

Sunny nodded. "I had to learn that lesson too. When you're young you think you'll live forever and that nothing can ever really be all that bad. Boy, was I wrong."

Debbie looked at her oddly. "How so?"

Sunny stiffened. "It's not important. There have just been some nasty bumps along the way. So who's left?" She did a mental tally. "What happened to Jasmine and Rachel?"

"Rachel's still here. She married and divorced Barry Sutton. He moved to Alaska, I think. She stayed here with her two kids and lives with her mom. Her dad died last winter. Jasmine left for California when you took off."

"Yeah, we were all going to go together with her sister and a couple of her sister's friends. Instead, I decided to stay in Las Vegas. I met up with her again in California, but lost track of where she went after that."

"Well, that's everyone. Not too many stayed and only a couple showed up for the ten-year reunion. I guess that's the way of it. The town is dying out. Some say if Hays grows big enough, Slocum will thrive again as a bedroom community."

"Is that likely?"

Debbie shrugged. "I suppose it's as likely as anything. Hays has grown so much since we were kids, I think it's possible."

"I did notice that," Sunny replied. "I was just there the other day."

"So what about you? Did you marry and have children? Where's your family?"

Sunny found herself back on the same topic she'd avoided with Kathy. "I did marry and have children, but I'd rather not talk about it right now. I'm sorry."

"No problem." Debbie got to her feet. "Why don't I show you around? The backyard is really incredible. My mother-in-law was a master gardener, as you probably remember. She planted the most amazing arrangements of flowers and shrubs."

Sunny appreciated Debbie's ability to let the matter drop. Most people would have encouraged her to talk or badgered her for answers. Debbie seemed content to let it go. Maybe that's why Sunny had always liked Debbie.

❧ ❧ ❧

Kathy was folding the last of her mother's clothes when she heard a car pull into the driveway. It was nearly supper-time, and she supposed it was Sunny. Within a few minutes that was confirmed by her sister coming through the front door, a large brown paper sack in hand.

"I got us Chinese food. I hope you still like it."

Kathy nodded in surprise. "You went all the way to Hays?"

Sunny smiled sheepishly. "I figured I owed you an apol-ogy and thought it might be better received with a gift of Cashew Chicken and Crab Wontons."

Kathy laughed in spite of herself. "Of course. That always makes it easier." She got up and led the way to the kitchen. "Let me get some plates."

Sunny put the bag down on the kitchen table. "I am sorry for the way I acted. I will talk to you about it all, but just give me a little time. Please."

Kathy turned with dishes in hand. She could see the ear-nest sorrow in her sister's eyes. "I'm in no hurry." She felt a tenderness for Sunny that she'd not yet experienced since her return. It was funny how her feelings seemed to be changing in stages. It was kind of like when her foot would go to sleep after she'd been sitting cross-legged for a long while. At first it was all numb and dead. Then as the blood rushed back in, it would tingle—even be painful. Then little by little the feeling would come back. That was how this felt. Maybe she did want the feelings to be restored.

"I'm starved," Kathy finally said, putting the plates on the table. "Time got away from me."

"What have you been doing?" Sunny asked as she began to pull things from the sack.

"I packed up all of Mom's old clothes. We can give them to Goodwill or the Salvation Army over in Hays. I've been packing up some of Dad's too. He wants to be buried in his overalls—just like he lived most of his life."

"I think that's the way it should be. And a baseball cap on his head."

Kathy smiled. "He already has it picked out."

Sunny laughed. "Why am I not surprised?"

It was almost like the old days, before Amy got to be so cantankerous and selfish. Kathy decided to plunge ahead. "Look, you might as well know what's going on," she began. "I pleaded last year with Dad to put the farm on the market. Sales were good around here and farms were surprisingly hot commodities. With the lower interest rates, everyone seemed to be able to go for something bigger and better, you know."

Sunny nodded. "I remember . . . we bought a house." She looked up at Kathy. "I'll tell you about it in a minute. Go on."

"Well, Dad didn't want to move. He figured he'd beaten the cancer and would get stronger. The doctors told him he had a fifty percent chance of it recurring, but Dad wanted to be optimistic. So instead of selling, we consolidated the debts and took out a bigger mortgage on the farm. The only problem was that the crop yields were poor and we went through the money pretty fast. One thing led to another, and I began dipping into my trust fund to pay the bills. Then the doctor gave us the news about Dad, and I realized things weren't going to get any better. Dad did too."

"So he let you put the farm on the market?"

"Finally. But it was too late to cash in on the boom that had been going on in the fall. By the time we listed it, several other farms were up for sale in the area, so local people had their choices."

"What's happening now?"

Kathy didn't try to hide her discouragement. "Nothing. No one has shown much interest. We're going to advertise in Kansas City and elsewhere, but I'm beginning to think it will take a miracle to sell the place very soon."

Sunny grew thoughtful. She appeared to be considering the matter for several minutes before she finally spoke. "I want to help with all of this. I know you have to get things put in order for the auction. I can help if you just tell me what to do."

"Well, I moved all that stuff out of your bedroom and into Mom and Dad's old room. We can start going through it later."

"You cleared out my room? I would have helped. I'm so sorry. I got caught up talking with Debbie this morning and before I knew it I'd decided to drive to Hays and get the food. If I'd known . . ."

"It doesn't matter. It wasn't a big deal. I just moved

everything out of there. It still needs some sprucing up—dusting and sweeping—but there are clean sheets on the bed. And you'll need to take your suitcases up. I didn't have time."

"I sure wouldn't have expected you to. Kathy, thank you. I really appreciate it."

Kathy spooned some rice onto her plate. It was good to be at peace with Sunny. Even if just for a little while. She knew their problems were far from resolved, but something was happening in her heart. Maybe in time, she could learn to forgive her sister for the pain of the past.

THIRTEEN

"AUNT GLYNNIS! UNCLE WILL! I'm so glad you're here." Kathy embraced them both and pulled back with tears in her eyes. "I don't know how much longer Dad has. He hasn't even asked to get out of bed in days and he's not eating at all. The pain is bad, but he doesn't want to take much in the way of medication, so he can stay coherent."

"Well, I'll talk to him about that," Glynnis said, in true big sister fashion. "He always was much too stubborn for his own good."

Glynnis was a beautiful woman. She had defied the years by taking good care of herself and living right. Dressed impeccably in a casual linen slack suit, she had just the right balance of makeup and jewelry to appear elegant, but not ostentatious. Kathy had always admired Glynnis and the way she presented herself.

Uncle Will, on the other hand, was more Kansas farm boy than pharmaceutical genius. He had gotten an education and became a pharmacist in Hays at a fairly young age. He worked there for several years before a growing interest in researching drugs had sent him to Jackson Pharmaceuticals. His interest had spilled over to spark Kyle's fascination about the industry one summer when Will and Glynnis had come to stay at the farm for a visit.

Kathy led them down the hall. "He mostly sleeps, but he insists that we come and talk to him as often as possible. I told him that I hated to wake him, but he always says there won't be time to talk later, and I know he's right."

Glynnis patted her arm. "You're doing the best for him. Letting him die at home like he wants is a huge blessing." She looked around as they stopped outside the den. "Where's Sunny?"

Kathy had forgotten to tell them. "She went to town. One of her friends invited her over. We didn't know exactly when you'd arrive, so she figured to go ahead."

"Of course she should. There'll be time for us to talk tonight. How's it going with her?"

Kathy shrugged. She could see the concern in her aunt's and uncle's expressions. "I think it's better. I don't feel quite so hostile all the time. I've started listening more."

Glynnis smiled. "God has a way of showing us what we need to see."

"We can talk more after you get in a visit with Dad."

"Good. That sounds just fine."

"I'll also start some lunch for us. We have some early tomatoes this year. How about BLTs?"

"Yum!" Uncle Will replied enthusiastically. "I think I could put away a couple of those."

"You got it," Kathy said. "And you?" she asked, turning back to her aunt.

"Just one should suffice for me. I'll get as fat as he is if I don't watch myself."

Kathy laughed and opened the door to the den. "Dad, look who's here."

He opened his eyes and smiled as recognition dawned. "Come to boss me around, did you?" His voice was raspy and weak.

"Somebody has to," Glynnis said, going to him. "Just

look at you. Lying around, doing nothing." She leaned down and kissed his forehead. "Still ornery as ever."

"Not for long." He met her eyes and Kathy could see he was trying to tell her that the end was near.

Glynnis nodded and squeezed his hand. "I know." She took the chair beside his bed and Uncle Will pulled up another.

"Looks like your girls are taking good care of you," Will offered.

Dad perked up at this. "They are. Did Kathy tell you about Sunny?"

"She sure did," Glynnis answered as Will nodded. "What a blessing for you."

Kathy backed toward the door. She figured it would do them good to have time to talk. Dad might want to say things to his sister that he'd rather not tell his children.

"I don't think I ever wanted anything as much as to see that girl again," Dad said as Kathy reached the door.

She felt a twinge of jealousy. She still couldn't understand how he could say things like that. Sunny had hurt him—and devastated Mom. How could he feel the same way about her? There was no pretense or sheltering of his heart. He gave his love to Sunny as freely as if she'd never disappointed him or caused him grief.

"What's she like now, Gary?"

"In the good ways, she's the same old Amy—even if she changed her name."

"Ah, a rose by any other name," Will said with a chuckle.

"Exactly. She's had a rough life, but her old sweetness and personality manage to come through."

Kathy contemplated this as she stepped into the hall. Dad said that in the good ways Amy was the same, but Kathy couldn't really see it. "Maybe because I don't want to see it," she chided herself.

Making her way to the kitchen, Kathy realized she felt a sense of relief just in having her aunt and uncle around. Her aunt had been very supportive when Kathy's mom had passed away. Even living in Colorado Springs, she had driven over from time to time to keep Kathy company. Kathy had always figured it was really more for her father's sake than her own, but having Glynnis around had done wonders. Glynnis had been quite unwilling to let either Kathy or her father slip away into sorrow and despair. She'd often told Kathy that was what family was for. They were to support and bear each other's grief. Sunny had promised to be there for Kathy, but they'd been children then. Could she be believed or trusted now?

Kathy sliced two large, juicy tomatoes. The aroma only served to make her hungrier. The bacon fried up nicely on the stove as Kathy completed the fixings. She had the sandwiches ready to slap together by the time Glynnis and Will rejoined her. They took seats at the table and reached for their iced tea at the same time. Glynnis took a long drink, then looked to Kathy.

"He's more gone than here, isn't he?"

Kathy brought a bowl of potato salad to the table and nodded. "I believe the end will be very soon. But I've been thinking that since the beginning of June, and the days just slip by with him hanging on."

"He's faded so fast," Will commented. "I didn't figure he'd be this bad."

"When he saw the doctor in May and realized there was nothing more to do, the fight went out of him. I can't say that I blame him. He and I talked about it on the way home from Hays. He even had me swing into the cemetery so he could visit Mom's grave. He talked about his own funeral the whole time. Told me how he wanted things done at the church."

"I think that was probably the only way for him to work through the finality of it all," Glynnis said. "We tend to want to do something reasonable and logical when everything seems so out of control."

"I hadn't realized how he was hanging on for Sunny until she got here. Now he's growing worse by the day."

"He has nothing left to wait on," Will said. "He's ready to go home."

They blessed the food and dug in while the kitchen ceiling fan clicked rhythmically overhead. Soon she heard the front screen door open. Apparently Sunny had returned. "We're in the kitchen," she called, getting to her feet.

Sunny came into the room, looking almost scared. Her eyes were wide. "Aunt Glynnis," she whispered as she stood at the door. Kathy saw her stiffen even more as she took in the cozy luncheon scene. It was almost like she was steeling herself against whatever criticism might be coming.

Glynnis got to her feet and went to Sunny without a single word. She opened her arms and pulled Sunny into a tight embrace. Kathy watched Sunny relax against her aunt's hold.

"Welcome home, darling. I'm so glad to see you again."

Will was on his feet still holding his napkin. He smiled as Glynnis led Sunny to the table. "Look here, Will. Isn't she the spitting image of her mother?"

"She sure is. You're a sight for sore eyes, Amy. Whoops, I mean Sunshine."

"Call me Sunny. Everyone does," she told them. "I would have come home sooner had I known you were already here. We didn't figure you'd be in until later today."

"We got a really early start," Glynnis said as they took their seats again.

"Sunny, are you hungry?" Kathy was already reaching for an extra plate before her sister could answer. She suddenly felt the need to make everything seem as normal as possible.

"I'm famished, actually." She smiled and sat down between her aunt and uncle. "So how was your trip?"

Glynnis picked up her napkin. "It was pretty nice. The weather has been beautiful and there wasn't much traffic."

"Have you visited Dad?" she asked, taking the plate that Kathy offered.

"Yes, we chatted with him a bit before sitting down to lunch. I hadn't expected to see him quite this far gone," Glynnis admitted.

"Kathy and I are actually surprised he's still hanging on."

"Your dad was always a strong man," Will offered.

Sunny picked up a couple of slices of bread and began to build her sandwich. "That's true."

"You don't suppose there's something else he's waiting to see happen, do you?" Glynnis questioned.

The thought pierced Kathy's heart. She had worried that maybe Dad was just lingering—waiting for her to make peace with Sunny. There were moments when Kathy thought that would be easy enough to do. But then as soon as she would explore the possibility and try to figure out how to go about the matter, something would happen and her heart would grow hard again.

But it's not really a hardness, she told herself. *It's fear. I'm afraid of what will happen if I open myself up to Sunny.* She looked at her sister for a moment before fixing her attention on the food. Sunny had fooled them all so many times. When she'd still been in high school she had come home sick one night after a party. She swore up and down it was the flu and for all intents and purposes it seemed to be. She promised her mother she hadn't had a drop of liquor, even though there had been some at the party. Kathy remembered they had all felt sorry for Sunny. The next day a group of her friends was planning a trip to a lake and Sunny couldn't go because she was still feeling so wretched. They had honestly believed she had the flu, but not long after that Sunny had admitted to Kathy she had been drinking, and quite heavily.

Then there was the time when Sunny came home with several purchases from Hays. Kathy had been amazed that she had gotten so much for so little. She had beautiful lacy bras and panties, expensive socks, a new purse, and several CDs. She had gone on and on to their mother about the sales she'd found. But again, Kathy later learned that her sister had shoplifted most of the items.

Yes, she'd been a child then. But from what Sunny had shared, her choices as an adult left a lot to be desired. Could Kathy believe her now? Were Sunny's words about forgiveness and making things right trustworthy?

After lunch Kathy slipped away to finish setting up her bedroom for Glynnis and Will. Rearranging the yellow roses she'd picked earlier in the day, Kathy looked around to see if anything else needed her attention. She was just placing the vase on a table at the end of the bed when Glynnis came in with a small suitcase.

"Will can bring up the rest after a bit. He's having another visit with your father."

"I'm sure Dad appreciates that. He loves you both so much."

Glynnis put the case on the bed and came to where Kathy stood. "These are beautiful. Did you grow them?"

"They're from Mom's bushes out back. They're the ones I told you I'd probably dig up and take with me when I move."

"Well, they smell glorious. I don't blame you." Glynnis straightened and smiled. "So you seem more comfortable with Sunny than I had expected."

"Things are better," Kathy replied. "I can't say they're perfect. I still find myself so angry. I don't know why, but it sort of spills out at the most awkward moments."

Glynnis chuckled. "I've been known to spill out on occasion myself. You've been through a lot—you're still going through a lot. Don't push yourself too hard. Just rest in the Lord. He has already taken care of everything. You might as well let Him have your worries and hurts, 'cause they'll do you no good."

"The people in town are as mad at her as I am. Oh, she has her friend Debbie, but otherwise, most of the folks at church and elsewhere are amazed that she had the nerve to come back at all."

"Well, sometimes people are afraid of the past returning. After all, we all have our secrets we'd just as soon remain hidden."

🌿 🌿 🌿

Sunny sat beside her father's bed and watched his chest as he drew slow, shallow breaths. How could anyone be so very sick and not yet die?

He opened his eyes and attempted to smile. "Sorry. I didn't . . . know you were here."

"That's all right. I just wanted to be near you. I spent so much time so far away, I didn't want to pass up a chance to share your company."

"What time . . . is it?"

"Past midnight."

"Why are you up?" He seemed a little more coherent— as if the time had suddenly startled him into clarity.

"I couldn't sleep. Sometimes I have trouble with that," she admitted. "Memories, you know."

He reached out to hold her hand. Sunny cherished the moment. "Past . . . can't hurt you, unless you let it."

"I don't believe that, Dad. I know God forgives, but I can't forget. The hideous things I've done—that were done to me—they haunt me. It's like Satan uses them against me."

"Of course he does."

"So how can you say that they can't hurt me?" She felt so vulnerable, almost like being a child again. Weak and scared. Why did this have to happen to her? Kathy always seemed so strong.

"Satan's a liar," Dad began slowly. "Bible says so. John . . . chapter eight—can't remember the verse—it says that lies are Satan's native tongue. He brings up the past . . .

to make you afraid . . . hoping you'll feel guilty." Dad rested for a moment and squeezed her hand ever so slightly. "He doesn't have any power over you, Sunshine. He can't touch you, because you belong to God."

"But there are still problems in my life. Things I have to go and face. I'd like to say that everything got perfect when I got right with God, but it didn't."

Dad nodded. "I know, babe. Lotta folks think it ought to. It doesn't change what's happened. There are still consequences. But it does change the future—how you deal with those consequences."

"I'm afraid, Daddy. I'm so afraid of everything. I don't want to be, but I'm just not strong like you."

"I'm not strong. Not strong at all," Dad whispered, grimacing in pain. "But He is, and that's enough."

🦌 🦌 🦌

Glynnis and Will stayed for two days, then made their way back to Colorado Springs with a promise to return for the funeral. Kathy knew they'd added the extra day because everyone felt certain that Dad's hours were numbered. He was slipping further and further away, and Kathy found herself drawn almost constantly to his side.

She sat beside him several days later, stroking his hand and remembering all the good times. Her favorite memories were of when she and Amy had been young. Dad had been a workhorse then, as he always had been, but he would sometimes take time out to spend with his girls. She remembered him teaching them to ride horses.

"Do you remember that?" she whispered. Dad didn't even stir. "You taught us to ride the horses. I was so scared because they were so big, but you just kept telling me not to think about their size."

After she and Amy had learned to ride fairly well, Dad would sometimes take them on long rides around the property. He would tell them funny stories about his childhood. She especially liked the one about Grandpa throwing Dad into the lake to teach him to swim. Dad had taken to water like a fish. Grandpa had teased that if he threw Dad into the air he'd probably just fly away. The memory made her smile.

"You always gave me good counsel, Dad." She studied his hand. The skin seemed so loose and pale. She thought of her aunt's observation that he was really more gone than here. It was true.

Kathy thought the house strangely empty without her aunt and uncle. How much worse would it be when Dad was gone? It was when she thought of that loneliness that she was glad to be leaving this big house. The memories of her life here could offer comfort, but they could also strangle her and leave her without hope. She could see this now.

"It would have been nice if Aunt Glynnis and Uncle Will could have stayed," she murmured. Kathy sighed. Glynnis and Will were a constant in her life that she desperately needed right now. With Dad dying and Sunny newly returned, their support was the only thing that helped to balance the chaos and confusion. Everyone else, even Sylvia, seemed at arm's length.

Renea Stover had called twice since her comments at church. She wanted to know how things were going and whether or not Sunny had left. Kathy had listened to the woman's vengeful, hateful words and realized that a few weeks earlier she had been saying all the same things herself. Was that how she had sounded? The thought made Kathy sick to her stomach.

"Oh, Dad. I know you'll soon be gone, and I wouldn't want you to stay—what with the pain and all." She leaned down and kissed his cheek. "I love you so much. You were such a good father."

"I tried." His response startled her. He opened his eyes and met her gaze. "I love you too."

She hugged him, placing her cheek on his chest. He put his arms around her and the action comforted Kathy in such a precious way. He stroked her hair the way he had when she'd been little.

"It's been . . . a good life . . . for the most part," he said. Then added, "But I'm ready . . . not sorry to go."

Kathy pulled up and looked into his eyes. "It's all right. I think I understand—maybe for the first time. You know where you're going. Kind of like when we'd take a trip to Hays when I was little. It seemed so far away—so foreign. But I knew where we were going, so there was such an excitement."

He nodded and closed his eyes. "Excitement," he whispered. "That's how it is."

"I'll let you sleep," Kathy said, straightening. To her surprise, Dad took hold of her hand.

"Don't waste time . . . never get enough."

She looked at him oddly. "I don't mean to waste it if I do."

"You and Sunny . . . are you working it out?"

Kathy squeezed his fingers. "Yes. I think we are. It's

taking some time, but I think things are coming around."

He smiled. "Good. Call Kyle?"

Kathy shook her head. "I . . . well . . . I've been afraid to call."

"Silly . . . he loves you."

"But that was twelve years ago."

"It doesn't . . . matter. Real love lasts. Call him."

Dad had tried several times over the years to encourage her to do just that, but Kathy always put it off. "I'll think about it, Dad."

❧ ❧ ❧

A heavy thunderstorm moved in that night. Kathy was glad to be back in her room after having slept on the sofa while her aunt and uncle were there, much to everyone's protest. She found solace in the familiar as she stared out the closed window into the rainy night. The house felt cooler with the rain so it wasn't quite so bad to have the window closed. She heard noises coming from the baby monitor that she used to keep track of Dad from her room. She strained to listen and realized it was just her father's moaning in his sleep.

"Soon, Dad. Soon you won't have to hurt anymore."

Hospice was scheduled to come out the next day, and Kathy fervently hoped they'd convince her father to start on the morphine drip.

Climbing into bed, Kathy sat with her knees up under her chin. She leaned her head down and closed her eyes, praying for wisdom and strength to deal with the days to come. She thought of Kyle and glanced at the clock. He would still be awake. It was only ten-thirty in Colorado. Glynnis had given Kathy his phone number, telling her she felt confident he would want to hear from her, but Kathy was skeptical. Could she dare hope to bring Kyle back into her life?

"I've been so stupid. I sent away the only man I would ever love because I didn't think I had enough love to share between him and Mom." She pounded her hand against the mattress. "Why did I think that solved anything? Why did I let him go?"

She remembered his promise to wait for her. To always love her. She knew from what Glynnis said that his interest in Kathy had never waned. The man had lived all over the U.S. and even in foreign countries, but her aunt said he always asked about her. Of course, Kathy always asked about Kyle as well. It was a silly game, she supposed. Glynnis said they talked to her so much about each other that she figured it was long overdue that they have a conversation of their own.

Kathy reached for the phone and dialed the number she'd already committed to memory. Her heart beat double time. As soon as the phone began to ring, she thought about hanging up, but then it was too late.

"Hello?" Kyle's voice was almost startling to hear. Twelve years faded away. She imagined his impish grin and the twinkle that always seemed to highlight his eyes.

"Kyle?" she questioned, but she knew it was him. For a minute there was nothing but silence. She feared it was too late. Would he hang up?

"Kathy," he said with something of a sigh in his tone. "It's been a long time."

"Maybe too long?" She tried to protect her heart from his answer but knew it was no use.

"No," he replied, reassuring her. "It hasn't been forever, and I promised I'd wait that long."

FOURTEEN

TALKING TO KYLE GAVE KATHY a sense of purpose that she'd not had for a long time. She told him about her mother's death and father's illness. She talked about the farm and her fears that no one would buy it. By the time they hung up, it was well into the night. They stopped then only because Kyle had to get ready to catch a plane.

Kyle told her she was lucky to have caught him. He was leaving that day for two weeks in England. It was business, but he intended to mix pleasure as well and enjoy a little sightseeing. Kathy couldn't help but feel a little sad. They had always talked of doing such things together. It did comfort her, however, when he added that he wanted to hear from her when he got back to the Springs and would call her if that was all right. She assured him it was.

She awoke the next morning feeling more refreshed and at ease than she had in years. It felt as if only days had passed since they'd communicated, rather than a decade. Of course, Kathy knew Kyle had kept up-to-date on her through Glynnis and Will, just as she had learned about him. Kyle had respected her requirement that he not call or write, but over the years Kathy had convinced herself that meant he didn't care. Now it seemed nothing could be further from the truth. In fact, he told her about a journal he'd kept since they'd parted. He hoped someday she'd read it and see that he'd never stopped loving her or thinking about her—even for a day.

"He still loves me," Kathy said with a sigh. Even the call from the Realtor didn't discourage Kathy that day. It seemed the only person interested in the farm wanted to know whether they would consider selling a two-acre patch of land along the road.

A knock at the door brought her out of her reflection.

"Hi, Luke," Kathy said, opening the door to the hospice nurse. She'd come to know Luke pretty well over the last few weeks. "How's your wife?"

"Due any day—any second." He grinned. "Gina's so tired. I sometimes wonder if he'll ever come."

"So it's definitely a boy?" She'd been following the pregnancy with great interest. Luke's enthusiasm made it impossible not to get caught up.

"Yup. They're pretty confident of that. We've picked the name. Samuel Douglas Johnson. How's that sound?"

"I think it sounds great. Will you call him Sam?"

"Probably. Gina says she'll call him Sammy while he's little." Luke pulled a stethoscope from his bag and draped it around his neck. "How's your dad?"

"Hurting. I think he's finally ready to allow for the morphine."

"Let's check him out."

Kathy led the way, then watched from the far side of the room as Luke examined her father. Dad cried out in pain every time Luke touched or moved him. It wasn't a pleasant thing to endure on her part or his.

"Well, Gary, the doc's been talking about you having something stronger for the pain. I think you're well overdue for it. So how about letting us help you?"

Dad nodded. "Yes."

Kathy forced herself not to cry. It was hard to see this stalwart man give in to his condition. He'd held out so long, and for what? She really couldn't understand.

"I'll call the doctor as soon as I've finished getting your vitals."

Kathy waited in the living room until Luke finished. He came out with his bag, cell phone to his mouth. "That's right. No, let me ask." He turned to Kathy. "Has he eaten or had anything to drink today?"

"No. He stopped eating the day his sister left. That's been nearly a week. And he's had maybe a tablespoon of water here or there. I keep trying to encourage it, but he just doesn't want it."

"Have his bowels stopped working?"

Kathy nodded. "He still urinates occasionally."

Luke relayed the information to the doctor on the other end of the phone. "Sure. I'll tell her. Yeah, I'm sure the same place where they've been getting the other prescriptions." He concluded the call and turned to Kathy. "He's ordering the morphine."

"What do we need to do? Will it be given through IV?"

"No. He doesn't think there's much time, so to put your dad through all that seems kind of cruel. He's ordering liquid that you can give to him with a dropper. You'll just squeeze some under his tongue every so often. It'll work like a charm, but it will also keep him pretty knocked out. I wouldn't look to have any more detailed conversations."

"He's not talking much anyway. Usually seems more out of it than with it," Kathy said. "I've seen him really slipping away these last two days."

"Yeah, I see it too. I'd say maybe another couple of days at the most."

Kathy choked back the lump in her throat. "How soon will they have the morphine ready?"

"You'll need to pick up the written prescription at the doctor's office. They can't just call it in because of it being what it is. Pick up the written order, then take it over to your regular pharmacy. The doctor's office said they'd call ahead to give them all the particulars, then when you present the orders, they'll have you sign for the medicine." Luke offered her a compassionate smile. "You've done a good job, Kathy. I probably won't see you again."

She drew a deep breath. "Thanks for your help with Dad, and blessings on you and your wife as you wait for your new baby."

"We'll send you a notice. Life ends and life begins. It's all a circle. A very fragile circle."

"But with Jesus, we know it goes on and on. The end here is only the beginning there," Kathy said, taking comfort in her beliefs.

Luke nodded. "And life there is bound to be something incredible. More than we can imagine."

Kathy gathered her things for the trip to Hays before going in search of Sunny. She found her sister working in the small garden. Kathy hadn't planted much, knowing she'd be busy with Dad's care and then leave before fall. There were a few tomato plants and onions, as well as a couple of bell pepper plants, but nothing more.

"I have to go to Hays. The doctor is ordering morphine for Dad, and I need to pick it up. He doesn't think Dad has much longer—maybe a day or two."

Sunny seemed to fight for control of her emotions. She finally drew a deep breath. "I could go for you." Sunny got up from her knees and dusted off her pants.

"No," Kathy replied. In the back of her mind she remembered Sunny's addiction to drugs.

"Seriously. I know you hate to leave his side, and he'll probably be more comforted having you with him than me. I could change clothes in five minutes."

"I said no. I'll go. They know me. I do want you to come in the house and be with Dad, however."

Sunny eyed her curiously. "What gives? You're acting strange. What's wrong with me going to Hays for the medicine?"

Kathy felt uncomfortable and looked away. "Look, I don't have time to argue about this. They're going to be very particular about who they give the morphine to. I don't want any delays."

"You think that because of the past—my drug addiction—that I might be tempted to use some of Dad's medication. Is that it?"

"Well . . . I wouldn't . . . I don't want you—"

"I can't believe this!" Sunny was livid. "How could you even think something so hideous? I should have never told you anything—you hold stuff against a person forever, don't you?"

Kathy became increasingly defensive. "Look, I don't know anything about you except for what you've told me. And I know nothing about drugs, except that they're hard to kick once you get addicted. Don't play the wounded victim in this. You are a liability I can't afford to risk."

"Boy, you said it there. That's exactly how you feel about me. It's how you've treated me since I walked through the front door. I'm sure glad God doesn't hold a grudge like you do."

Kathy was dumbfounded by her sister's statement. Maybe she had responded poorly to the situation, but it didn't merit Sunny's anger. "Look, I haven't got time for your wounded feelings. I need to get that medicine so that Dad can be out of pain. Will you stay with him or should I call someone else?"

Sunny clenched her jaw and folded her arms against her chest. "Just go. I'll be here, and I'll handle things just fine without you."

Kathy stood facing off with Sunny for another few seconds before turning to go. "I'll be back as soon as I can."

❧ ❧ ❧

From the moment she reached the doctor's office in Hays, things started to go wrong. Kathy was frustrated when the nurse couldn't locate the written prescription. The doctor had gone to make a hospital call, so he couldn't just write out a second order. Finally someone thought to look in her father's chart and found it clipped to the outside.

With the paper in hand, she hurried to their regular pharmacy only to get more bad news.

"Sorry, Kathy. We don't have the liquid oral morphine on hand," the pharmacist apologized. "I've called around for you and Dillons has it. If you take the prescription there, they should have you set in no time."

But that wasn't the way it went at all. Kathy presented the prescription only to have the woman look at her as if she were a drug dealer trying to pull a fast one.

"Who are you to the person this medication is intended?"

"I'm his daughter. My father is dying from cancer."

"I see."

But it clearly sounded as though the woman didn't see. "I'll need your identification—something with a picture."

Kathy pulled out her driver's license and handed it to the woman. She looked at the card, then at Kathy and back at the card. Finally she asked, "Do you have anything else?"

"Good grief. My father is dying. I just want to get him some medication to ease his pain. Didn't you talk to Brad at Wilcox's? He said he called over here to let you know what was happening. He knows me. I've been dealing with him ever since Dad got sick."

The woman looked at her blankly. Clearly she was unmoved by Kathy's plea. "Do you have any other form of identification?"

"Nothing else with a photo. I have a credit card and insurance card. Oh, and I have a checkbook." Kathy dumped the contents of her purse on the counter. "I have a hairbrush; maybe you could do DNA testing." Her sarcasm was not winning any friends.

"Look, we have our rules. I don't know you," the woman said in her authoritative manner. "For all I know, you've set this entire thing up to get the drugs for yourself."

Kathy suddenly wondered if this was how Sunny felt. Kathy hadn't even given her sister a chance. She'd just pre-sumed Sunny would be a risk where the morphine was concerned. Her shoulders slumped in defeat. All she wanted was to get her father some medicine to cut the pain. Tears spilled from her eyes as she gathered the things from her purse.

"Call the doctor's office. I've spent a good portion of the last year there. I was just there today. They know me, even if you don't. I'm going to sit over here in your waiting area."

She was glad that the woman said nothing further. It seemed to take forever before the pharmacist called her name. He was a tall older man with great compassion in his expression.

"I'm sorry for the difficulty in getting this filled," he began. "We have to be careful."

"That's fine," Kathy said. "Just tell me what I have to do so that I can get back to Dad. He doesn't have much time, and I've wasted enough of it here."

The man gave her instructions on the dosage and use. Kathy quickly signed the paper work and paid for the medicine. She was well on her way home when she broke down. Why did it have to be so hard?

"They made me feel like a criminal—and I haven't done anything but come to get medicine for my father."

She thought again of Sunny. *That must have been how I made her feel. I stood there with my accusing attitude and had no reason to believe it would have been a problem. Just because she had a problem in the past doesn't mean she has one now. She's done nothing to make me suspicious. I was unfair.*

Kathy drove well over the speed limit all the way home. The two-lane road to Slocum wasn't the best in the world, but Kathy didn't care. She thought only of getting the morphine to Dad so that he could rest peacefully in his final days—hours.

"Lord, I was wrong. I should never have made Sunny feel that way. I had no reason to act like I did. I was suspicious based solely on the past. Just like I don't want to trust her because of the past. I need to change my heart, Lord, but I don't know how."

She drove down the gravel road to the farm, slowing only enough to keep the car under control. The house was soon in sight and Kathy eased off the gas with a sense of accomplishment. She sighed. She would apologize to Sunny and let her know how wrong she'd been, just as soon as she gave Dad his medicine.

Kathy hurried into the house and made her way to the den. She heard Sunny crying, but the meaning didn't register until she came into the den. Sunny was sitting with her head on Dad's chest, sobbing.

"Sunny?" she asked apprehensively. "Are you all right?"

Her sister straightened and wiped at her tears. "Kathy. Oh, Kathy. He's gone."

"What? Are you sure?" Kathy tossed her things aside and hurried to the bed. She reached for Dad's hand and felt for a pulse. Her own heart was racing like a trip-hammer.

"He stopped breathing about ten minutes ago. I waited, thinking he would take another breath, but he didn't. I called hospice and they said they'd send an ambulance and the sheriff."

Kathy collapsed into a chair. She couldn't believe Dad had died without her being at his side. She hated to admit it, but she felt jealous that Sunny got to share his last moments.

She waited for her tears to come, but they didn't. She was cried out. She'd spent the last few months mourning her father's dying. Perhaps there was nothing left to offer his death.

FIFTEEN

NEARLY EVERYONE IN SLOCUM, KANSAS, turned out for the funeral of Gary Halbert. The man had been a friend to everyone, and no one could remember him ever having an enemy. Dad had died on the second of July, but Kathy had delayed the funeral until the seventh, hoping Aunt Glynnis could attend. Glynnis had taken a rather bad fall in her garden and the result was a twisted back that left her in a great deal of pain. Uncle Will said it wasn't possible for her to make the trip, and while Kathy understood, she was still very disappointed. She had hoped to lean on Glynnis for support and understanding, but instead, the only family member present was Sunshine.

Things at the house had been strangely quiet. Sunny seemed to have withdrawn into her own little world, and Kathy was busy with telephone calls and final preparations for the funeral. She could hardly believe that an era of her life had come to an end. Dad was really gone. Everything from this point on would change.

As she stood at the graveside listening to the pastor's final prayer, Kathy couldn't help but steal a glance at her sister. Sunny stood with her head respectfully bent and eyes closed. She had dressed in a dark blue suit and white blouse and looked rather out of place. Others had worn their Sunday best for the event, but they seemed lackluster and almost shoddy compared to Sunny. There was just something about her that made her different. Maybe it was the cut of her clothes or the brand. It could be the way she styled her hair and wore her makeup. Whatever it was, it emphasized the fact that she didn't belong in this group.

Kathy hadn't given her own dark plum pantsuit much thought. She had fully intended to wear a lightweight dress to the funeral but, noting a strong wind that morning, changed her mind. Now as the hour approached noon, she was getting hot and wished only to put an end to the ordeal.

There's still the funeral dinner at the church to get through, she remembered. *People are going to expect me to be there for them—to assure them that all is fine and that they did enough.*

Funny how funerals were in honor of the dead, but they were really about making sure the living felt vindicated of any negligence of which they might be guilty, or comforted because of the personal loss. Even Kathy found herself mentally calculating whether she'd done enough—said the right things—bought the proper flowers. She lowered her head as Pastor Butler ended his prayer.

"Go now with this family, Lord. Go also with the friends who have come here today. Ease their sorrow and let them reflect on the good times and blessings shared with them by our departed friend Gary. Amen."

The crowd echoed the amen and waited momentarily, as if to be dismissed. The pastor came and took hold of Kathy's hand. "We'll certainly miss your father."

"Yes, we will," she agreed. "Thank you for a lovely service. I know he would have been pleased."

The pastor turned rather awkwardly to Sunny. "And may God be with you in your grief."

"Thank you." Sunny seemed just as uncomfortable as the pastor. It was one of those moments that reminded

Kathy of two people meeting for a blind date. Neither one was quite sure of what the other expected or needed. The thought made her smile, because the pastor was nearly seventy and married, and Sunny looked like she might bolt for home any minute.

"That was a real nice service," Renea Stover said, coming to shake the pastor's hand and offer Kathy her condolences. "This town just won't be the same without you and your family."

"It will be hard for me as well," Kathy said. "I've never lived anywhere else, so Colorado Springs will be something completely different."

"When do you go?"

"Well, that depends," Kathy began. "I had fully expected to be out of here by the end of summer, but no one has bought the place yet. The Realtor said there was a bit of interest, but so far nothing has developed."

"Pity. It's such a nice place."

"I know. I've always loved it here, but I'm not equipped to farm it myself."

Renea eyed Sunny with contempt. "Will she go now?"

Kathy was glad that the pastor was still talking to Sunny. "Dad asked her to stay with me at least until the sale of the farm."

Renea shook her head. "He didn't take your feelings into consideration. I suppose it was the sickness." She smoothed her black dress and leaned toward Kathy. "You know, given that his mind probably wasn't what it should have been there at the end, you wouldn't have to honor his request. No one would blame you if you sent her packing right now."

"I'd blame myself," Kathy replied, trying not to sound

too harsh. "The Bible says blessed are the merciful, for they shall receive mercy. I'd rather be kind to my sister and honor my father's wishes than demand my own way and show no mercy."

Renea patted her arm. "That always was like you. Just give, give, give. Never with any motive."

But Kathy knew Mrs. Stover was wrong. She had motives like everyone else. Over the years Kathy hadn't realized it, but she was coming to understand them now. Funny how it should be Sunshine who helped her to see the truth.

But seeing the truth doesn't mean I know what to do with myself or my thoughts. Kathy grimaced. Seeing the truth was just the beginning.

Kathy soon found herself surrounded by people. She recognized everyone. Most were longtime friends of her parents, some coming from as far away as Salina to pay their last respects and remember him.

"You look like you could use a nap," Sylvia said as the bulk of the crowd eventually moved away.

"I'd love that," Kathy admitted. "I'd like to sleep for about a week, but there's too much to do."

"Well, you know I'm at your disposal. If you need help with the house, just holler."

Kathy looked around to see who else might overhear her. Satisfied that they could talk without any eavesdroppers, she continued. "This might sound strange, but I realized the day after Dad died that I felt this tremendous sense of relief. Like I could finally relax and let down now that he was gone. Does that sound awful?"

"Not at all." Sylvia's sympathetic smile was reassuring.

"Kathy, you're worn out. You've sacrificed the past dozen years for your parents—far more than most adult children are called to give at your age. You've sacrificed having a family and life of your own. You've watched first your mother and now your father deal with ravaging illnesses. Of course you're relieved. Don't feel guilty about that."

Kathy lowered her voice even more. "I didn't have a chance to tell you, but I called Kyle."

"You did?" Sylvia gave a chuckle. "Well, it's about time."

"He was taking off for England, or I'm pretty sure he would have been here." Kathy raised her gaze to meet Sylvia's. "It was like we'd never been apart. We talked so easily."

"You never should have been apart. I'm glad that at least this part of your life can be altered and corrected."

Kathy frowned. "I know most people didn't understand me, but I always felt you did."

Sylvia shifted her purse and crossed her arms. "I did to a point. But really, there's no use rehashing the past. What I want to know is what is the future going to look like?"

"I'm hoping it will look like a wedding in Colorado Springs," Kathy said rather boldly. It wasn't like her to make such predictions, but Kyle's sweet spirit and obvious desire to pick up where they left off made her hopeful.

"You'd better give me plenty of warning. I'll need time to warn Tony. Better make it a winter wedding too, so we can have things wrapped up enough on the farm to leave for a few days."

"Anything else?" Kathy teased.

Sylvia grinned. "If I think of it, I'll call you immediately.

Tony has already arranged for us to have one of those unlimited long-distance plans. He very sweetly told me that with you moving to another state, he knew it would be hard on me."

Kathy squeezed her hand. "I know you're right and that things will change, but I'll never stop loving you like a sister. You were always there for me."

"And I always will be," Sylvia promised.

A few more townspeople made their way to Kathy and offered their condolences. Most were older folks who had known her mother and father on a first-name basis. Kathy knew them as Mr. This and Mrs. That. She had been raised to show the utmost respect, and even now, even as an adult on equal footing, she couldn't bring herself to call them by their first names.

Kathy was saying some final good-byes when she caught sight of her sister. Sunny stood off to one side of the highly polished oak casket. She seemed uncertain of what she should or shouldn't do, so she did nothing but stand there, twisting her hands and looking at the ground. Kathy noted that hardly anyone was stopping to speak to her.

"Excuse me," Kathy said, pulling away from the collection of people.

She walked to where Sunny stood. "I think Dad would have been pleased, don't you?"

Sunny looked up rather surprised. "I . . . uh . . . yes. Yes, I think he would have been very pleased."

"I saw you over here by yourself and thought maybe we should head for the church dinner."

"They hate me," Sunny said, meeting Kathy's gaze. "They hate me and blame me for Dad's cancer and Mom's heart attack. They blame me for keeping you from getting married like Sylvia—married with a bunch of kids."

"Now's not the time, Sunny. We can talk about all of that later. Just be brave and deal with the situation. You knew it wouldn't be easy, but this day is about honoring Dad's memory. Let them think what they will. It doesn't change the truth."

"I know," she whispered, tears in her eyes. "That's what bothers me the most."

🐦 🐦 🐦

For Sunny, her father's funeral had been harder than any other funeral. She had buried Randy and baby Gary in the midst of tragedy, and the shock of the time had kept her from feeling anything too deeply or keenly. Each time the feelings had returned weeks later and caused severe depression, whereas this time the sorrow and depression were her staunch companions.

Now three days after the funeral, Sunny felt the stupor begin to lift just a bit. The farm still hadn't sold, but Kathy had decided to move as soon as possible. As she pointed out to Sunny, she wasn't able to even earn money in Slocum to pay the mortgage. At least in Colorado Springs she could get a job and try to pay the bills with what she earned.

Sunny knew Kathy was worried, however. She would never talk about what the farm was worth or how much the mortgage amounted to, but Sunny knew it had to be quite a bit.

Kathy seemed to bear it all with such strength. Sunny

had thought about telling Kathy that she was leaving. There were things Sunny needed to take care of, but she'd made a promise to their dad that she would stay. He had hoped Sunny would help Kathy bear the load, and Sunny was willing to try. She wasn't so sure about Kathy's willingness, however. Sunny wondered if her sister resented the promise they'd made Dad. Would she have shown Sunny the door if their father hadn't insisted on them promising to get along?

Returning to the house after taking an early morning walk, Sunny was surprised to hear a commotion coming from upstairs. She made her way up and found Kathy already at work in their mother and father's room.

"Good morning," Sunny announced.

"Morning," Kathy said from where she knelt in front of a plastic tub. "I thought I'd better get to sorting through this stuff. The auction people will be coming to assess everything in a few days."

"Can I help?" Sunny didn't want to start the day off by irritating Kathy, but she felt rather useless.

Kathy looked around and shrugged. "I don't know what to tell you to do. We need to organize things into groups. Clothes with clothes, knickknacks with knickknacks, books with books. Like that."

"Well, I can figure out what goes together." Sunny walked to the dresser and picked up a framed photo of their parents on their wedding day. "They looked so young—so hopeful." She couldn't keep the regret from her voice.

"We all had our hopes," Kathy said simply.

"You blame me for Kyle and your broken engagement, don't you?"

Kathy seemed taken aback. She quickly turned her

attention to a box of books. "I don't think I want to talk about that with you."

"Why?" Sunny didn't want to make things worse, but she felt almost driven to ask.

Kathy stiffened. "I'm trying hard to put the past behind us. I'm willing to try to sweep it aside, but I can't do it by wallowing in the ugliness of the past."

"There's a difference between dealing with the past and pretending it never happened," Sunny said. "I had to learn that one for myself. You can ignore the past—hide it away—and never have dealt with the issues at hand. It then becomes like a cut that's gotten infected. It might heal on the outside, but down deep it's still festering."

"So you think that if we don't hash out all the gory details, I'll go on harboring ill feelings and anger toward you? Is that it?"

Sunny could hear the defensive tone in Kathy's question. "I just think it would do us both good to at least talk through the last twelve years."

"You weren't so willing back in June when I asked about whether you had someone waiting for you somewhere—if you had a family."

"I know. I was wrong to react the way I did. It's just that things are very complicated right now." Sunny put the photo back on the dresser. "When I married Randy, I finally knew what it was to be loved and cared about just for being me."

"We loved you that way," Kathy said matter-of-factly, "but that wasn't good enough."

Sunny hated the way the conversation was going but didn't know what else to do but push ahead. "I thought I would always be happy. I thought that at last I'd found what it was that was missing at home, and then Randy died. I wanted to die too. I told you they put me in rehab, but what I didn't tell you was that for the first thirty days I was on suicide watch. I didn't care about life—it just seemed too painful."

Kathy opened her mouth, then must have decided not to comment. She dusted a couple of books while Sunny tried to figure out how to share the truth of her life.

"Rehab was hard. Not so much because I had to give up the drugs, but because I felt that I had no one. I had to make this work on my own. I had to care enough to quit and stay clean, or it wasn't going to do any good. The problem was, I hated my reality. Being clean wasn't pleasurable to me, because when I was clean I could see my miserable life for what it was."

"But why should you be any different than the rest of us?" Kathy asked. Her tone had softened and the look on her face suggested she genuinely needed an answer to that question.

"Didn't it ever dawn on you, Kathy, that some people just can't take the pressure? Not everyone is cut out to succeed. Not everyone has the ability to be the next president or Einstein. I always hated it when they'd tell us in school that if we worked hard we could be anything we wanted to be. That's not true and you know it. I could have worked as hard as humanly possible and I still wouldn't have ever been able to be a doctor or a scientist. Those things weren't in me."

"But they told us we could be anything we wanted to

be," Kathy reiterated. "*Wanted* to be. You didn't want to be a doctor or scientist."

"Maybe not, but what if I had wanted to be the president of the United States? There's nothing that says that by trying my best, as suggested, I could do that. We only get one president every four years. So far most have been lawyers. What are the chances that it could be me—an uneducated woman? One percent? Half a percent?"

"But if you give up, the chances are zip—zero."

"That's how I felt when the doctors told me I could have a great life if I got clean. Nothing felt great. Nothing looked good. I felt the chances were so small on recovering that I was my own worst enemy."

"So what happened?" Kathy put aside the books and gave Sunny her full attention.

"I was in my last week of rehab. I had kicked my habits and could honestly say that I had no desire to go back to them. Why bother to get high? You'll just come down and have to get high again in order to keep from facing the truth of the situation. So I felt it was all in vain. Life. Death. Family. Independence. Totally in vain."

Sunny walked to the window and pulled back the dusty drape. Outside, rain clouds were gathering to the west. She knew farmers were hurrying to harvest the last of the wheat and murmured a silent prayer that they could complete the job before the weather turned bad.

"I was sitting outside the rehab center, reading a book, when a man approached me. It turned out to be another doctor. He was there visiting a friend who was kicking heroin."

She dropped the drape and leaned against the wall

beside the window. "Brian Dennison was unlike anyone I'd ever spent time with. He was educated, gorgeous, kind, and gentle. He really seemed to have it all. And to my surprise, he wanted to know me better. He helped me get an apartment when I got out of the hospital. I had been pleasantly surprised to realize I had money left. Between Randy's funeral and my rehab, I had figured to be broke. I sold our house and felt like I could manage financially for a time— at least a short time. California prices are outrageous and leave a great deal to be desired."

Kathy watched her with intent interest but said nothing. Sunny wondered how she'd take the news she was about to share. "Brian and I dated and had a whirlwind romance. He was very well off. He came from old money, and his practice as a Beverly Hills plastic surgeon was making him wealthy in his own right. Before I knew it we were planning a wedding. A Beverly Hills wedding that spared no expense. I think the final count on all the bills came to over $450,000."

Kathy gasped. "For a wedding?"

Sunny laughed, but there was no joy in it. "Yeah. Sounds pretty crazy, doesn't it? My dress alone cost $50,000, and it was hardly more than a strapless tube created by a designer who everyone wanted for their next creation."

Kathy shook her head. "I can't even begin to imagine such a thing. When did this happen?"

"Five years ago. I was twenty-five and he was forty."

Kathy wasn't about to leave it there, and Sunny had known she would want more information. Maybe that's why it was so hard to be honest about this part of her life.

"So what happened?" Kathy finally asked.

Sunny frowned. The pain threatened to take the very air from her lungs. "I didn't get to be president."

Sixteen

SUNNY'S MEMORIES PASSED BACK through the years once again. She could easily place herself back in the elegant Beverly Hills home her husband had bought for them. It was a safe and welcoming home—one that made Sunny feel completely happy. Life had seemed so good. She wore Christian Louboutin shoes and carried an Hermès bag. She was courted by every important designer, often finding herself traveling in private jets to have fittings and see new ideas. It was a privileged life that she had only dared to dream of— a life that Sunny found both exciting and foreign.

Pacing impatiently, Sunny waited for Brian to come home from work. He was married to his job as a plastic surgeon, every bit as much as, if not more than, he was to Sunny. When they had married, he'd promised to cut back and spend more time with his new wife, but that hadn't happened. Sunny had tried to be patient as he cancelled one getaway or evening out after another. She knew that what he contributed to the world was important—much more important than anything she had to offer. But Sunny had news that she hoped would change all of that: she was pregnant.

The thought of having another baby brought her both joy and sorrow. Baby Gary's memory still brought her to tears. When she talked about the baby she'd never had a chance to know, it tore at something deep inside. Sometimes it was easier to pretend that part of her life had never happened.

Now she was pregnant once again and all the old worries and fears came to the surface. What if something happened? What if she lost this baby too? Brian knew all about Sunny's past and would understand her fears. He would be gentle and loving, because that was the kind of man he was. He would also tell her not to worry, that nothing would happen to cause them grief.

The sound of the garage door opening stirred excitement in her heart. Sunny had dressed carefully, wearing one of Brian's favorite outfits. The red Donna Karan dress and strappy sandals had been a gift for her birthday two months ago. She supposed now she wouldn't be able to wear it for long, but it would always be there after the baby was born.

The baby.

Putting her hand to her stomach, Sunny could scarcely believe it. She was going to have a baby. Now Brian would have to spend more time at home. Now things would have to be different. Sunny smiled. He would be so pleased.

Brian walked in from the garage looking for all the world like he'd just accomplished the most amazing feat of his career. He threw her a grin and tossed his jacket to the nearest chair. "Mmm, you look fantastic."

Sunny crossed the room and fell into his arms. "I feel fantastic."

"Me too. We should celebrate."

"I think we should."

He nibbled on her ear in the affectionate way Sunny had come to love. "What shall we celebrate?" he asked before trailing kisses down her neck.

"That we're going to have a baby," she whispered.

Brian pulled back and looked at her in disbelief. "A baby? Are you sure?"

Sunny giggled. "Yes. Yes, I'm sure. I took two tests just to prove it to myself."

He picked her up and twirled her around. "That's incredible! This is definitely worth celebrating!"

She laughed and cherished the feeling of being in his arms. "I thought you'd be pleased."

"I'm more than pleased. This is the best possible news."

When they'd married, Brian had been forty, and now a year later he saw time passing rather quickly. Most of the time it was the woman who worried about her clock ticking, but in this case Brian had made it clear from the start that he wanted children, and wanted them soon. Sunny was happy to oblige him. Despite her fears, she'd longed for a baby since losing Gary.

"When?" Brian questioned, pulling away from Sunny. "When is the baby due?"

"Well, you're the doctor in the family, but by my calculations it should come sometime in late December."

"Wow, this is all so fantastic." He dropped his hold and grabbed his jacket. "We need to go out and have a very expensive night of it."

"I'm hoping this will also mean you'll cut back on your schedule and give more of your work to Rick." Rick Anniston was Brian's partner of two years, but so far Brian really wasn't inclined to share his client list. People came back to Brian because they trusted him, and often Sunny saw Brian risk his own health and well-being to accommodate patients who could have just as easily been handled by Rick. All it would have taken was one word from Brian and things could have been different. She had no idea why he hesitated. It wasn't like they needed the money. Brian wouldn't have even had to work if it hadn't been for his love of surgery.

"Of course. I'll talk to Rick tomorrow. I know I've been really swamped since we got married, but I promise you, Sunny, things will be different."

But when Lucianna Noel Dennison was born on Christmas Day, Sunny endured the birth with no one from the family at her side except Brian's mother, Nancy. Two floors down, Brian was caught up in some emergency surgery and missed the birth of his daughter. Sunny felt a strange sensation that this was a forerunner of things to come.

Brian showed up an hour after his mother went home. Sunny held Lucianna in her arms, marveling at the tiny child—wondering how their lives might play out in the future.

"I'm so sorry, Sunny." He approached the bed with a dozen pink roses. "I had to take the surgery. It was a child—a little boy who'd run through a plate glass window. It wasn't easy, but I think he'll end up looking pretty close to normal. Please forgive me."

Sunny smiled. She'd been angry at first, but how could she stay mad when his reason was so altruistic? "I forgive you. I also have someone I want you to meet."

Brian leaned down close. "She's beautiful—just like her mom."

"Lucianna Noel, you should open your eyes and meet your father. It might be one of the last times you get to see him."

Brian placed a kiss on the baby's forehead. "No way. I told you I was going to cut back, and I meant it. Rick is going to start taking a third of my patients. I've already been talking to some of my people about it and they understand."

Sunny felt a surge of happiness. "So maybe we can take that getaway trip? Just you and me and the baby?"

Brian nodded. "I think you've more than earned it."

The telephone rang, disrupting the memory and Sunny's train of thought. Kathy looked at her, as if suggesting they forget the phone, but Sunny suddenly felt rather vulnerable. Now Kathy would ask about Brian and the baby and where they were now.

"Shouldn't you get that?" Sunny asked. She got up and fled the room without waiting for Kathy to answer.

Slapping her hands against her sides, Sunny fought back the urge to scream, thoughts of her daughter nearly bringing her to the edge of hysteria. Lucy was just three and a half and so mature already, speaking full sentences before she was two years old. The ache in Sunny's heart built with every thought of the little girl, whose dark blue eyes and blond curls were so much like her daddy's.

"Oh, Lucy. I'm so sorry." Sunny ran out the front door and down the driveway. She wanted only to get away. Get as far away as she could from the memories and the pain. The only problem was she took those things with her wherever she went. She couldn't leave those things behind, because they were an intricate part of who she was and why she was here.

Kathy will think me completely daft. She'll wonder how in the world I could possibly be so messed up. But chances were better than not that Kathy had already thought those things long before Sunny had come to Slocum.

Kathy answered the phone with a great sense of regret. "Hello?"

"Kathy, it's Glynnis."

"Oh, how are you feeling?" Kathy had called Glynnis the day of the funeral but hadn't talked to her since.

"I'm feeling much better. Slow goes it, but I see progress."

"I'm so glad to hear that," Kathy said, sitting on the edge of her parents' bed.

"You sound upset. Are you okay?"

Kathy wondered how much to tell her aunt, then decided to let her know the truth. "Sunny was telling me more about her past. She's married—at least I think she still is. She married about five years ago and had a daughter named Lucianna. I don't know much else. He's a plastic surgeon in Los Angeles and very wealthy."

"Oh my." Glynnis sounded as dumbfounded by the news as Kathy had been.

"I'm not sure what's going on with her or why she hasn't said anything about them until now. Maybe she isn't married to him anymore. I don't know. It seems like all summer she's had nowhere to be or go. I just assumed she was alone."

"When I think of the things you've told me about Sunny, it's easy to see she didn't get the wonderful life she thought she was buying into when she left home."

"I know. It was always so easy to imagine she was either dead or living it up. I would get so mad when I'd imagine her living this wonderful dreamlike life while the rest of us suffered, longing for some kind of news. I feel so confused, Aunt Glynnis."

"I can well imagine. You're having to come to terms

with so much in a matter of a few weeks."

"First just finding out that my sister was alive," Kathy began, "then learning that Dad knew where she'd been at one point and had done nothing to try to force her home— or even tell me. Then there's all the information Sunny has shared: an abusive marriage and death of a child, a second marriage and drug addiction—having her husband overdose and die. It's all too much to imagine, much less make sense of. I honestly don't know what to do."

"The only thing we can do is love her, Kathy. There's little else to be accomplished. I mean, you could turn your back on her. You could tell her all the things you've dreamed of saying and walk away from any further relation-ship, but I don't think you'd ever be happy."

"No, I know I wouldn't. I can't walk away from her . . . she's my sister. Yet, on the other hand, I feel so betrayed and angry at times. When I think I might finally have a grip on the situation, something new pops up. I found myself even resenting her help this morning."

"How so?"

"I was sorting through Mom and Dad's things for the sale. Sunny came in to help, and I wanted to send her away. I wanted to tell her not to touch anything."

Glynnis said nothing, so Kathy continued. "Sometimes I want to throw my arms around her and hold on to her and never let go. Other times I want to tell her it hurts too much to have a relationship with her. That knowing she was alive all these years—yet never caring enough to let us know—is too much to expect anyone to overcome."

"And if you tried to do it on your own, you'd be right. This kind of thing can't be battled in the flesh. It's a spiritual and emotional war as well. You'll exhaust yourself in trying to make it right."

"I know. But what I don't know is how to keep from making the same mistakes. I'm not sure how to be honest with Sunny—or even if it would matter if I were."

"I believe understanding each other's feelings is paramount to resolving this situation in your life. You need to understand why Sunny made her choices, and she needs to understand why you made yours."

Kathy shook her head. "But understanding why someone did something isn't going to alter the fact that the deed is done. It will hurt just the same—with or without explanation. Not only that, but what if Sunny told me that the choices I made were stupid? It would make me really mad."

"Yet she's supposed to take that from you?"

Kathy fell silent. *It isn't the same*, she told herself. *There's a difference.*

"She might not want to take it," Kathy finally said, "but her choices were stupid."

"So were yours," Glynnis said matter-of-factly.

"What are you saying?"

"I'm saying what you're saying," she replied. "Sunny's choices made no sense to you, so you call them stupid. Your choices made no sense to me, so I do the same. If this were a contest, you'd both come in first place—a tie."

"How can you say that?" Kathy felt so hurt she could hardly speak. "I did what I was supposed to do. I stayed home and took care of my loved ones."

"Kathy, I don't discredit what you did for your parents. It was a loving act. But you made other choices that made little sense to me. Sending Kyle away was one of those. How much easier it could have been for you with his love and support! In my mind your choice to send him away was just as foolish as Sunny's was to run away.

"Oh, don't you see, Kathy? I just want you to realize that it will do you no good to harbor grudges and keep the past alive. You and Sunny have the chance to make a new start. Forget that which is behind, as the Bible advises. Figure out what it is you want—need. Find what it is you need from Sunny in order to set things right."

That night, Kathy lay awake for a long time pondering exactly that question. *What do I need from Sunny? What do I need from any of this?* She thought of her father's desire to see his family knitted together—his continual prayer that God would bring home his prodigal daughter. He knew what he wanted from Sunny, but for the life of her, Kathy couldn't figure out what she wanted. Worse still, what did Sunny want from her?

Morning came much too soon and brought no answers. A rumble of thunder in the distance left Kathy little doubt that rain was soon to be upon them. She pulled on some work jeans and an old white oxford shirt. Looking in the mirror, Kathy pondered the reflection she saw there. She brushed her long hair and tied it into a ponytail, all the while contemplating her appearance. She looked so old—so tired. She had allowed the grief and misery of her life to age her. She was only thirty-two, but she looked much older. There was a hardness in her expression that made her appear unapproachable. Was that how everyone saw her? Was that the picture she wanted to portray?

Glynnis had reminded her of her lack of appreciation for the safety and love she'd known at home. Kathy had no idea if it was too late to appreciate such a thing or not, but she had to find a way to try. She was grateful for all she'd had. She was grateful for the time with her parents. She was grateful God had given her at least that much time.

Glynnis had also said that the choices Kathy made could be considered equally as foolish as the ones Sunny had made. That was hard to admit to. Kathy felt her reasons for sending Kyle away had been for his benefit as much as hers.

"Only I never asked him if he felt the same way," she muttered to herself.

Downstairs Sunny was already fixing breakfast. Kathy walked to the porch and glanced outside. "Looks like a storm's moving in."

"Yeah. I closed most of the windows." She turned from the stove. "I'm making eggs in a basket. Want some?"

"I haven't had those in years," Kathy said, warming at the memories. "I remember when mom would cut the little circle out of the bread and give that to us to munch on while she fried the rest with the egg."

"I do too, only I liked it better when my circle of bread was fried up with butter. It's a wonder we didn't weigh twice as much as we did." Sunny laughed and flipped the bread and egg combo. "Remember how Dad always called them eggs in a frame?"

"I do," Kathy said, nodding. "And Grandpa Halbert called them fire in the hole."

"Yeah, he said the yoke of the egg looked like a fire, but I told him, 'No it doesn't, it just looks like an egg.'" They both laughed at the memory, then fell silent.

Sunny brought the food to the table, then went back for the coffee pot. "Look, I want to say something." She paused a moment. "I want us to be friends, Kathy. I know I may be asking too much, but I really want you back in my life. I guess I just need to know what it is you want from me— what it is you need so that we can make this right. This isn't about Mom or Dad anymore—it's about us."

Kathy felt the impact of her statement. "I know. Believe it or not, I spent half the night awake thinking about the same thing."

Sunny sat down. "Soon we'll go our separate ways, but I don't want that to be the end of it. I want to be a part of your life. I want us to be a family again."

For some reason that statement caused Kathy to immediately feel defensive. She had never once tried to be anything but a family. It was Sunny who had left them. Sunny who had torn them apart. Now she demanded to have back what she'd thrown away in such a cavalier manner years ago.

Kathy knew if she didn't leave now, she'd say something that would only set back their recovery. "I need to go." She got up and looked at Sunny, hoping—praying—she might understand.

"I need to be alone. Please understand."

"But you just got here. I have breakfast for us."

"Sunny, please. If I stay, I might say something I shouldn't. I still feel angry, and I need desperately to find a way to let that go. You don't understand how hard this is. I gave you up for dead. Gone for good. I thought I'd never see you again, and believing you were safely in heaven was the only way I ever got through the most painful days." She paused and fought to control her trembling voice.

"You always knew where I was," she continued. "You

could have come back at any moment you chose, but I didn't have that luxury. I didn't know what had happened to you. I didn't know if you were dead or alive, and the thought of you suffering nearly drove me half crazy. Please . . . I can't stay just now. I'm not strong enough for this."

Seventeen

"AND THAT'S HOW I LEFT IT," Kathy told Sylvia as they shared lunch the same day at the Slocum Café. "I just couldn't stay there and talk about all of this. Something happens to me when I'm left alone with Sunny."

"What do you mean?" Sylvia picked up her glass of soda.

Kathy sat back against the booth and sighed. "When I'm alone, I pray through things and feel that I have control of my emotions. Then I see Sunny face-to-face and the past comes flooding back. All the hurt—bitterness—fear—desperation. I really feel angry at Sunny. I pray about it and think I've dealt with it, then it resurges. I try to push it back down, but it keeps coming back. Then you add my stress over the farm not selling, and I'm just not fit for company."

A couple of old farmers came into the café. The bell hanging from the glass door jingled to call attention to their entrance.

"Howdy-do," one of the men said as he nodded to Sylvia and Kathy. Kathy recognized the man as Mr. Bennett. He owned a farm to the east of town. The other man was Mr. Blevins. Both had been good friends of her father.

Kathy smiled. "Hello."

"Meant to tell you I thought the funeral was real nice," Mr. Bennett said. "Sure gonna miss your dad."

Mr. Blevins nodded. "God didn't make too many as good as Gary."

"I agree," Kathy said.

"Have you sold the farm yet?"

She shook her head. "No, there's not been much interest. I'll probably have Tony keep farming it and see about renting out the house until I can get a buyer."

"I told my nephew about it. He was kind of interested, but now's not a real good time for him." Mr. Bennett seemed disappointed. "Wish it could be otherwise."

Kathy sighed. "Me too."

The men moved to the counter and nodded in affirmation as the waitress held up a pot of coffee. Around there, all farmers started meals, important conversations, and sometimes even arguments with a stout cup of coffee.

Kathy pulled her attention away from the men and looked back at Sylvia. "What were we saying?"

"You were talking about how your feelings of anger keep resurfacing. I think it keeps coming back because you aren't really dealing with it. At least that would be my guess—I'm no psychologist." Sylvia grinned. She and Kathy had been psychoanalyzing each other for years. They always joked about saving each other a fortune in therapy bills.

Kathy smiled. "You're as close to one as I'll ever need. I guess I just want to protect myself. In some ways, I'm afraid of Sunny."

"But why? What is there to be afraid of?"

Kathy toyed with her silverware. Her cheeseburger sat untouched on the plate. "You know how I felt when we were younger. I thought Sunny . . . no, Amy and I were very close. See, it even feels like I'm dealing with two different people. Amy died and Sunny was born. Amy changed her name and identity and Sunny took her place. Amy ran away from home, but it was Sunny who came back."

"And what if I said you weren't the same Kathy? You aren't, you know." Sylvia frowned. "The Kathy I knew in high school had a positive disposition and could take on the world. She loved the Lord and knew that no matter what happened she could count on God to always be there for her. The Kathy I knew twelve years ago had dreams and ambitions—romance and plans for the future. You may have stayed here in Slocum, but you've changed."

"I suppose so." Kathy nibbled on a french fry and sat back once again.

"You doing okay?" Marcy Atchison, a slender sixteen-year-old, asked. She refilled their water glasses and waited for their response.

"We're doing fine," Sylvia offered. "Tell Marvin the burgers are perfect."

The teen grinned. "You'll just make his head swell. He already thinks he's the best in the west ever since he won that award at the hamburger grilling contest in Hays."

Kathy and Sylvia laughed. Marvin was nearly seventy years old and had run the Slocum Café most of his life. It had been handed down from his father, and Marvin thought himself rather the expert on his specialty—hamburgers.

They ate in silence until Kathy suddenly announced, "But it isn't just about changing. It's about thinking things existed that never did. I thought my sister and I were close. I thought we could talk about anything. I thought we'd always be there for each other. I misjudged her, Sylvia. I misjudged what we had."

"So what? Things get misjudged all the time."

"What if I'm misjudging her again? What if this time my

misjudgment of the situation only serves to set me up for more pain?"

"What if it does? Are you going to go through life never attempting to love or trust anyone because you might get hurt?"

Kathy shrugged and offered a weak smile. "Seems like a plan I'd come up with, doesn't it?"

"No. It's not like you at all. That's why you're struggling with this situation. You are a loving and giving person. You want to trust your heart again to Kyle and have him trust you with his love. That's asking a lot as far as I'm concerned. When your mother got sick you turned away from me to a degree, but if you had treated me the same way you did Kyle, I'd be hesitant to let you have a second chance."

It was like a light going on for the first time for Kathy. "I did exactly to Kyle what Amy did to me. He thought we had something special—and we did. Yet I shoved it all away from me because . . . because I couldn't see any way to deal with it and have what I needed in order to survive."

Sylvia nodded. "It does sound familiar."

Kathy felt overwhelmed with guilt. Excuses immediately came to mind. "But I didn't lie to him. I told him how much I loved him. He told me he'd wait forever. He knew that my love for him was true. I didn't know that with Amy. She was always lying to us. Lying about her actions. Lying about her needs. I completely misjudged her motives and may be doing the same thing now."

"Why do you have to judge her motives at all? Why not just love her? She is your sister, after all. I know you have your aunt and uncle, but otherwise you don't have any family except Sunny."

"But what if she's playing me for a fool?"

"To what purpose? Kathy, she's in the same boat you are. She's lost both of her parents and is estranged from her only other close family members."

"But how can I trust her?"

"I suppose you are the only one who can answer that. You're the only one who can decide what it is that you really need from Sunny in order to make this worth your time and trouble."

"What I need from her? That's exactly what she asked me. She wanted to know what I needed from her to make this work—to make things right enough that we could be a family again."

"And?" Sylvia questioned, leaning closer.

Kathy looked at her inquisitive expression and shook her head. "And what?"

"And what is it that you need?"

"I don't know. I don't know how a person goes about figuring that out."

"Oh, come on now, Kathy. You know better." Sylvia sounded more like a mother chiding her daughter than a woman speaking with her friend. Her tone set Kathy's defenses on full alert.

"Kathy, what is it that you need from our relationship? I know what I need. I need someone I can trust to keep my confidences. I need someone who will love me no matter what. I need someone who will forgive me when I take advantage of her and who will go the distance with me when I'm being stubborn and can't see matters the way they really are. I get all of that with you. I get it with Tony. I couldn't be best friends with either of you if I had anything less in our relationship. So I'm asking you again—what do you need from Sunny?"

Kathy thought for several minutes. The one thing that kept coming to mind was the one thing she felt she had no way of proving for certain.

"Truth." Kathy spoke the word in a whisper. "I need the truth. I need to know that she's being completely honest with me—that there will never be another lie between us. I need to know that the feelings we're sharing are the real deal."

"And if she told you that she would always give you the truth—would you believe her? Would you be able to feel confident of her word? Or would you just have to give it time and let her actions speak for themselves? Would you have to take a chance that this time things might be different?"

Kathy could see exactly what Sylvia wanted her to see. "There are no guarantees, are there? You keep telling me that, but I keep pretending it's not true."

Sylvia laughed. "Pretend all you want, but it won't change a thing."

"That seems so lame."

"But it is true," Sylvia countered. "We live in a world where lies are the norm. Where cheating and deception are actually rewarded. You can't judge Sunny's heart. You can't know how sincere she is—but you can know your own heart and its sincerity."

"And that's really all I have. Isn't it?"

Sylvia nodded. "It's all any of us have."

Kathy thought about that long after they'd finished their lunch. She went to the grocery store and picked up a few things for supper and tried to sort out her feelings. She would need to talk to Sunny when she got home. It was difficult to know exactly how to say what she needed to tell her. Their relationship was like a razor-sharp sword balanced on its tip. If it fell either way it could cut one or both of them to ribbons.

"Oh, Kathy. How are you holding up?"

It was Renea Stover—the last person Kathy wanted to deal with right now. Kathy forced a smile. "I'm doing pretty well. How about you?" The woman looked very pale and tired. There were dark circles under her eyes.

"I've been terribly worried about you. I must say I've even lost sleep. I just keep thinking about how awful it is for you to have to endure that woman in your house."

"You mean Sunny?"

"Yes. Sunny. Sunshine. Amy. Whatever she calls herself these days. There's nothing in a name to her. She has no respect for anything precious."

"Now, Mrs. Stover, I have to say in Sunny's defense that she's a changed woman. She's not the same person she was twelve years ago."

"It's good of you to defend her." Mrs. Stover gave a look suggesting she thought Kathy the perfect balance of martyr and saint.

"It's not because I'm good that I say that. Sunny has changed, and we should be willing to recognize it."

"Bah. No one changes that much. She can't possibly be as deserving as you say."

Kathy thought of something she'd once heard Pastor Butler say. "But isn't that what grace is all about? Getting what we don't deserve? I can't say whether Sunny deserves a second chance or anyone's respect, but I can say that if I were in the same fix, I would hope people would extend me grace—and mercy."

"She killed your mother." The woman's voice rose in volume. Then as if realizing her tone, Mrs. Stover stepped closer. "Your mother loved that child and she the same as killed her."

"Yes. Mother loved Sunny. Mom's dying words were love for Dad and me . . . and Sunny. She left Sunny a beautiful letter that told of her love . . . and of her forgiveness." Kathy felt as though she could have been arguing with herself. The same accusations had come out of her own mouth.

Kathy gently took hold of Mrs. Stover's shoulder. "We have to understand that Mom loved Sunny with a mother's heart. A heart that you know very well would never with-hold love because of something her child did or didn't do." Tears came to the older woman's eyes as Kathy continued. "To hate Sunny is to hate someone Mom loved dearly. Mom would have died for Sunny. It didn't matter to Mom that Sunny's indifference had led her into a state of poor health. It didn't matter to Mom that Sunny took advantage of her family. It only mattered that Sunny come home—that she know she was loved."

"Marg was such a good woman." She began to cry softly.

Kathy put her arm around Mrs. Stover. "She was a good woman, but so are you. You can't let this go on eating away at your heart, causing you to lose sleep. And neither can I. We have to find a way to let God help us through—to heal us."

"I know you're right, Kathy. I thought I'd let go of it, but when I saw her again—it all rushed back. I thought of your mother lying there so sick and sad. She used to say, 'Renea, if I could just see her again—just hold her and kiss her face—then I could be at peace.' I wanted so much for her to be at peace. I wanted her to die knowing that peace."

Kathy nodded. "I think in a way she did have that peace. I think at the end God gave her a peace that we knew nothing about. He can give us that peace too. I have to believe He can."

The older woman straightened. "I know He can. I'm sorry, Kathy. I've admired you for a long time, just as I admired your mom. I guess I took up offense for you both. It was wrong. I can't say that I'll be able to set it all aside overnight, but you've humbled me, and I see what I need to do."

Kathy drew a deep breath. "I think God is humbling us both."

EIGHTEEN

SUNNY DIALED LANA'S FAMILIAR NUMBER and waited as the telephone rang. Just as Sunny was about to give up, Lana answered the phone.

"Hello?" She sounded breathless.

"Lana, it's Sunny."

"Oh, goodness. I'm so glad to hear from you. I was just heading out to do some shopping but heard the phone ring and thought I ought to come back. Now I'm glad I did. Where are you, and how are you?"

"I'm still in Kansas. My father passed away, and Kathy and I are trying to get the house in shape. We're having an auction to sell off most everything."

"How are you handling your father's passing?"

"Well, for the most part, I think I'm in shock. I knew he was dying, but I guess I still wasn't really ready for it. I wasn't ready for anything I found here." Sunny toyed with the metal cable that connected the receiver to the pay phone. "It's so hard knowing they're both gone. The grief is fierce, but like most of the grief in my life, I'm afraid to let it come to the surface."

"But why, Sunny?"

"I guess I'm worried about it overwhelming me. I don't feel that strong. I worry that I'll turn to drugs or alcohol for help. I don't want to and I don't plan to, but it's always there in the back of my mind because that was my old nature."

"But it's not your new nature. You know that God has a plan for your future. He has promised to never leave you or forsake you. You don't have to be afraid."

Sunny looked down the long dusty road that led out of town. There were very few trees beside it and no curves to the road, so it looked as though the thing went on forever. It seemed endless and empty, and that was exactly how Sunny's life felt at the moment.

"How are things going with your sister?" Lana asked.

Sunny sighed. "I don't know. Sometimes I get hopeful that we can work through things. Then something happens or one of us says something, and I feel like we've gone back to step one. We both seem to have a lot of frustration in dealing with each other."

"Give it time. You may have to take two steps forward and one step back for a while."

"I know, but I really wanted to make this work before leaving Kansas. Kathy's trying to sell the farm, but even if it doesn't sell right away she plans to leave within a couple of weeks. That's all the time we have. Then she'll go to Colorado."

"And where will you go, Sunny?"

The question caused tears to come to Sunny's eyes. "I don't know."

"Look, I don't want to divulge confidences or create false expectations, but you really need to call your mother-in-law. Nancy has been so worried about you, and I think it would be encouraging to you to just talk to her. Please promise me that you'll call her as soon as we finish talking."

Sunny thought about it for a moment. She had wanted to call her mother-in-law for some time but wasn't at all sure her contact would be welcomed. "I . . . uh . . . I want to."

"Then do it. It's important that you stay connected. Sunny, she's half sick with worry about you."

Sunny loved her mother-in-law. Nancy had been nothing but supportive and kind. Even when Brian had treated her with contempt and suspicion, Nancy had shown Sunny unconditional love.

"I'll call her as soon as I hang up."

"Good. Why don't we just postpone any further conversation so you can do that right now? You can always call me tonight and discuss things further if you'd like. I have the day off."

"Okay. I guess I'll do that."

Sunny hung up the phone and found herself tempted to forget about the second call. Her nerves were on edge and her emotions felt raw. How would she ever be able to talk in a normal manner and not reveal her misery and pain? But what if she did reveal those things? Why shouldn't Nancy know that she was unhappy? It wasn't like she'd brought any of this on herself.

Looking at the phone, Sunny contemplated the call. What if Brian answered the phone? He could be visiting his mom and then . . . well . . . then nothing. He'd hang up on her. Sunny was certain of this.

The phone seemed to beckon her. Reaching for the receiver, Sunny decided she could always be the one to hang up. If Brian answered the telephone, she would end the call. He'd need never know it was her. At least this was what Sunny told herself over and over as she punched in the numbers of her calling card.

The phone began to ring. Sunny drew a deep breath and

gripped the telephone so tightly her hand ached.

"Hello?"

Sunny let out her breath and steadied her nerves.

"Hello?"

"Nancy, it's Sunny."

"Oh, Sunny! Oh, sweetheart, I'm so glad you called. I've been so worried."

Tears streamed down Sunny's face. "I'm . . . sorry. I didn't . . . mean . . ." She fought to keep her voice even, but it was no use. She sobbed softly. "I'm sorry."

"Sunny, it's all right. You have nothing to apologize for. Just tell me that you're all right. Where are you?"

"Didn't . . . Lana tell you?" Lana was Nancy's best friend in all of California. In fact, when Sunny's world had fallen apart yet again, Nancy had sent Sunny to stay with Lana.

"Lana told me you'd asked her not to reveal where you were going. She respects people's confidences, Sunny. She told me that you were all right, but not where you were."

"I came to Kansas. I wanted to see my mom and dad— and Kathy, of course."

"And did you?"

Sunny gave a deep sigh as the tears continued to pour. "Mom is dead. She died not long after I left. Dad just passed away on the second of July. Cancer."

"Oh, Sunny. I'm so sorry, honey. How awful for you. What about your sister?"

"She hates me. Well, maybe not as much as she did. We're trying to work through things, but she's . . . she blames me for most everything, and in truth . . . I blame myself."

"I can't imagine what you must be feeling."

"How's Lucy?" Sunny could no longer keep from asking the question. She longed for news of her daughter. Craved it like the air she breathed.

"She's right here. You need to talk to her. She asks about you constantly. The day care has been beside themselves. Lucy goes on and on about you. Wanting to know where you are and when you're coming back."

"Oh, please put her on. I'd love to talk to her." Sunny could hardly draw a breath. She fought to control her tears, not wanting to upset Lucy.

"Mommy! Mommy!" Lucy yelled into the phone.

"Hi, baby. Mommy sure loves you." Sunny trembled from head to toe. The precious voice of her daughter, not yet four years old, filled her with a joy she'd not known since coming to Kansas.

"Mommy, you come home right now."

"I wish I could, baby."

"You can. Just come right now."

Sunny closed her eyes. "Oh, Lucy, I want to. I miss you so much. Please don't forget that I love you."

"Mommy, please come home."

Lucy's pleading was Sunny's undoing. She began to cry in earnest. "Oh, Lucy. Lucy, I'll come soon. I promise. Mommy loves you, Lucy. Please . . . please remember . . . Mommy loves you."

Sunny hung up and fell against the pay phone hood for support. She felt as though all strength had left her body. Crying uncontrollably, Sunny made her way blindly to the car. The heat inside was unbearable, but Sunny didn't care. She turned on the ignition, then laid her head against the steering wheel and let the pain of the last few months wash over her.

Oh, God, I've made such a mess of everything. Why do you let me live? Why do you allow me to go on when I can't even make the tiniest thing right?

Sunny thought of her daughter standing there holding the phone, listening to the disembodied voice of her mother. Did she understand at all what had happened? Could she possibly believe in Sunny's love for her—when Sunny hadn't seen her for nearly two months?

I try so hard, Lord, but it seems no matter what I do, I hurt people. I don't want to hurt them. I didn't want to hurt Mom and Dad when I left. I knew I was being selfish, but I didn't think it would hurt them like it did.

She thought of Kathy and the relationship she'd once known with her sister. At one time they'd been very close. Kathy had been the one person Sunny could turn to in her young life. Everyone and everything else was prone to change. Even when Sunny really messed up, Kathy always forgave her and even seemed to understand.

But not this time.

Everyone had their limit, and apparently she had found Kathy's. Sunny was certain that Kathy could never forgive her.

The air-conditioning cooled the interior of the car and helped to settle Sunny's unstable emotions. She straightened and pulled on her seat belt. She didn't want anyone to find her in this state. She thought of the only place that might offer her any comfort, and despite the building storm clouds in the west, she threw the car in gear and hit the gas.

Gravel flew as the tires fought for traction. The car easily maneuvered onto the short run of pavement on Main Street. Sunny tore through town faster than she knew she should. She didn't care. There was no real law here. Someone might call her on it later, but it wasn't like anyone would pull her over.

She glanced at the skies, remembering the brutal storms she'd experienced as a child. Spring was usually the worst time for violent thunderstorms and tornadoes, but she'd seen them come to the area during most every month of the year. Kansas weather was notorious for its flexibility and quick change. There was no telling what they might be in for today.

I don't care. Let the storms come. Maybe they'll take me away—take my life and give me some peace.

Kathy was just climbing into her car when Sunny's car went streaking past. Sunny looked very upset, and Kathy couldn't be certain, but she thought her sister might be crying. Without giving it further thought, Kathy got into her car and decided to follow Sunny.

"What can she be up to?" Kathy muttered as she accelerated to catch up.

Sunny was well ahead of her, but as she turned her car onto a narrow gravel side road, Kathy knew where she was headed and slowed her car.

Countryside Cemetery was located at the end of the road. In fact, the road just sort of dead-ended at the cemetery gates. You could either enter the tiny fenced-off cemetery by driving through the closely set wrought-iron gate or you could turn around and head back to town.

Sunny had chosen to enter, as Kathy had known she

would. Slowing even more, Kathy followed. Row after row of ancient white stones marked the oldest part of the grave-yard. Here the final resting places of old pioneers could be found. Slocum had been settled in the late 1880s and shortly thereafter had endured a measles epidemic that had taken the lives of half the settlement. Kathy remembered walking in the cemetery with Kyle and noting so many stones that showed the deaths within days of each other. It seemed unnatural.

The cemetery progressed in years the farther Kathy drove onto the grounds. At the very back rows, she spied her sister's car. Sunny had already parked and gotten out. Kathy couldn't see her but knew she'd find her sister on the other side of the car, where their parents' graves were.

Kathy parked her car and prayed for strength. The air outside was heavy. The weather report had called for the possibility of thunderstorms, and Kathy could see that thick gray clouds had already formed and were darkening the sky in the west. If they spent too much time out here, they might well find themselves drenched.

"I don't know what to say to her," Kathy whispered as she reached for the door handle. "Lord, I need your help."

NINETEEN

"DO YOU MIND IF I JOIN YOU?" Kathy asked.

Sunny was nearly sprawled on the ground. She was reclined against their parents' headstone, her head bent in sorrow. When she looked up, Kathy saw her tears.

"You looked upset when your car passed me in town. I thought maybe I should follow you."

"Go away. I'm no good to anyone—especially right now."

Kathy knelt on the ground beside Sunny. "I want to help, but I don't know how. I don't feel like I even know you anymore—in fact, I'm not sure I know myself."

Sunny shook her head. "There's no way to help me. I've been making messes of my life and everyone else's for years now. It's what I seem to do best."

"No it isn't. You aren't half as bad as you tell yourself." Kathy shifted to sit on the ground. "Sunny, I don't know what's got you so upset, but I do wish you'd talk to me about it. I know I haven't been good to you, but I do want to try. I'm finally starting to understand some things."

"You've been very good to me, Kathy. I have no complaints where you are concerned. I can't even imagine how hard it's been for you. Like you've said to me over and over, I knew where you all were. I knew that you were probably safe and sound, but you had no idea about me. Now I come back here trying to amend the past, and all I end up doing is hurting the people I love."

"That's not true. Dad died experiencing a peace that he'd not have had if you hadn't returned. You know that very well."

"But I should have come back years ago. We both know that and it sits between us like a wide canyon. There's no way to bridge it."

Kathy heard thunder rumble in the distance, but she chose to ignore it. "I can't imagine anything too big for God to bridge."

Sunny looked at her for a moment, then shook her head. "But even God says no sometimes. This may be one of those times."

"I doubt that. I can't think of a single verse that says that when a person repents of their sins and asks to be forgiven, we're supposed to ignore them and say no. I think this is just a whole lot harder than either of us could have imagined."

Sunny began to cry fresh tears. "You can . . . say that . . . again."

Kathy thought the storm appeared to be moving near them. She hoped she could get Sunny to calm enough to move this conversation home. "Sunny, I really want to work things out with you. I know that it's just as much my responsibility as yours to overcome the past. And I want you to know that I'm trying."

"I appreciate that." Sunny buried her face in her hands and seemed to fight to control her tears.

"Can you tell me what's brought all this on? Was it what I said at breakfast this morning?"

"No," Sunny said, raising her face. "I . . . no . . . it wasn't that." She met Kathy's gaze. "I miss my daughter. I miss Lucy."

Kathy knew she would have to proceed carefully. "Where is she?"

"California. With her father."

"Why aren't you with them?"

"Because Brian told me to leave and never come back."

Kathy frowned. "But why? Why would he do that?"

"Because like most everyone else in my life, I've disappointed him. He believed something of me that wasn't true."

Kathy said nothing for a moment, then gently touched Sunny's shoulder. "Please tell me about it."

Sunny seemed resigned. She closed her eyes. "It started around Thanksgiving last year."

Sunny felt pretty good about the upcoming holidays. It was a few days before Thanksgiving, and she hoped she might convince Brian to take a little vacation. Just the three of them. Lucy was almost three and quite easy to travel with. Sunny had been looking into accommodations in Mexico, thinking they could fly down on a Thursday and be back on Sunday night. She was hopeful that if she suggested just the short getaway, Brian would allow for it. And if not—if this was simply too soon to give him time to change his schedule—then she had in mind to suggest a little longer trip at Christmastime.

She heard him come into the house through the garage and squared her shoulders. It was never easy to convince him to take time off, but she felt it was absolutely necessary this time. He had promised after Lucy's birth that he wouldn't work so much, but he'd never honored that pledge.

"Hi . . . you look tired," Sunny said as he came into the kitchen. She leaned back against the counter. "Rough day?"

"You could say that." He reached for a glass and went immediately to the refrigerator. Opening the door, he pulled out a carton of orange juice. He poured himself a glass and drank a good portion before adding, "Everybody was in a bad mood. You'd think with the holidays coming up and the fact that we closed the office for Thursday and Friday, they'd be a little happier."

Sunny thought this the perfect time to bring up her ideas. "Speaking of which, I was checking online and found some great deals to Mexico. Just tiny trips—no more than three or four days. I thought maybe we could take Lucy and go. You know, get a little sun and fun."

"The sun's bad for your skin and you know it," he countered.

She laughed. "Well, I didn't say we wouldn't go without our hats and sunscreen." She came to him and put her arms around his neck even though he held the glass of orange juice.

"It won't work. I have too much paper work I've been putting off. I planned to use this time to get caught up."

Sunny tried not to show her disappointment. She let go of her husband and backed up a few steps. "How about at Christmastime then. We could do something special. Maybe take a week."

"How do you think we pay for all of this?" he questioned. "I have to work, Sunny. Money doesn't just fall off trees."

"I know that, Brian, but neither does good health.

You're wearing yourself out. Besides, you promised me. You promised you'd spend more time at home with Lucy and me."

He grimaced. "Yeah, well you promised me more kids. I don't see you trying to get pregnant."

This had been an ongoing argument with them since Lucy turned a year old. Brian wanted a son. In fact, he wanted several sons. Sunny wasn't opposed to more kids, but she felt it unfair to bring them into a home where their father was never around.

"Brian, I've tried to talk to you about this. You're never home. I feel like this is the first time I've seen you in weeks. Even when you're here you're so worn out you don't know which end is up. You go for a swim or lift weights, take a shower and read, and then go to bed. I'm not sure when we'd make another baby even if I thought it was a good idea."

He slammed the glass down on the counter. "Maybe I'd be home more if I thought there was something to be here for." He stormed out, not even bothering to look back.

Sunny found his attitude confusing. She'd done nothing but baby and pamper him since they married. She tried always to be considerate of his schedule. Maybe she'd been too considerate.

Three weeks later, as Christmas and Lucy's birthday drew near, Sunny found herself facing another argument. She'd cornered Brian as he got ready for work. She was determined to get his promise that he'd be a part of Lucy's third birthday.

"It's just one day. Christmas and your daughter's birthday. Everyone takes Christmas off."

"Doctors can't. People are still sick and injured. You know how it is, Sunny. Some of the worst accidents we've seen have happened around the holidays. I can't make big plans because I promised to be on call in case there are emergencies. Lucy is a baby. She doesn't care what day we celebrate her birthday."

"Fine. Then tell me which day you'll take off, and I'll plan her party around that."

Brian finished knotting his tie and shook his head. "It doesn't work that way and you know it. Look, Sunny, my patients need me."

"Your family does too," Sunny replied, her voice edging on hysteria. "You don't even care that we need you. You don't care how often we want to spend time with you. I've thought about making appointments for Lucy and me, just so we'd get at least fifteen minutes of your undivided attention."

He rolled his eyes. "You're such a drama queen. Why can't you be happy with what you have? Go shopping—put Lucy in day care and get a job. I don't care. Just find something to do that doesn't involve me."

"But I got married to you because I wanted to be involved with you," Sunny countered. Tears began to fall, and she knew Brian would despise her for them. He thought tears were a woman's game to control men. He said his mother had always used tears to manipulate his father—before she got religion.

"Look, I'm not going to fight anymore about this. I can't take time off and you need to accept it."

"Then you need to accept that there will be no more children. I won't bring another baby into this house."

"Are you threatening me?" Brian asked, crossing the room in three steps. Sunny cowered instinctively, which seemed to take him by surprise. Then he grew angry. "I've never touched you in anger. Why do you dodge away from me like I'm about to hit you? You know better."

"Then why stomp across the room like some kind of force to be reckoned with?" Sunny straightened and wiped at her tears.

He shook his head and waved her off as a complete irritation. "You're a child, Sunny. Grow up and realize that you can't run the world or me. If you want to take a trip, take one, but leave me out of it."

Sunny followed him from the room, her anger sufficiently stirred. "Maybe I will take a trip. A nice long trip—just me and Lucy."

"Leave Lucy out of this," he said over his shoulder as they went down the stairs.

"Why should I? I'm the only parent she knows." Sunny was thankful her mother-in-law had kept Lucy overnight for some extended time together. She wouldn't have to witness their angry words.

"Lucy knows I love her, unlike you. You're so insecure, you have to be constantly fed a line of praise and compliments." He cursed and went from table to table in the foyer as he searched for something. Probably his car keys.

Sunny smarted from the insult but knew there was some truth to the matter. She fought to keep from crying, but it was impossible with him acting this way.

"You know, I figured you'd be difficult. Drug addicts always are."

"I've recovered," she protested.

"Once an addict, always an addict. You're weak, Sunny. It's why you ran away from home. It's why you ended up married to a wife beater. You draw tragedy to you like ants to ice cream. I despise it and you know it."

"Stop throwing the past in my face. You have your problems too," Sunny said, her voice breaking. "I . . . I'm . . . doing the best I can. I thought you cared about my needs."

"Maybe I'd care more if there weren't so many of them." He finally located the things he'd been looking for and headed for the attached garage.

Sunny couldn't help herself. She followed after him like a lost puppy—a kicked-in-the-ribs, lost puppy.

"Look, stop smothering me and putting demands on me that I can't fulfill. I'm not going to put up with this. I'll divorce you before I put up with much more."

His declaration stopped Sunny in her steps. Brian continued to the garage, however. She heard his Jag roar to life, then listened as he peeled out of the garage and down the drive.

Sobbing uncontrollably, Sunny sank to the kitchen floor. Why did he have to be so mean? How could he possibly say the things he had said if he loved her?

No more than ten minutes had passed when the doorbell rang. Sunny rose slowly from the floor but figured to ignore it. She had no desire to see anyone. Then she worried that it might be Nancy bringing Lucy home. Something might be wrong. Composing herself as best she could, Sunny went to the door and answered it as it rang a third time.

"I was beginning to think nobody was home." It was Rick Anniston, Brian's partner. That is, if *partner* could even be used to describe the relationship those two shared.

Rick frowned. "You've been crying. What's wrong?"

Sunny pulled back and shook her head. "It's nothing." She tightened the sash on her robe. "Brian's already left."

"Seriously, Sunny. What's going on?"

"We fought. That's all."

"I'm a good listener if you want to talk about it." He flashed her a smile.

"I appreciate that, but you can't fix this. It's the same old thing. Brian won't take any time off to be with Lucy and me. I called him on it and he blew up." She shrugged. "It's that simple."

"I'm sorry, Sunny. I guess we're both suffering from Brian's drive to be all things to all men. I've been turning to spiritual renewal for my peace of mind. Maybe you should consider the same."

"I was raised religious," Sunny said. "I didn't care for the hypocrisy. I certainly don't need to listen to one more speech about how bad I am."

"He said that?" Rick took a step toward her. "He said you were bad?"

"He threw my past in my face and accused me of things." Sunny began to cry again. "It's all so unfair. I love him so much, and he treats me like dirt. I don't understand. In the beginning he really seemed to care. I guess I'm just a trophy wife to him." Blinded by tears, she turned to find a tissue, but instead found Rick's strong arms around her.

"I'm so sorry, Sunny. You're a good woman and he should never have hurt you like that."

Sunny resisted his touch, then gave in. It had been so long since anyone had held her—just hugged her or offered words of encouragement. Now Rick was here, and he seemed to know all the right things to say.

Mindless of wetting his suit with her tears, Sunny let her emotions drain. Neither one said a word. Rick simply held her and let her cry. There seemed to be something almost paternal in his touch. She thought of her father and cried all the harder.

"I should have known something like this was going on."

Brian's angry words caused both Rick and Sunny to jump. Neither one had heard him come back. Sunny raised her tearstained face to her husband. His rage was clear. He called her a string of ugly names, then grabbed her arm and pushed her to one side and faced Rick.

"Is this how you repay me for the support I've given you? For allowing you to come into my clinic and practice under my reputation and name in this community?"

"You don't allow me to do much of anything in your practice," Rick declared. "You've misjudged this situation, just as you generally misjudge everything. Sunny's done nothing wrong. I came here a few minutes ago and found her crying. I didn't come for some illicit affair."

"Then why are you here?" Brian's face grew beet red. "Why are you here with her dressed like that?" Sunny pulled at her robe self-consciously.

Rick reached into his pocket. "I came to give you this. It's my resignation. I had my lawyer draw up papers. You can buy out my investment. I've decided to join another group."

"Get out of here. I should have known you'd pull something like this. You never were worth trusting—that's why I didn't turn over my patients to you."

"I was completely trustworthy, Brian. Just like your wife."

"I said get out here. Both of you. I want you both out of my house."

"This is my house too," Sunny shot back. She took a step forward then halted at the look Brian threw her.

"Not anymore. I want you out of here. Go get dressed and pack your things."

"You can't just throw her out," Rick protested. "She's done nothing wrong."

Brian threw a swing and narrowly missed connecting with Rick's nose. "If you don't go on your own, I'll put you out myself."

"Don't fight. Please," Sunny said, her mind a blur of unanswered questions. "I'll get some things and leave. I just don't want you to fight." Desperation made her voice thick, and she knew something had happened that day that could never be fixed. Never be overcome. It was the end of the fairy tale, and no one was living happily ever after.

TWENTY

A LOUD CRASH OF THUNDER brought Sunny into the present. She looked at the ugly sky and shook her head. "Guess we'd better head home, huh?"

Kathy looked up as if seeing it for the first time. "I was so engrossed in your story that I lost track of the weather. I think you're right. We'd better get out of here."

They hurried for their cars and headed back out the way they'd come in. The greenish sky swirled with thick billowing clouds. Sunny knew from her childhood that this usually meant hail—probably wind too. And sure enough, just as they reached the farm, the sky started chucking pea-size hail. The orange and yellow marigolds that lined the walkway were already drooping from the barrage.

Sunny got out of her car and started to make a dash for the porch, but Kathy called to her. "We need to get to the storm cave. Didn't you hear? We're under a tornado warning."

Sunny felt a chill go through her. All of their young lives they'd lived with the threat of violent weather. She had to admit in the years that she'd lived in California, she hadn't missed it. The threat of earthquakes was unnerving at times, but tornadoes were horrific storms that Sunny had hoped to never again endure.

"I didn't have the radio on," Sunny told her sister.

They ran for the backyard as the hail grew in size. Kathy opened the shelter door and motioned Sunny inside.

"There's a flashlight at the bottom of the stairs," she called and pulled the door down just as Sunny managed to locate the piece.

Sunny turned on the flashlight and felt an eerie sensation wash over her. Overhead the hail beat down on the metal door, but otherwise there was no sound.

"I didn't realize the storm was so close—or so bad." Kathy secured the latch before coming down the stairs to find the battery-operated lantern. "There, that helps," she said as she switched on the light. "You can turn the flashlight off. Now for the radio." She went to the small cupboard and took down the weather alert radio they'd used for years.

"I'd almost forgotten what this was like," Sunny said, turning off the flashlight. She placed it back where she'd found it. "At least I tried to forget. This place has always scared me. You've made it nice in here—well, at least nicer than I remember." She motioned to a metal rocker with a plastic-covered cushion. "That's definitely new. Better than the old wooden benches." She noted they were gone. Other cushioned metal chairs were in their place.

"We've probably been down here at least once a year since you left. One year, I can't remember now which one," Kathy said, "we were down here almost every night from April through June. It was one storm after another, and most were tornadic. Dad even put cots down here, because there were nights when it was just a good idea to grab some sleep while the storms raged."

Sunny heard the wind pick up outside and sighed. "I suppose it wouldn't have been a fitting trip home if I hadn't endured a good old Kansas storm."

"What about—"

The weather alert radio cut off Kathy's words, the dull drone of the weather service's computerized voice announcing that an important message was about to be delivered.

The news wasn't good. The sheriff had sited a tornado touching down just southwest of Slocum. If it continued in the path it was on, it would pass very close to the farm. Sunny whispered a prayer for their safety.

"Remember when Mom would sing 'Shelter in a Time of Storm' when we'd have to come down here?" she asked her sister.

Kathy nodded. "I do. That's a pleasant memory in light of all of this."

"Sounds like the hail stopped."

"I'm glad for that," Kathy said. "The farm will be even harder to sell if there's a lot of damage. I'd hate to have to replace the roof. Dad and I just did that a couple of years ago. We had a storm come through with baseball-sized hail that totally destroyed the windows and really beat up the roof."

Silence engulfed them for several minutes. Sunny felt a nervous tension that always came with storms, while Kathy seemed calm. Or maybe she was just bored. After all, there was nothing they could do but wait out the storm. Perhaps that was the most maddening thing. All they could do was sit and wait to see what destruction they might face.

"What were you going to say before the radio went off?" Sunny questioned.

Kathy looked a bit uncomfortable. "I guess . . . well . . . I was hoping you'd tell me what happened after you left Brian. If you don't mind."

Sunny nodded. She was actually glad to be focused on something else. "Things calmed down a bit, but I realized things had changed. I went to stay at his mom's because I didn't have anyplace else to go. The thing that made me saddest was that Lucy never asked about Brian. He wasn't home enough to miss. She thought staying at Grandma's was such a great treat, and nothing else really mattered.

"I got tired of waiting to hear from him, so I took Lucy and went home on Christmas morning. He was there— quiet, but at least not angry. I figured with Lucy in tow, he wouldn't be as likely to make a scene, but I hated risking her comfort. We said very little. He had bought a large red rocking horse for Lucy and she thought it was the best thing in the world. She practically rocked herself to sleep on it. After I put her to bed, I tried to talk to Brian, but he didn't want to talk. He said talking wouldn't fix what was wrong with us."

"I'm sorry. That must have been so frustrating—being accused of something you didn't do."

Sunny felt the pain of the memory threaten to strangle her. "No matter what I said, he didn't want to listen or talk. His mother tried to talk to him too. That only made him mad. He accused me of putting her up to it, but I told him I'd said very little to her about anything."

"What happened to Rick?"

"Brian bought him out and he went to a firm in Houston. Before he left, he came to the house one night to talk to Brian. I'd already gone to my room—Brian and I had separate rooms by this time. Anyway, I'd gone upstairs, but I heard the sound of voices and went to investigate. Rick was telling Brian he'd misunderstood everything. That was when I found out about Anita."

"Who's Anita?"

"She's Brian's office manager. It seems she was jealous of me. She had thought she had a chance with Brian prior to his marrying me. From what I could discern, she had all sorts of things planned, but then Brian connected with me and we married very quickly."

"Did Brian have an affair with her?"

The weather radio went off again. This time the news sounded better. They were still under a tornado warning, but the storm system was shifting north and the tornado that had been spotted earlier was no longer on the ground.

"Well, at least the storm will pass mostly over open ground," Kathy said, resetting the radio. She turned back to Sunny. "So did he cheat on you?"

"Brian didn't have an affair as far as I know. But Anita planted thoughts in Brian's mind, and he thought I was having an affair with Rick. She'd been telling him for months, probably years, that the two of us were sneaking around behind his back."

"That probably explains his reaction when he came home and found you together."

Sunny nodded. "I know he figured the worst. Nancy came over one day and we talked about everything. I told her I hadn't cheated on Brian—that I loved him. She believed me, and that comforted me in a way I can't even begin to explain. I felt that everyone suspected me of the worst, but not Nancy. In fact, she told me she was worried that Brian was going down the same road as his father. Brian's dad had divorced Nancy when Brian was about fifteen. He left her for another woman and married soon after the divorce was final. He was actually into his fourth marriage when a heart attack caught up with him."

"So are you divorced?" Kathy asked.

"Not yet. Things went along in a strange kind of unspoken agreement. We didn't talk about anything. We didn't share meals or time together. I lived at the house, but in a separate room. I took care of Lucy as I always had, but Brian wanted nothing to do with either of us.

"Then on Valentine's Day the doorbell rang. I thought maybe Brian had sent me something—you know, a sort of 'starting over' gift. It was cold and rainy that day—strange weather, if I remember right. It felt almost like winter might here, instead of Southern California. I remember shaking uncontrollably even before the man served me with divorce papers. Brian had filed for divorce and was requesting full custody of Lucy."

"Full custody? What made him think he was entitled to that?"

"Probably because he was rich and felt powerful."

The weather radio announced an all-clear, but neither sister made a move to leave the shelter. Sunny tried not to get emotional at the memory of that night.

"Brian came home early with an older woman, probably midfifties. Her name was Mrs. Cartwright. He'd hired her as a nanny. He told me in front of her that he wanted me to collect my things and get out of the house. He told me Mrs. Cartwright would care for Lucy and that he was suing for full custody. I told him there was no way he deserved it and I would fight him tooth and nail."

"What happened then?" Kathy was completely engrossed.

"He told Mrs. Cartwright to wait in the living room while we went upstairs. Lucy had been playing happily in her room, but when she heard us she came to investigate. Brian asked her if she wouldn't like to live with him for a while—just the two of them. Lucy told him no. She came to me and wrapped her arms around me. I'd never seen Brian angrier. He accused me of turning Lucy against him. He said I had caused him nothing but pain.

"Lucy began to cry and he called for Mrs. Cartwright. The woman came upstairs looking quite uncomfortable with the situation. He commanded her to take Lucy to her room. Lucy screamed as he wrenched her from my arms. She kept calling for me." Sunny's voice broke. "I wanted to take her back and run. Run as far as I could, but when I made a move toward her room, Brian took hold of me and pushed me up against the wall. He said that if I did anything to interfere with him and what he wanted, he would see to it that I never saw Lucy again. He told me he had everything he needed to secure his desires—that my past alone would keep a judge from granting me custody of any kind."

"I'm so sorry, Sunny. That must have been hideous."

"You can't even begin to imagine. Brian wasn't anything like the man I'd married. He seemed so changed. His attitude was completely foreign to me. I worried that maybe he was on drugs, because he was so altered."

"It's so strange," Kathy said, growing reflective. "I sat here all these years believing you were either dead or living the good life. I hated you for either one. Every time someone talked about you, I systematically disassociated myself. I told myself feeling nothing would be better than the pain."

"I've certainly done that enough times myself," Sunny admitted. She could see that Kathy's defenses were down and she longed to keep things under control. Her head throbbed from all the crying she'd done. The storm outside had nothing on the storm that raged within her heart.

"You asked me why I was here and not there with them," Sunny began again. "That's the reason. Brian told me if I left and cooperated with him, he'd see that I had regular visitation with Lucy and a maintenance stipend—a very generous one.

"I didn't know what else to do. I couldn't put Lucy through the misery of fighting over her. I suggested to Brian that we get counseling and work things out, but he didn't want to even discuss it. I think Anita had completely convinced him that Rick and I were scheming behind his back. She evidently had been telling Brian that Rick planned to take over his business and patients. That's why Brian wouldn't give up any of his people or take time away from the office. I'm sure of that now."

"What an awful woman. And all because of not being able to have something she wanted." Kathy shook her head. "To destroy a marriage—a family. How in the world could that woman even live with herself?"

"Some people don't care who they hurt. They only want what they want—at any price. I know, because I was that person. I've told myself over and over that I got what I deserved for treating people the same way."

"I don't believe that. I don't think God works that way. Yes, we have to bear the consequences of our actions, but I can't see Him wanting to hurt a little girl in the process."

"I talked to Lucy today. I called my mother-in-law and Lucy happened to be there. Nancy doesn't hold me responsible for any of this, and for that I'm most thankful. She let me talk to Lucy." Sunny wiped at her tears. "She . . . she . . . begged . . . No, she demanded," Sunny said with a harsh laugh, "that I come home."

"Nancy did?"

"No. Lucy." Sunny could still hear the pleading in her daughter's voice. "I'm telling you, Kathy, it nearly killed me."

TWENTY-ONE

KATHY STRUGGLED WITH HER feelings. One side of her felt great sympathy for Sunny, but the other side felt Sunny had probably brought on part of her problems. *After all,* Kathy thought, *look at all the trouble she's caused our family.*

Sunny said nothing for several minutes. The weather alert radio went off again, this time telling of another tornado in the county to the east of them. Apparently the storm was moving off at a quick pace. Kathy didn't know whether there was another system heading their way, but she was tired of the storm cave.

"Why don't we go up and see if we got any damage," she suggested. "I need some fresh air."

She got to her feet and headed to the door. "Would you switch off the lantern when I get the door open?"

Sunny nodded while Kathy unlatched the shelter entrance. They went up the stairs and found the skies clear overhead. The sun was already out and everything seemed clean and refreshed by the rain. Kathy didn't spot any damage and breathed a sigh of relief. The last thing she wanted was a delay in selling the farm and getting that part of her life laid to rest.

As much as she regretted leaving Kansas and the only home she'd ever known, she had a true restlessness that urged her forward. The last twelve years were becoming increasingly confusing to her. What she had once thought was an act of selfless love seemed somehow clouded by thoughts that she was breaking out of bondage. *Why should I feel this way? I loved Mom and Dad and wanted to help them.* She frowned and opened the back porch door.

They turned on the television and found the weather clear to the west. "Why don't we sit on the porch and you can finish telling me about California and the divorce," Kathy suggested. Somehow Sunny's story didn't seem finished, and Kathy wanted to know what had happened to her sister after Brian kicked her out.

Sunny followed her outside rather reluctantly. They took seats, Kathy in the glider swing and Sunny in a rocker. Kathy knew that Sunny was deeply troubled by the conversation with her daughter. Kathy tried to picture the child as a miniature of Sunny. It seemed so crazy to imagine that Sunny had a daughter—that Kathy had a niece. Kathy shook her head.

"Have you talked to Brian since leaving?"

"No." Sunny fixed her gaze in the distance. "I doubt he'd even take my call. I tried to talk to him over and over before I left, but he wouldn't speak to me. His mother said his pride was wounded. She believes he knows the truth but is too proud to admit it."

"So he'll just destroy his family for the sake of his pride? That's a bit ridiculous, don't you think?"

Sunny frowned but still didn't look at Kathy. "I think a lot of things are ridiculous." She began to rock back and forth. "For so long I believed I didn't have a right to question anything or anyone. I felt like the mistakes I made were so severe I'd lost any right I had. I believed I was so bad that even God couldn't love me. But Lana believes it's typical of people who've been abused. They convince themselves they

got what they deserved and they don't have a right to anything better. I keep trying to work on that, but sometimes
it's really hard."

Kathy felt uncomfortable with the topic. Hadn't she told
herself that Sunny didn't deserve anything better? Hadn't
she been as harsh about the situation, convinced that
because Sunny had made poor choices she deserved to bear
the consequences—no matter how painful? *How could I be
that cruel?* She suddenly felt a mixture of shame and guilt.

"Tell me about Lana." She hoped Sunny's comments
would steer her mind away from the negative thoughts.

"Lana's a wonderful woman. She's a widow who works at
a hospital in Anaheim. She's a registered nurse, and she's
also best friends with Nancy, Brian's mom." Sunny shifted
in the chair and crossed her legs. "They're a funny combination. Nancy is so wealthy she'll never have to worry about
anything, and Lana barely makes enough to treat herself to
an occasional dinner out. They're an odd couple, but they
are closer than any two friends I've ever known.

"When Brian demanded I leave, I went to Nancy. I
didn't have anyone else. It's funny, but I didn't make any
real friends in California. We knew people, of course, but
they weren't what I would call friends. There are those
people in the world who are happy to be close to you when
things are going great, but just let one thing go wrong or get
ugly, and they either desert you or hang around long enough
to see how badly you're going to crash and burn."

Kathy nodded. "I know the kind."

"Well, I didn't have anyone to go to that I cared to let
know the situation. So I went to Nancy. I told her what had
happened. I told her I knew I couldn't stay with her—after

all, Brian was her son and he wouldn't be comfortable to come to her if I was there. Nancy agreed, but suggested I could stay with a friend of hers. She called Lana and told her the situation. Lana was happy to have me. She had a three-bedroom house to herself and was rather lonely. I went to live with her but had no idea what I'd gotten myself into."

"What do you mean?" Kathy's curiosity was once again triggered.

"Lana is a woman with a strong faith in the Lord. She lives her faith like nobody I've ever seen."

"What about Mom and Dad?" Kathy felt defensive and crossed her arms. "They had strong faith."

"Yes. They did, but this went even beyond what we grew up with. Lana lives in a way that suggests she's actually seen God face-to-face. I know she hasn't done that in a physical way, but she certainly has in a spiritual sense. She's at peace all the time. She never questions God's ability to resolve a matter or deal with things fairly. She doesn't fool anyone by suggesting that getting right with God equals freedom from pain and problems, but she makes it clear that by experience she knows that a closeness with God equals a peace of mind that cannot be had anywhere else."

The rhythmic beat of the glider moving back and forth was the only sound for several minutes. Sunny seemed to be considering her words carefully, almost as if she knew Kathy was feeling a certain tension from the unspoken suggestion that Lana had something the rest of them didn't.

"Mom and Dad trusted God for sure. They were always encouraging us as kids to read our Bible and pray. They wanted us to be in church and to know who God was and what Jesus had done for us in dying on the cross. I knew all of that and still walked away. I knew the stories. I knew the routines. I had even stood up in church when I was twelve and asked God to save me from my sins. I did everything that tradition called for."

"You mean that the Bible called for, don't you?"

"Some of it was what the Bible called for. Some of it was what we the people in the church had attached to it. Do you realize how difficult we make it for someone to accept that Jesus died for their sins and that they can be saved for all eternity by accepting His sacrifice?"

"What are you saying?" Kathy shook her head. "You make it sound as if Christians don't want people to get saved."

"Well, I don't know if they do or don't as a whole. I just remember how severe people could be with each other. I know how hard they've been on me. All I want is forgiveness and to be able to move forward with my life, and instead I get negativity and ugly comments."

"Now wait a minute." Kathy stopped the glider and leaned forward. "You can't just do whatever you want in life and then expect people to overlook it."

"I wasn't suggesting that. There are always consequences, good and bad. Lana helped me to see that God's love is unconditional, while most people put conditions on their love. They'll accept you or care about you so long as you do things their way. Some people do whatever they can, even to their detriment, all in order to please someone else and earn their approval. That's what I was doing with Brian. I really loved him—I still do—but I wasn't being myself. I was living in a way that I thought would please him, until I saw what it was doing to our daughter. When he started pressuring me to have more kids, I knew I couldn't just please him without counting the cost. Lana suggested that my standing up to him probably fit in with one of the stories Anita was feeding him at the office."

"How does she figure that?" It frightened Kathy to realize that she wanted to challenge her sister at every move.

"Well, if Anita was telling him that I was having an affair with Rick, she was probably also suggesting that I wasn't willing to have any more kids or get off the birth control pills I insisted on taking, for fear I'd get pregnant while having my fling."

"Seems strange that Brian should have even confided in Anita about wanting more kids."

"I know, but I'm sure he doesn't see it that way." She sighed.

"Lana sounds like a good friend," Kathy said after several minutes of silence.

Sunny got up and leaned against the porch rail to face Kathy. "Lana has helped me to see things in a different way, but I don't suppose I ever would have cared about what she had to say if I hadn't seen her live her convictions firsthand. She's not just a Sunday Christian—she really lives her faith daily."

"Mom and Dad weren't Sunday Christians either. Neither am I." Kathy knew her tone was edged with irritation, but she didn't try to disguise it.

"I'm not going to judge anyone," Sunny said defensively. "I just saw Lana live her faith rather than just speak it. She helped me to see that I could have something different too. It's more than what I had when I attended church as a child.

It runs so deep and true. I'm sure you're right, that Mom and Dad had it, that you have it, but remember ... I left not caring to recognize that kind of behavior in them. I'm not trying to say Lana is better than anyone, but she has a friendship with Jesus—a deeply rooted love and trust in Him that keeps her solid when things around her seem shaken to the point of destruction. I want that for myself—more than anything."

"More than Brian and Lucy?"

Sunny stood biting her lip for a moment, then nodded. "Yes. Because I now see that if I don't have that kind of real relationship with God, none of the rest will matter. None of it will last. I'll have no solid foundation to build on."

Kathy could finally see what Sunny was saying. "I guess I understand what you're saying. It's kind of that place where life can no longer shake you. I want that too."

A large four-wheel-drive vehicle came down the road in front of the farm. Kathy recognized it as Sylvia and Tony's Suburban. She waved and saw Sylvia wave from the passenger seat at they drove toward their farm. Sunny waved too.

Silence shrouded them for several minutes. Sunny again took her seat in the rocker while Kathy thought on all they had discussed. It was like a door had opened just a little wider. They were making progress, but it was coming in baby steps.

"I knew it would be hard coming back. I figured I'd have a real time of it with Mom and Dad," Sunny said softly. "Lana helped me to see I needed to mend the past before I could move forward, and I really wanted to do that. I guess in most respects, I have. I have Mom's and Dad's forgiveness. I thought that would be hard earned, but instead it came in such unexpected ways. Mom's letter. Dad's open welcome." Sunny turned and faced Kathy. "But what I don't have is your forgiveness. And, as strange as it sounds, I never thought I would have to work for it like I have."

"What do you mean work for it? I'm not making you work for anything."

"You may not think you're doing anything, but you are. You've withheld yourself from me in so many ways. I kept telling myself I didn't have a right to talk to you about it— to challenge you to face it or change it, but I can't stay quiet. You treat me as if I'm a stranger. As if you have to be cautious of me and what I might do."

Kathy stiffened. "Why should I be any different than anyone else? You hurt me."

"But I thought we had something different."

"I thought so too, but then you ran away." Kathy felt her defenses rising. "I felt like everything I had believed was a lie."

"But why? I was the one who messed up."

"But I felt betrayed. You asked me what it was I needed from you, and I figured it out earlier today. I need honesty. I need truth, because, Sunny . . . Amy, I thought I had the truth when we were girls. I thought we were close—and what you did by leaving the way you did, by staying away without any word for twelve years . . . well . . . it negated the relationship I thought I had with you."

Kathy fought to keep back tears. She didn't want Sunny to think she was weak. "Everything I believed was true changed almost overnight. Some by my hand, but mostly because of you. The family changed. My relationship with Kyle changed. I changed. The only constant I had was God.

I clung to Him like a drowning rat, and while I may not fully understand what it is to have complete peace in Him, I'm trying."

"That's all any of us can do. Lana told me that her relationship with God didn't come overnight. It's been developing over years of getting to know Him better and learning that He is faithful—that we can trust Him not to hurt us like we hurt each other."

"I believe that," Kathy said, calming a bit. "It's the same with human relationships. When we put our faith and trust in someone and they prove themselves to be false, it hurts." She felt the tears slip down her cheeks. "You hurt me, Sunny. You hurt me more than I can say."

Sunny nodded, her expression betraying that she too was close to tears. "But you won't let me make things right?"

"You can't make things right!" Kathy declared a little louder than she'd intended. "You can't give me back the wasted years—the lost relationships and life that I might have known—that we might have known."

"No. I can't. I can't do anything about the past except say I'm sorry—and I am genuinely sorry. Hopefully I can do something about the present—the future." Sunny got to her feet. "But first, Kathy, I need you to forgive me."

TWENTY-TWO

KATHY REMAINED QUIET for a long time. Forgiving was the right thing to do, and in truth, Kathy knew it was what she wanted to do. She stared out past Sunny to the road. The light was fading and nearly gone.

So many years stood between them, the past a vast wasteland that seemed impossible to cross. Yet Kathy knew that with God, all things were possible. Either she honestly believed that or it was nothing more than a quaint saying, hollow in its promise.

She looked at Sunny and saw nothing but sincerity in her expression. "I want to forgive you. I know it's the right thing to do, but my heart screams for protection. I want to trust you again," Kathy finally said. "Please understand, though, I can't do it overnight. I mean, I can say the words, but it's going to be a process—a journey."

"Most things in life are," Sunny replied. "I don't mind waiting, Kathy. I just want you to forgive me so that we can start over."

Kathy nodded. "I want that too. I really do." Yet still she wasn't saying the words. What was wrong with her? Why was her heart so hardened against giving Sunny her forgiveness? Was it that Kathy thought forgiveness somehow equaled approval? Was forgiveness saying that it didn't matter what Sunny had done—that she shouldn't feel bad or responsible for the problems she'd caused? Kathy felt her head begin to throb. She thought of what Paul said in

Romans seven, "I do not understand what I do. For what I want to do I do not do, but what I hate I do."

Hating Sunny wasn't what she wanted to do. Holding a grudge and focusing on the bitter past weren't what Kathy wanted either. Yet most of her adult life, Kathy had focused on exactly that.

But what child of God—what honest-to-goodness Christian woman—would refuse someone forgiveness when they asked?

The thought startled her. She wasn't refusing Sunny forgiveness—was she? But she was using the excuse that it would take time—that Sunny would have to prove herself. *It's a good thing God doesn't treat me like that*, Kathy thought. *How would it be if I asked God for forgiveness and He said, "I want to forgive you, but it's going to take time"?*

❧ ❧ ❧

The next morning Kathy woke up thinking about Sunny's stories about the past. She thought too about Sunny's desire for forgiveness. It had taken a lot of courage for Sunny to come home again.

"And I haven't made it easy for her in any way." She thought of the way she'd wanted to slam the door in Sunny's face on that first day. Dad had welcomed Sunny with open arms, thanking and praising God for answered prayer. But not Kathy. Kathy had been angry and frustrated by the entire situation.

Why? Why couldn't I have just opened my arms as well? Sylvia must be right. My love for Sunny is shallow—based on her doing and being what I need her to do and be.

Kathy stretched and threw back the sheet. She had a lot to get done today, and she knew she shouldn't waste any time. She glanced over at the clock and was surprised to find that it was already a quarter till eight. Thoughts of Sunny fled.

"Oh, good grief." She jumped up from the bed and scrambled to find her work clothes. Knowing the day would probably be plenty warm, she donned capris and a tank top.

Kathy grabbed her hairbrush and took several minutes to force her hair into compliance. For the kind of work she knew she'd have to face, it was best to pull it back and braid it out of the way. Finally satisfied, she slipped into sandals, then made her way downstairs.

"I thought I'd find you already at work," Sunny said as Kathy entered the kitchen. She was busy making coffee. "I just got down here."

"I slept crazy last night. I'd sleep hard then wake up, then go back to sleep. I think it's the stress and excitement of all that needs to be accomplished."

"Yeah, time's passing pretty quick."

"We've got to finish sorting things out today and tomorrow for the auction." Kathy went to the fridge and grabbed a container of yogurt. "And of course there's a ton of cleaning."

"Of course," Sunny said with a smile. "I think we'd better get some of those storage tubs too. You know the plastic ones?"

"Yeah, those would be easier to move. You know, I've pretty well decided I'm not taking much with me. I'll take my clothes and whatever knickknacks and furniture that I feel are important.

Sunny nodded. "That makes sense. Starting fresh will be good."

"We always just kind of lived in a hodgepodge. I hope it will bring something at the sale. The auction people told me we could expect the biggest money from the farm equipment, obviously, and then the tools and antique dishes and collectibles." She ate for a minute while leaning against the kitchen counter. "Are you sure you don't want some of the Depression glass?"

Sunny shook her head. "No. That will bring some good money and you deserve to have it. Besides, I don't know what I'd do with it. I don't even have a home right now."

Kathy frowned and tried not to let Sunny see her reaction. She didn't know how to comfort Sunny in this situation. Kathy knew if the roles were reversed, she wouldn't be looking for sympathy.

"So do you want me to run over to Hays and get some tubs? I can go right away and get back in a short time. I can also pick up some planters for the roses."

"That would be a great idea. We also need trash bags, cleaning supplies, and more boxes if you can get them. The grocery store's been most accommodating, but you have to catch them before they cut them up."

"I'll do it then." Sunny checked the coffee maker. "Coffee's done. I'll grab a cup to take with me."

"There are some travel mugs under the sink. Dad and I sometimes took them when we went back and forth to the doctor. The red one was his favorite."

Sunny opened the cabinet and took out the plastic mug.

She held it with an expression that suggested something between love and regret. Kathy felt sorry for her.

"You can have it if you want it. Otherwise the auction gets it."

"I'd like to keep it. At least for a while." Sunny popped the lid and poured coffee into the cup. "I can just imagine Dad sitting in the car with it." She smiled. "I'm guessing anytime you bought coffee when you were out somewhere he complained that it wasn't as good as you could get at home."

"Or from the old percolator types," Kathy said with a laugh.

"Ah, the good old days."

Fifteen minutes later Sunny was on her way to Hays and Kathy was back to work in their parents' room. She had her piles sorted. Books, clothes, bric-a-brac, photo albums and framed pictures, odds and ends that didn't seem to fit any particular category. It was the stuff of their lives.

Digging through her parents' closet, Kathy was amazed to find a lot of things that she hadn't even realized they had. Old cameras, a slide projector, two shotguns, three worn leather suitcases, antique hatboxes. She was even more amazed to find the latter still contained hats.

She got most of the stuff packed and marked in short order. Soon Sunny would return and they could work together to break down the bed. With a sigh, Kathy got to her feet and decided to clean the floors of the stark room. She went to Sunny's room, where she remembered they'd decided to store the vacuum.

Crossing the room, Kathy couldn't help but notice Sunny's Bible was open atop her bed. A letter lay beside it.

She knew it was wrong to snoop, but she felt compelled to see what the letter was. She unfolded the paper slowly and recognized her mother's handwriting. This was the letter she'd written to Sunny.

An aching grew in Kathy's heart. She had no such letter to read and find comfort in. She was jealous. Mom had often told Kathy some of the same things that were in Sunny's letter, but Kathy had no proof of them as Sunny did.

"Just proof in my own heart."

She folded the letter and sat down on the bed. "I don't want to envy her. She's suffered more than I have. I had Mom right up until the end. I have to remember that I had time with both Mom and Dad that Sunny forever forfeited."

But the past was still haunting. Accusations sprung to mind regarding Sunny—accusations that only weeks ago Kathy would have relished as great companions. Now she only wanted them to leave her in peace.

Looking down at the Bible, Kathy saw the book was opened to the forty-third chapter of Isaiah. Her gaze fell to the eighteenth and nineteenth verses, and it seemed that God was speaking the passage directly to her.

Forget the former things; do not dwell on the past. See, I am doing a new thing! Now it springs up; do you not perceive it? I am making a way in the desert and streams in the wasteland.

She pondered the verses for a time. "'Forget the former things,'" she murmured. "'Do not dwell on the past.'"

Kathy looked around her at the room. She thought of the house and all its contents—relics of a past that had long outgrown its usefulness. It wasn't about the things anymore. It wasn't about the farm and the land she'd grown up on. Suddenly everything around her seemed worn and tired.

"He's doing a new thing," she said, putting the Bible back down. "'A way in the desert and streams in the wasteland.'"

Kathy heard the sound of a car pulling into the drive. She checked her watch. It was too soon for Sunny to be back. Hurrying downstairs, she reached the bottom step just as a knock sounded on the front door. It was definitely not Sunny.

Sylvia stood on the other side, a casserole in hand. "I knew that even if you didn't need my help in cleaning, you could probably use it for supper."

Kathy laughed. "Of course. I love your cooking." She took the towel-wrapped glass dish. "What'd you make?"

"Chicken with that rice and stuffing combination you like so much."

"Oh, I can hardly wait. I might have to have some for lunch."

"It works for that too." She glanced around. "It looks like you're making progress. Everything seems a little more sterile with each visit."

"Yeah. Sunny went to Hays to pick up some plastic tubs and cleaning supplies. I thought when you showed up that she might have made it back, but it seemed too early." They made their way back to the kitchen and Kathy put the dish on the stovetop and unwrapped it from the towel. "You might as well take this towel back so that I don't accidentally put it in the auction."

Sylvia nodded. "So how are things going?"

"Really much better. We've had a nice breakthrough." Kathy related the events that had led up to the day. "I suppose sitting in the storm cave forced us to deal with each other, but it was more than that. I really started to care. It felt good."

"That's wonderful news. It will help you to overcome all the bad."

"I know it will," Kathy agreed. "Sunny asked me to forgive her, and I didn't lie. I told her I wanted to, but that it would have to come little by little. I suppose not so much the forgiving part. I can forgive her . . . I realize that now. But the trusting and the recreating of our relationship—that's going to take some time."

"And did you ask her to forgive you?" Sylvia asked matter-of-factly.

Kathy felt her pride rise. "What do I have to ask forgiveness for? I didn't do anything wrong."

Sylvia gave her a smirk that Kathy had only seen her use when dealing with her children. Usually it was in reaction to something they were lying about or when they were trying to pull the wool over her eyes.

"Well, I didn't!" Kathy declared.

Sylvia crossed her arms. "Kathy, don't ruin it now. You've come so far."

"What have I done that I should ask her forgiveness?"

"What about your bad attitude? What about the bitter, hateful way you reacted to her coming home? What about—"

"Hold on now." Kathy gripped the back of one of the kitchen chairs. "Everything I felt and did was borne out of response to things Sunny did. My attitude was bad only because she ran off and didn't let any of us know whether she was dead or alive."

"An unpardonable sin to be sure." The sarcasm in Sylvia's

voice was softened by the slight smile on her face. "Take a deep breath, Kathy, and think. You know it's not Sunny's fault that you reacted the way you did. You have to own this one."

Kathy didn't know what to say. She hadn't meant to explode like that. She did take a deep breath and tried to form a rational, unemotional thought. "Well, okay, my reactions were my own, but I still don't see that they constitute a need to ask for forgiveness. I mean, I've put aside the pain and misery of those twelve years and agreed to forgive her— isn't that enough?"

Sylvia raised a brow. "Is it? Is it enough?"

Sunny felt good about the way things were going with Kathy. Her heart felt lighter than it had in weeks, despite the ever-growing ache to see Lucy. In her dreams she saw herself returning to California to find Brian frantic for reconciliation. She liked to imagine that he would take her into his arms and apologize for the past. But in reality, she knew that wasn't going to happen. Their divorce would be final in August—possibly September. He would take Lucy from her—as he already had. He would take away the last pretense of their being a family.

She'd talked to Nancy again and begged a favor. Explaining the situation at hand, her mother-in-law had been more than gracious. Nancy had agreed to purchase the farm. Sunny had explained the situation and how desperate her sister was to get the place sold. Nancy understood and promised to contact the real-estate office immediately. Whatever they were asking, she'd buy it and see things expedited to have the sale closed within as short a time as possible. She also promised to keep the transaction a secret. Sunny hoped Kathy would be pleased. Surely it would ease her sister's worries.

Looking out across the vast open fields of wheat stubble, Sunny felt it a good representation of her life. Only the good parts had been taken away. Now all that was left were the bits and pieces of what had once been a profitable crop. Nothing but crumbs for the birds and deer. And after a time, even that would be plowed under and the fields replanted for the next crop.

The time was rapidly approaching when Sunny would have to leave Kansas and her childhood home behind. She needed to be back in Beverly Hills for the divorce. She thought it strange that her lawyer hadn't contacted her to let her know when they were to meet in court. Sunny supposed she should call him and see what was going on.

The road to home came into view and Sunny slowed the car and made the turn. Things would be different now, she thought. Everything would wind down here and come to an end. She and Kathy would say their good-byes, promise to write or call, and go their separate ways.

"And then what?" Sunny asked. "What do I do then?"

TWENTY-THREE

"WHAT DO YOU THINK of this one?" Kathy asked, holding up a snapshot. She and Sunny had been poring through old photographs for over an hour.

"That was the spring pageant at church when I was eleven," Sunny remembered. "The children's department was doing a play about Easter. Didn't we call it something like 'How the Easter Bunny Stole Easter'?"

Kathy sat back. "Yeah, I think we did. You know I vaguely remember that."

"I don't think you were in it. You were thirteen then and in the junior high group."

Kathy nodded and put the picture in Sunny's stack. "You might as well have it then."

"Here's one of us at the lake." Sunny held up the picture and smiled. "Remember when Mom and Dad would take us up to the lake?"

"Yeah. We had to have all our chores done or we couldn't go. So we'd hurry home from school on Friday and work like crazy and get everything done in half an hour."

Sunny laughed. "Mom would always say if we'd just do that every day we wouldn't be dragging around until supper to be done with our tasks."

"I remember." Kathy looked at the picture. "I remember this trip pretty well. I think I was only nine or ten."

Kathy and Sunny were watching their father as he worked on a large kite. The girls were focused on him with such intensity that it must have amused their mother enough to snap the shot.

"I remember Dad trying to get that silly kite to fly. He would run and run and nothing would happen. I laughed so hard at that," Sunny admitted.

"And I got after you because I was afraid Dad's feelings would get hurt."

"You were always worried about people's feelings." Sunny picked up another photograph. "I never was. I was just a bad person."

Kathy looked at her oddly. "I don't believe that."

Sunny shrugged. "Well, I never cared enough. When I wanted something I went after it and didn't worry about anybody else. We both know that's true. I imposed my will on everyone around me. Like you said a while back, I even got the piano teacher to change the recital. I knew it wasn't convenient for everyone else, but I didn't care. I saw it as my needs being more important."

"Like when you left home."

Sunny put the picture down. "Yes. Exactly that. But you have to remember, I honestly didn't understand Mom's tears. I figured she and Dad were both upset because they were losing control over me. I felt like everyone in my life was playing some giant control game."

"Where did it all go wrong? How did we go from happy little girls whose only concern was getting an oversized kite to fly and then come to this place?"

Sunny blew out a deep breath. "I don't know. I just know that I needed something more than what I felt I was getting. From the time I became a teenager on I had a rest-lessness in me that I cannot explain. Maybe I should have been on medication or gotten therapy. I don't know. The pain was so intense sometimes. I felt like the odd man out."

"But why? Mom and Dad adored you. I felt so jealous sometimes of the way they favored you. You were so accomplished. You did everything perfectly."

Sunny laughed. "I swear you're talking about another sister."

"Sometimes I think I am," Kathy said with a smile. "You seem like two different people."

Sunny thought back to her childhood. "It was all about being in control and having that edge over everyone else. I felt safe there. When I was performing well, it was like no one could touch me. I wanted to be a take-charge kind of girl. I guess high school was the worst. I saw my friends falling in love and making plans for a future in Slocum or Hays. I even listened to you make those plans."

"What was wrong with making plans?" Kathy seemed genuinely confused.

"There was nothing wrong with making plans," Sunny replied. "It was making them for this place. I hated Slocum. I hated the farm. I'm still not that crazy about it. The only reason I even came back was for you and Mom and Dad. I'm not a farm girl. I love the city, the energy there. I wanted to get away from here, while you seemed to want to carve your initials into it and make a permanent place for yourself. I couldn't relate to that and I feel like it drove a wedge between us."

"You could have talked to me about it."

"I tried. Don't you remember all the times we'd talk about the future? Especially as you headed off to college. You wanted to help Dad have this super farm. You and he talked about raising horses and breeding them along with having the crops. I wanted to scream. I hated the smell of the farm—I hated this house."

"Why the house?" Kathy's confusion only seemed to grow.

"It's old and worn out. You've never known anything but this house, so maybe I can understand why you find comfort here, but it felt like a tomb to me."

"I find comfort here because it reminds me of good times—some bad too, but mostly good. It reminds me of Mom and Dad. Even our grandparents. I think of all the family events we had here when we were younger and it makes me feel good."

"When I think of this house, I think of the mice running in the walls. I think of the uneven flooring upstairs. I think of the desperation I had to paint those kitchen cupboards white, just to have a change in this house. I didn't paint them for Mom, I did it for myself."

"I didn't know." Kathy shook her head. "It's hard to believe that we could have such diverse opinions of the same thing."

"I know. I used to think you were crazy, but then I came to realize that there was nothing wrong with you."

"Gee, thanks." Kathy laughed, but it sounded stilted.

Sunny didn't want things to head down the wrong road, so she thought maybe it best to let things drop. "Oh, look, here's a picture of you and Sylvia when you were in high school."

Kathy took the picture but gave it only a cursory glance. "Sunny, don't change the subject. This is the best talk we've had since you arrived."

"I'm afraid that I'll say the wrong thing, like a minute ago."

"You didn't say the wrong thing. I'm glad to know what you thought. I'm really trying to let go of my anger."

Sunny smiled. "Thank you. I'm more grateful than you'll ever know. I've got so much to deal with. It would really comfort me and help to know I had resolved something in my past."

"Go on with what you were talking about. Thinking me crazy and all."

Sunny looked past Kathy to the clock on the kitchen wall. It was the same clock that had been up there for the last twenty years. "Nothing ever changed here. I felt like I was dying here. We would talk in class about other places. Do you remember that World Cultures class we had in high school?"

"Sure. The one taught by Ms. Daniels."

"Ms. Daniels. Remember, she was a women's libber." Sunny chuckled. "How she ended up stuck here was something I always wondered about. Anyway, she had traveled quite a bit, remember?"

Kathy nodded. "She was the one who got me thinking about traveling to Europe. I told Kyle that I wanted more than anything to go to London. We even made plans to do just that. He's been there the last few weeks. He thought he'd just have to go for two, but I got a postcard the other day saying he might have to be there for as many as four."

"Ms. Daniels made me think about a life outside of Slocum. It was like she awoke something sleeping in me. Something that had always been there, but just lying dormant. I listened to her talk about big cities, and the excitement she had for them gave me an excitement as well. I wanted to see them all—especially Los Angeles. But I didn't just want to visit—I wanted to live there. I wanted to let it engulf my entire world. After that, the restlessness I knew continued to grow. I felt everything here was stupid—my name, my life, my boyfriend. When Todd told me he wanted to stay here and farm forever, I knew I couldn't go on. I really cared about him. He was probably my first true love, but I knew that I could never be happy with his love so long as it meant living in my mother's shoes."

"I'm sorry, Sunny. I really never understood."

"No one did. I tried to talk to Mom about it once. She was all offended because she thought I was insulting her and the choices she'd made. She never did understand that it wasn't her I had a problem with. It was me. I was just so unhappy."

"And did all the travel change things?"

Sunny shook her head and sorted through several pictures. "You know, it didn't. I needed God, not LA. I needed to know the reality of Jesus, not the facades of Beverly Hills."

"You talked yesterday about Lana's relationship with God. I've thought about that ever since. I realize that some people are happy just to know the truth and to go to church and to read their Bibles on occasion. They are content just to be saved from the fires of hell. Then there are others who want something more."

"And not only want it," Sunny interjected. "They demand it out of desperation."

"Exactly. Mom and Dad were content here. Their world wasn't filled with a whole lot that rocked their boat."

"Until my escapades," Sunny said sadly. She hated that she had somehow burst the bubble that was her parents' perfect world.

"It did shock them. Shocked us all," Kathy admitted. "It made us feel vulnerable. It showed us that the world we'd created for ourselves wasn't as stable as we thought it was."

"Nothing ever is." Sunny picked up a picture of her mother. She looked young and pretty, holding Kathy, who couldn't have been more than three. Sunny immediately thought of Lucy. How the small child felt in her arms. The scent of her hair after a bath. The feel of those tiny arms wrapped tightly around her neck.

The pain was so fierce it nearly stole her breath, but still Sunny refused to push aside the memories. Maybe she'd run enough. Maybe it was time to realize that this would always hurt. The loss of her daughter and husband would always tear another little piece out of her heart with every memory—every reflection.

"I'd forgotten about these pictures," Kathy said, handing a stack over to Sunny. "They were taken a few months before Mom died. We were trying so hard to live as if nothing was wrong. It's kind of like living with a dead mouse in the room. You know you ought to take it out before it starts to smell, but you don't want to have to deal with it."

"Boy, do I ever know how that is." Sunny took the photos and gasped. Mom was a mere skeleton of her former self. Her skin hung sallow and loose on her tiny frame. Her eyes were sunken with huge dark circles that made her almost seem like she had been punched in each eye.

"She looked so bad," Sunny murmured.

"She was. Her heart wasn't functioning enough to keep

the blood circulating properly. Her liver and kidneys deteriorated so rapidly. She couldn't breathe well because of the
increase of fluids around her heart. It was pretty awful."

Sunny shook her head as she thumbed through the pictures. There was one of her mother and Kathy that caused
her to pause. Kathy too looked more dead than alive. Her
face was pinched, as if she were in pain. "Where was this
taken?"

Kathy leaned over. "University of Kansas Medical Center in Kansas City. The doctor had told us that day that
Mom was too far gone for a transplant. We now understood
it was just a matter of time—that all our hard work had been
for nothing. All the counting of sodium and the special
meals, all the medicines and routines were for nothing.
Mom's body simply couldn't do what it needed to do to keep
her alive."

"How awful."

"It was. A part of all of us died that day."

"How you must have hated me then."

Kathy looked up and shook her head. "No. Not exactly.
That came later. Right then I think I envied you more than
anything. I was screaming inside for the courage to run as
far and fast as I could. To leave the death and dying behind
me." She paused and met Sunny's expression. "I didn't hate
you in that moment. I wanted to be you."

Just then the telephone rang. Kathy got to her feet and
glanced at her watch. "Wonder who's calling." She picked
up the phone. "Hello?"

"Kathy, it's Marion."

Kathy covered the receiver and turned to Sunny. "It's
the Realtor."

"Kathy, I've got great news. I've sold the farm."

"What? But no one's even been out to look at the property. What kind of price did you have to take?"

"That's the funny part. I got our original asking price. I told the agent we'd dropped the price, but he said the woman he was working for said to purchase it for the original price. And here's the real kicker. She's paying cash. We can close immediately on the property."

"Cash? Nobody has that kind of money. Do they?" Kathy felt as though she might actually faint. She rubbed her forehead. "I just can't believe this."

"Neither can I. It's like nothing I've ever seen. Look, I'll get all the papers together and we can meet in Hays for the signing. I'll let you know what day."

"Thanks, Marion." Kathy hung up the phone. "Someone bought the farm. Sight unseen—for the original asking price."

"That's great," Sunny said, smiling. "God answered your prayers."

Kathy nodded. "I can't believe it. All my worries are gone." She looked up and met Sunny's joyful expression. "I guess my faith just isn't what it should be."

"Why do you say that?" Sunny asked.

"If it had have been, I wouldn't be so shocked by all of this. If I'd had the faith of a mustard seed, I would have expected this instead."

Sunny sobered. "We're always so capable of accepting bad things—as though we deserve nothing more. Why is it so hard to take the blessings God offers, much less learn to expect them?"

TWENTY-FOUR

THE DAY OF THE AUCTION arrived with pleasant weather and surprisingly cool temperatures for Kansas in July. The sisters ate breakfast off of paper plates using plastic knives and spoons they'd bought in Hays a couple of days earlier and joked about living out of suitcases. It hadn't dawned on either one until the auction drew near that most of the household things they took for granted would be sold.

After a breakfast of bagels, yogurt, and bananas, Kathy and Sunny went outside to find the workers had already arrived. They worked furiously to set up tables for displaying the goods. Kathy and Sunny had brought most of the boxes and furniture to the front rooms of the house so they would be fairly easy to retrieve. They watched in silence as fifty-odd years of memories and sentiment went out the door.

The entire farm was abuzz with activity. Two women set up the area where people would pay, while several young men assembled a small stage. A couple of other men were bringing up the farm equipment from the barn.

Kathy startled as an older man drove the tractor. He looked so much like Dad that she had to do a double take. The man smiled and waved and Kathy could almost imagine it was Dad on his way out to the fields. He loved that tractor. Kathy had to fight the feeling that selling the machine was akin to selling her father's memory.

"They sure have a way of getting things done," Sunny said.

"Yeah. It's not going to be easy to watch it all go out the door—off the farm."

Sunny reached out to take hold of Kathy's arm. "I know, but I'll be here for you. It's not much, but you don't have to bear this alone."

"Thanks, Sunny. It's worth more than you could imagine."

By nine-thirty everything was in place. There were probably over a hundred people present by the time the auctioneer started the proceedings. With each piece sold, Kathy thought of her parents. Would they be pleased at the outcome? Did the monetary value match the sentimental value her folks had once placed on the various items?

Sets of the Depression glass were sold for such outlandishly high prices that Kathy was afraid some mistake must have been made. The woman who bought almost every piece was representing a wealthy collector from back East. How she found out about the sale was beyond Kathy.

Some other pieces also sold for far more than Kathy had predicted. The shotguns turned out to be antiques and quite collectible, as did the old cameras. Her mother's collection of china was also a remarkable find for one woman. She declared it some of the best early twentieth-century Doulton available. One little double-handled cup, called a loving cup, brought nearly three hundred dollars by itself, as two different antique dealers went head-to-head to purchase the piece. The entire eight-place setting fetched several thousand dollars, leaving Kathy speechless. Where had her mother gotten hold of such valuable china?

"You looked as if you'd seen a ghost," Jason Bridger, one of the men from the auction house, told her while the auctioneer was selling the farm machinery.

"I think I'm in shock. I had no idea that china was so valuable."

He laughed. "I figured someone had told you it was an exceptional set. I hope it was a pleasant shock."

"Yes, but . . . well . . . I have no idea how my mother ended up with such expensive dishes."

"You'd be surprised at the valuables we uncover in rural Kansas. In the old days people thought, 'Oh, it's nothing more than an old farm sale. Can't be worth much.' Then antique stores started realizing that some of those old farmers were sitting on a lot of antiques passed down from mother to daughter, grandmother to granddaughter, father to son, and so on. We've uncovered antiques from the colonial period here, as well as a few pieces that go back even further."

"I had no idea." Kathy watched as the auctioneer brought the gavel down and called the final numbers for the sale of the combine. It was a very good price. At this rate there would be more than enough money from the sale of the auction and farm to pay off all the debts and have a nice little inheritance for herself.

Kathy had lost track of Sunny. Her sister had been fairly close to her side through the early hours of the sale, but as the day wore on, Sunny had disappeared. Kathy was pleased with the discussions they'd been having. Last night they had gone to Hays for a steak dinner, and Kathy had really enjoyed her sister's company. It was a start of a new relationship, she told herself. Something new to build the future on.

"How are you holding up?" Sylvia asked as she came to

join Kathy by the large walnut tree in the Halberts' front yard.

"I'm not doing too bad. It's hard to see it go," she said with a sigh. "It's like losing a piece of Mom and Dad."

Sylvia gazed out across the yard. "I can understand that. I hope you kept the things that were most important to you."

"I did. Sunny too." Kathy shook her head. "Did you see the price Mom's old china brought?"

"I was stunned, I have to tell you. Makes me want to go through my cupboards and see what's what. I may have thousands of dollars worth of dishes and not even realize it. I'll probably cringe every time the kids break something and wonder how much it was worth."

"I can see it now," Kathy teased. "Everyone will be eating on paper plates."

Sylvia laughed. "I was also surprised by the value of the old canning jars."

"I guess sometimes things that don't look like much can be the most priceless. Some of Dad's tools turned out to be old enough to have belonged to his grandfather and great-grandfather. Little bitty things that I had no use for and probably would have tossed brought hundreds of dollars. It seems crazy to me. Sunny thought so too, and she's been living in California, where expensive pieces are the norm."

"She's probably never shopped for antique tools," Sylvia said with a grin. "But since you mentioned Sunny, how's it going with her?"

Kathy stopped and turned to face Sylvia. "Really well. I thought a lot about what you said—about whether it was enough to just agree to forgive. I thought about how I would want to be treated, and I thought about how God would treat me if the shoe was on the other foot."

"And what conclusion did you come to?"

A laugh escaped as Kathy replied. "I concluded that I was very glad God didn't act like me."

Sylvia laughed as well. "I've thought that about myself on several occasions."

"Sunny and I have had some great talks. I realize that she's suffered so much in life. I don't know why this place was so hard for her to endure, but I really tried to put myself in her place and see things from her perspective."

"She seems a lot more at peace," Sylvia said. "You must have done something right."

"Not me . . . God. I think back on these last few weeks, and I know I have nothing of myself to recommend in this situation. I wasn't kind or loving. I wasn't even civil. I'm ashamed of how I reacted—especially when it came to her asking for forgiveness."

"We all make mistakes. Sunny's were just so much more visible."

"Isn't that the truth?" Kathy murmured. "I take great comfort in knowing that many of my mistakes or faults have been hidden from the public eye."

She fell silent and watched as yet another person she didn't know bought her parents' bed. Personally, Kathy had never cared for the piece, but at this moment she felt like some kind of traitor for letting it go.

Desperate to change her thoughts, Kathy turned back to Sylvia. "I received a postcard from Kyle. He's still in England; as a matter of fact, he has to stay as long as another two weeks. However, he wanted me to know that everything about his life is so much happier since I called. He said that he had felt like he was on a perpetual hold all these years and now could finally move forward again. He said he was looking forward to our future together." Kathy couldn't help the girlish giggle that came out. "Our future together."

"It's amazing, Kathy. I always knew Kyle loved you, but he's more than proven the depth of his love. You can never ever doubt it now."

"I know. I was so wrong, Sylvia. The way I treated him was wrong, and it just caused me to be more miserable than I had to be. You were so right about that. I wish I could have seen it sooner."

"Bitterness and anger so often blind us, Kathy. It's a hard-learned lesson, but one I hope neither of us is quick to forget."

"Me too."

"Have you heard any more about the sale of the farm—like who bought it?"

"No. I only know that it was a woman and that she's sending her agent tomorrow to handle the papers and paying cash so we don't have to worry about waiting for going through a bank. Cuts the time considerably."

"That's amazing. I wonder if she'll move here."

"I don't know. I plan to ask the agent she's sending. I want to let him know that Tony could farm the land if they wanted him to."

"Well, let us know. He'll want to prepare the ground for the winter wheat."

"I promise as soon as I know something, I'll let you know."

Sylvia glanced at her watch. "I'd better get. You two are still coming for supper, right?"

Kathy turned back to see what piece the auctioneer was offering. It was a set of some of the more modern tools. The auction people had put various things together for optimum sale, and this was one of those sets. "We'll be there," she said, her thoughts focused more on the tools than on the food. In her mind she saw her father working to make or mend something on the farm.

I'm going to miss you, Dad.

Sylvia checked her watch one more time. "I'm going to get home and get supper started. Come as soon as you like. And don't forget—if you change your mind and want to sleep at our house until the sale of the house is finalized, you're more than welcome."

"It's just the one night."

"Well, something could go wrong; it's been known to happen. My sister thought she was closing on her house at a certain time and ended up delayed by two weeks, remember?"

"We'll be fine. Sunny and I are going to finish cleaning the place and get our stuff loaded into the cars. We'll be able to leave in the morning and head to the title company in Hays and that will be that." She shook her head. "It's going to seem so strange."

Sylvia hugged her. "No," she said, pulling back to meet Kathy's teary eyes. "It's going to be so wonderful."

❧ ❧ ❧

Sunny wandered the property for the last time. She knew tomorrow she and Kathy would head to Colorado Springs. Aunt Glynnis had suggested Sunny stop there for the night on her way back to California.

While she was glad for the invitation and the decision to head back, Sunny had a gnawing fear that refused to let her go. What awaited her in California?

Sunny entered the barn and gazed around as she drew in the heady aroma of hay. How many girlhood adventures had she had in this place? She and Kathy used to get Dad to help them make tunnels with the hay bales. The girls would crawl around for hours and even made a little area in the hay where they could keep some of their things. They called it their hideout, although Dad and Mom knew exactly where it was.

She passed the stalls where they had milked their two cows, Numbers and Deuteronomy. The cows had been named by their grandfather, who had kept Genesis, Exodus, and Leviticus for himself. Many had been the cold morning she'd come out to milk those cows. She hated when it was her turn to do the milking. Her hands always ached from the strain, and inevitably she'd get kicked or stepped on. Numbers had even broken her finger once. She gently rubbed her right-hand ring finger, remembering the event.

"There are good memories here," she whispered. "It wasn't all bad."

Glancing up at the loft door, she remembered times when they would break up bales of straw and jump into the stack from the loft. The straw would always tear them up, scratching their arms and legs, but the fun of flying through the air always negated the pain.

"I wondered where you'd gone," Kathy said, entering the barn behind her.

The shadows of the darkened room played tricks on Sunny's eyes. She saw her mother in Kathy, even though most people commented about Sunny's appearance being more like Mom's. Mom had a strong influence on them both, Sunny decided.

"I needed a little alone time. It was all starting to get to me."

Kathy smiled sadly. "A little like watching them tear things apart, piece by piece."

Sunny nodded. "We probably should have taken the auctioneer's advice and spent the day in Hays."

"Maybe. I think we would have regretted that though."

Sunny sighed. "I suppose so. I was just thinking about some of the fun times we had here."

"Oh, like mucking out stalls?" Kathy teased.

Sunny appreciated her light-hearted comment. There was no sense in getting too maudlin. "Yeah, that and staying up all night with sick animals."

"Or how about dealing with the walnuts?"

Every year when the tree would bear nuts, there was the inevitable job of getting the green hulls off and putting the nuts to dry. The hulls stained everything, and if the girls didn't wear gloves, their hands would bear that same discoloration for weeks.

Sunny hugged her arms to her chest. "I'm so glad I came home when I did. It would have killed me to not have this place to come back to."

"Why? I thought you hated it here."

"I did. I don't think I do so much anymore." Sunny felt

her eyes grow damp. "I have some good memories, but I pushed them so far back that I convinced myself the times were all bad."

"The bad comes with the good. It's just a part of life." Kathy cast a glance at the ceiling and then to the loft. "I had convinced myself the times were all good, but seeing you reminded me of times that were less than perfect." She frowned and quickly followed it with an explanation. "Oh, Sunny, that sounded awful, and I certainly didn't mean for it to."

Sunny understood. She knew what it was to carefully consider each word before it came out of her mouth. She hated word games, but everyone seemed to want to play them at one time or another. Yet this wasn't one of the times Sunny wanted to see the rules of the game engaged. "I understood exactly what you meant."

"I'm glad. I don't want to hurt you anymore. I realize how wrong I've been. You asked me for forgiveness and I told you you'd have to wait. That was stupid—heartless. I was afraid, but no more. I have to trust that God has a plan in all of this and that His grace is enough for us both. Honestly, I need to ask you for forgiveness of my horrible attitude. Can you forgive me, Sunny?"

This confession completely stunned Sunny. She had not expected her sister to make any such declaration. "You know you have my forgiveness, but I don't think there's much to forgive. I think even when you were angry with me, you still loved me. Look, there's something you need to know. I hope it won't make you mad."

Kathy's brows furrowed. "What is it?"

"My mother-in-law is the one buying the farm."

"What?!"

Sunny nodded. "I knew you were worried, and I wanted to help. Everything I have is tied up, and until the divorce, I won't know how much I'll have access to. Nancy is rich and I knew it wouldn't even put a dent in her funds. I told her what was going on and how you really needed the place to sell. Oh, Kathy, I'm sorry if I overstepped my bounds. I just wanted to help so much. I've made you so miserable over the years, I wanted to give you something good. Please don't hate me."

Kathy began to cry. "Oh, Sunny, I don't hate you. I can't believe you'd do something so generous. Worrying about this farm was eating me up inside. I hadn't wanted Dad to fret over it, because he knew we should have put it on the market last year. I didn't want you to worry about it, because I wanted to be . . . the strong one. This was such an act of love. How could I ever hate you for that?"

They embraced and held each other for several minutes. Tears streamed down Sunny's face. She didn't know what would happen in the future, but she knew it would take a great deal to match the importance of this moment.

Sunny heard someone step into the barn and pulled away from her sister to wipe her eyes. She didn't want to be seen crying.

"I'm sorry," Kathy said in an authoritative manner, "the barn is off limits for the sale. You'll need to return to the auction."

"I came here to see Sunny," the man explained.

Sunny knew the voice immediately. She looked up, knowing the shock must have been written on her face.

He stepped forward, and with him came a rush of thoughts and feelings too overwhelming for Sunny to know what to say. She could only breathe one word.

"Brian."

TWENTY-FIVE

KATHY WATCHED THE COLOR PASS from Sunny's face. Her sister looked as if she might faint. "Why don't we go into the house?" Kathy suggested.

She took hold of Sunny's arm in a possessive way. "Come on, Sunny."

Sunny moved hesitantly, but Kathy pulled her along. "We don't have much in the way of furniture, but there's still a small table and chairs in the kitchen." Kathy had long ago promised the set to Sylvia and was planning to take it to her at supper that evening. Everything else was packed in the trailer Kathy planned to pull.

It felt strange to have her brother-in-law show up. She stole a quick glance at him. He was quite handsome. Sunny always did have a way with picking her guys. No doubt Mitch and Randy had been good-looking as well, but Brian almost had movie-star good looks. From his wavy blond hair to his broad shoulders and athletic build, the tall man seemed nearly perfect. She looked at her sister and back to Brian. They made a very handsome couple.

Kathy pushed Sunny through the open back door. "Sunny, why don't you go wash your face and freshen up a bit." She leaned close to her sister's ear. "It might help you feel better. I'll take care of Brian."

Sunny met her sister's gaze and nodded. "I'll be right back."

With Sunny gone, Kathy turned to Brian. "I'm Kathy,

Sunny's sister. Why don't you have a seat and tell me what brings you here."

Brian took a chair, looking around the stark room. "I . . . well . . . I came because of Sunny. My mother told me where she was."

Kathy frowned. "I see. Well, you should know this day has been really hard on both of us. I hope you aren't here to make it that much harder."

"I promise you, that's not the case."

"Then why are you here?" Kathy tried not to sound accusing, but she worried about what this visit might mean to her sister.

"I need to talk to my wife," he said rather defensively.

Kathy crossed her arms. "You aren't going to berate her with more of that nonsense about cheating on you, are you?" Kathy was surprised to suddenly realize she completely believed Sunny's story. Her sister would never have cheated on this man—of that she felt confident.

"So I take it she's told you everything?" he asked in a manner that suggested embarrassment.

"Yes. Or at least enough."

"You must have a pretty bad opinion of me." He met her gaze in an almost pleading manner.

It was easy to see he felt terrible, and Kathy didn't know what to think. Sunny came back from the bathroom looking a little better—at least not quite so pale.

"I have things to do. You two feel free to talk here. No one should bother you." Kathy turned to Sunny. "Unless you need me to stay?"

"No, I'll . . . be . . . all right." She drew a deep breath and let it out slowly. "Thanks."

Kathy casually walked from the room in no hurry to leave. She actually hoped she might hear some of the conversation between the couple, but no one was talking. Reaching the front porch, Kathy paused to whisper a prayer.

Lord, Sunny needs you—maybe more than ever. Brian needs you too. I don't know what you have planned for this family, but I know you hate divorce and lies. Please help us, Lord, to get beyond both.

Sunny tightly gripped the back of the kitchen chair. She had told herself over and over in the bathroom that she could handle this situation, but now that she was face-to-face with him, Sunny was certain she could not. Tears came to her eyes and rational thought fled. When she looked at Brian, she saw nothing but the loss. The loss of her marriage—her happiness—Lucy. It was more than she could bear. She lowered her head and began to cry in earnest, even knowing it would probably irritate him to no end.

Brian didn't rebuke her for her tears. Instead, she heard him get out of his chair. For a moment Sunny feared he would leave, but she had no power to stop him. She could barely breathe for the tightness in her chest.

Without warning, Brian pulled her to him, turning her gently so that she could put her face on his chest. "Sunny, I was wrong."

The words poured over her like a refreshing rain. It was all that she had hoped for, but she couldn't bring herself to believe it might actually happen. She pulled away to look into his eyes.

He took her face in his hands. "I was wrong. I was so very wrong. I know you didn't have an affair. I know I should have spent more time with you and Lucy. I failed you in so many ways. Sunny, please forgive me."

"I can't believe this is happening. What changed?"

He wiped her damp cheeks with his thumbs. "I did. I finally saw how stupid I'd acted. Just tell me I'm not too late."

"Of course you aren't." Sunny felt her tears come anew. "I want to hear what happened."

Brian let her go. "I guess the most important thing I did was learn the truth. I was working late one evening and happened to overhear a call. Remember Anita?"

Sunny nodded. "I do."

"Well, she'd been telling me for months that you and Rick were an item." He held up his hands. "I can't believe I fell for her lurid tales. I knew better. I knew you loved me, and I knew that you wanted me at home. Anita suggested that you and Rick were in league to destroy me. She told me Rick wanted to take over my practice and with you and him both pressuring me to give up patients, I figured that was the truth of it."

"I'm sorry. I never thought of it that way." She motioned to the table. "Let's sit."

Brian nodded and held out her chair. Once they were both seated he continued. "Anita told me that you and Rick were having an affair, and that I should even question whether Lucy was mine. I had confided in her about wanting more children and how you didn't want to have another baby yet. She told me that was because Lucy was Rick's child and you only wanted his children."

"That's awful. And why would she say that? I mean, I know she was jealous of me, but still, she would have to know that Lucy's paternity could be tested."

"Sunny, I'm so ashamed to say this, but I had her tested."

"Oh, Brian."

"I was so crazy over the whole thing. I finally just felt like I was losing my mind. I wanted to talk to you, but you were gone. Mom didn't know where you'd gone, and Lana knew but wouldn't say. Mom finally sat me down and started talking to me about the past. She told me things about my father that I'd never understood. She told me things about her as well. She started talking about her faith in God and how everything had changed the day she'd realized she couldn't cope with life on her own—the day she turned to Jesus."

Sunny sat motionless, hardly able to believe Brian would be receptive to such a message. At least not the old Brian. *The old Brian would never have admitted he was wrong either.*

"Mom told me she knew I was miserable because I really loved you and knew I'd falsely accused you. But more than that, she knew I was miserable because I needed to find God for myself."

"I had to find Him too," Sunny offered.

Brian reached out and took hold of her hand. "I didn't want to hear any of it at first. I felt like it made no more sense than the rest of my life. I asked Mom to take care of Lucy for a while, because I honestly felt I couldn't be anything she needed me to be. The weeks dragged on, and I felt my misery grow even more acute. I knew something had to give. I even thought about suicide."

"No!" Sunny gasped and gripped his hand more tightly. "I couldn't bear that."

"I just couldn't see any hope—any light. When I really felt most desperate, I called Mom and she called her pastor. He came over to see me."

"Pastor James?"

He nodded and smiled. "The very one. He didn't cut me any slack. I figured he'd give me all sorts of sympathy and compassion, and instead he asked me point blank if I wanted things to be right. Not better. Right."

"I know. He asked me the same thing."

"I told him things were so wrong they could only go right. He told me I was wrong—that they could get much worse. I think that scared me more than anything."

Brian let go of her hand and leaned back in the chair. "I met with him faithfully for two weeks, every day. He never once babied me along. He was firm, spoke the truth, and listened to me, but he wouldn't allow me to wallow in self-pity." He paused a moment. "I heard that your mom and dad are dead. I'm really sorry that I wasn't here for you."

"As hard as it was to lose them, it was nothing compared to losing you and Lucy. Oh, Brian, how is she? I miss her so much."

"She's doing pretty well, but she misses you. She won't stop talking about you. I left her with Mom, because . . . well, I wasn't sure you'd even see me."

"Of course I'd see you. You were the one who wouldn't deal with me, remember?" she asked in a teasing tone. She suddenly felt that no matter what else they discussed, everything was going to be all right. The peace that rushed over her was like no comfort she'd ever known.

"I stopped the divorce, Sunny."

"You did?"

"I don't want a divorce. I don't want to lose you."

"What do you want?" She hesitated to ask the question, but knew she needed the answer. If Brian wanted life to go on as it had, they would still have a lot of difficulties to overcome.

"I want everything to change. I think we should even leave Beverly Hills."

"Truly? Where would we go?" Sunny had never considered that he might be willing to move. Of course, she'd never considered that Brian might admit his mistakes and come looking for her. She felt even more of the burden lift.

"I don't know. It doesn't matter so long as we could all be a family. You know there's no problem with the money. I figure we could just start over. I could even take a month off so we can work on our family."

"It sounds too good to be true." Sunny got up from the table. Her nervous energy wouldn't allow her to sit any longer. "I've prayed so much for this. I knew God could do it, but I wasn't convinced He would."

Brian got up and came around the table to where Sunny stood. "The way your sister stood guard over me, I wasn't sure she would allow for anything more than my departure."

Sunny laughed. "We've been through a lot this summer. She was so angry with me. She had given me up for dead and yet there I was demanding to be recognized."

"She seemed very protective of you a few minutes ago."

"We've just now started to work through things."

"I didn't expect to see the auction taking place," he told her. "What's going on?"

"Kathy is moving to Colorado Springs, where she hopes

to pick up with her life. The guy she gave up twelve years ago is still waiting for her."

"Wow. That's pretty incredible. It must be true love."

Sunny thought of her sister and Kyle. "I believe it is. He's built his career all these years while waiting for her."

"What does he do in Colorado Springs?"

"Works for a pharmaceutical company. I'm not sure what all he does for them. My uncle was involved in research there. Anyway, we're selling off everything that we didn't want to keep, because it's time Kathy got her inheritance. She closes on the farm tomorrow and then we were heading out."

"You were going to Colorado Springs too?"

"Just for a night or two. My aunt and uncle live there and had invited me."

"Then what had you planned to do?"

Sunny looked up into her husband's eyes. "I didn't know. I knew I had to see Lucy, so I figured to come back to Los Angeles. After that, I didn't really have any hope."

"I'm so sorry, babe. I know that was my fault." He reached out again to touch her face. "I've missed you so much. I've missed a great deal the last few years."

"You have, but we can't live in the past. It's time to put it behind us and start fresh," Sunny said.

"Then you'll let me take you home?"

She smiled as warmth engulfed her heart. Home. That one single word held so much power. All of her life she'd looked for the sense of home, and it wasn't until finding her way to God that she'd realized His was the only home that would last.

Stepping into her husband's arms, Sunny sighed. "Yes.

Please take me home. Take me where my heart belongs."

Kathy stood on the back porch, crying. She had only returned a few minutes earlier, but the words she'd heard spoken kept her from turning to leave. Things were going to be all right for Sunny. Brian still loved her and she still loved him. Everything was as it should be.

Composing herself, Kathy sniffed back her tears and knocked lightly on the open kitchen door. Sunny and Brian pulled out of a passionate kiss that made Kathy embarrassed to have interrupted.

"We're supposed to go to Sylvia's for supper," she said sheepishly. "I also need to take her the table and chairs."

"Do you suppose she has room for one more?" Sunny asked. It was clear by the way she smiled that she knew Kathy comprehended the situation without explanation.

"Sylvia would have room for fifteen more. That woman always has room for guests." Kathy looked at Brian, remembering his moneyed background. "It won't be anything fancy, however. You'll have to deal with Clancy at the door and the table."

"Who's Clancy?"

"Their Irish Setter." Kathy grinned. "She's very fond of people and handouts."

He laughed, as did Sunny. "I think I can handle it."

"I think you probably can." Kathy met Sunny's eyes and smiled. "And I think you probably have a place for those roses now."

Her sister nodded, but Brian looked confused. Sunny took hold of his hand and gave it a squeeze. "I'll explain after supper."

TWENTY-SIX

"WELL, I'M SO GLAD TO meet you," Sylvia said as she passed Brian a big bowl of potato salad.

"I'm just glad you agreed to include me," Brian replied. He helped himself to a big scoop of the salad before passing it to Sunny.

"I would have been offended had you gone anywhere else," Sylvia admitted.

"This is so good," Sunny said, tasting the fried chicken. "How come when I try to do this it never tastes the same?"

Sylvia laughed. "Probably because I've been doing it nearly every day since I was ten."

Kathy took the bowl from Brian. "Yeah, Sunny always hated to cook. Mom would try to teach her something in the kitchen and we'd just end up with a small disaster every time. Once she even set the kitchen on fire, but Mom was ready for her."

"She told me that," Brian said, reaching for the iced tea Sylvia had poured minutes before. "That's why I hired a cook."

"It was that or starve," Sunny added.

"Or get smoked out," Brian teased.

They all laughed at this, but Kathy couldn't imagine the world Sunny had known in California. Nannies, cooks, gardeners, and maids. The idea of so many strangers in your own home didn't appeal to Kathy at all. Of course, she thought, those people probably don't remain strangers for long. Still, it wasn't a life she would want. She would hate the invasion of her privacy.

"So are you two headed right back to LA?" Tony asked.

Brian shook his head. "Sunny had planned to overnight in Colorado Springs. I've asked to join her there."

Kathy reached for a slice of Sylvia's homemade bread. "Aunt Glynnis and Uncle Will are going to be thrilled. We've decided to just surprise them."

"I'm sure your aunt will be excited. This is really the best news any of us could have prayed for." Sylvia turned to Brian. "I'm glad you're here and that we got to meet you."

Brian reached for Sunny's hand. "I never knew much about Sunny's life here in Kansas, so I'm glad to experience it."

"It's not a life for everyone," Tony said in a serious tone. "My boys have little interest in staying here, and frankly, the way things are going with farming, I'm just as glad to see them move on to something else."

"What do they want to do?" Kathy asked. Sylvia had never said much about the boys wanting to leave the farm.

Tony put his fork down. "Tim wants to go into the Marines. It's all he's talked about this year. He's just nearing fourteen, but he seems to have his mind made up on the matter. Justin doesn't know exactly what he wants, but he's been involved in debate at school. The teacher mentioned that he might want to get involved in the law, so he's been talking about checking that out."

"And Missy wants to be a ballerina fire fighter," Sylvia said with a grin.

Kathy laughed. "You can never have too many of those."

"Where are the kids?" Sunny asked.

"Oh, you were still outside when I told Kathy they were spending the evening with Tony's mom. We wanted to have you to ourselves."

Kathy toyed with her glass of ice water. "But what about carrying on the tradition? The family farm and so forth. Don't you feel they'll lose a sense of connection?"

Tony shook his head. "I hope we've given them a sense of that through their family. I want the kids to always be close to each other—not a place."

His statement startled Kathy with its simple wisdom. She could see now that the farm—home—wouldn't matter nearly as much as finding a way to keep a strong connection with her sister.

"You have to remember, Kathy, your father never minded the idea of your leaving the farm or of Sunny having a life elsewhere," Sylvia reminded.

"That's true. Dad always wanted me to go back to college and finish my degree. I didn't need that many more credits to complete it, and he always felt sad that life had interfered."

"Well, maybe you can do that in Colorado Springs," Sylvia suggested.

"What were you majoring in?" Brian asked.

Kathy smiled. "Animal husbandry and business. Dad always wanted to get away from just farming. He wanted to bring in quality horses—good bloodline animals that would be excellent for breeding."

"Would you still want to do that?" The question came from Sunny this time.

Thinking about it for a moment, Kathy finally shook her head. "No. I was only doing it for Dad and Mom. I knew

Dad had the dream, and I wanted to help see it come about. That's all it was ever about."

"So if you went back to college, what would you want to study?"

Brian's question pierced her heart. What she really wanted—all she'd ever wanted—was to marry Kyle and have a family "I'm not sure . . . I want to study . . . anything," she said rather hesitantly. She looked at the gathering of friends and family. "I guess I'd really like to just settle down, marry, and have a family. Anything else can come another day."

Sunny nodded and reached over to pat Kathy's hand. "I think it sounds perfect. You'll no doubt be great at being both a wife and a mother."

"Oh, I nearly forgot." Tony dug into his pocket and pulled out a folded paper. He opened it and tried to flatten it out. "Here's your share of the wheat money. Gary said to make it out to you, as it would be part of your inheritance."

Kathy took the check and glanced at the amount. "Wow. This is a lot more than last year."

"We had a great crop. Weather was good last winter and spring. It was one of the best yields we'd ever had. Your dad even noticed that. He was pretty excited."

"I'll bet he was." Kathy tucked the check into her pocket.

"So will everything be finalized when you close the sale of the farm tomorrow, or do you still have to go pay this and that?" Sylvia asked as she offered Brian more of the green bean casserole.

"Everything will be done. Dad borrowed against the farm to pay Mom's medical debts as well as his own. He paid off all the other bills with that loan as well. The bank will get their share off the top and cut me a check for the balance. I won't be mega-rich, but I'll be very comfortable." Kathy looked at Sunny and smiled. "Can I tell them?"

Sunny laughed. "I suppose so, since you'll probably need to get Tony to go ahead and farm the land at least another year."

"What's she talking about?" Sylvia asked.

"Sunny knew I was worried about the farm not selling, so she called her mother-in-law to get help. Brian's mother is the one purchasing the farm."

Sylvia clapped her hands together "How wonderful! So it will stay in the family?"

"I'm not sure what will be done at this point," Sunny said, looking to Brian.

He shrugged. "Might be nice to have it as a place to come and get away from it all. Maybe make some good memories with a new generation."

"Can't you see Lucy there?" Sunny laughed. "She'd be all over the place. And no doubt she'd want a pony."

"She wants one anyway, and we live in Beverly Hills."

"Oh, I'm so happy to hear this," Sylvia said, looking to her husband. "And of course, we'll still farm it for them. Won't we?"

"I don't see why not," Tony said with a shrug.

"So we have a happy ending," Kathy said, toying with her glass.

"Well, you deserve much more than that," Sunny interjected. "I for one appreciate what you've done more than I can find words to tell you."

Kathy turned to her sister. "Thank you." Sunny's

acknowledgment meant a lot. Her sister had truly changed; it was easy to see, now that Kathy could look at her without anger clouding the image.

"So will you buy your own place right away?" Tony questioned.

Kathy shook her head. "I had thought that's what I'd do, but now things are different."

"Because of Kyle," Sylvia said, grinning.

Nodding, Kathy felt a giddy sense of anticipation. "Yes."

"Does he already have his own place?" Brian asked.

"As I understand it," Kathy began, "he's lived in a very small house all these years. He plans to use it as a rental if we . . . well, when we . . ." She let the words trail off, feeling awkward in speaking about something that still seemed more hope than reality.

"When they get married," Sunny said, laughing. "It's still too much for her to even put into words."

❧ ❧ ❧

Back at the farm, Sunny and Brian walked around the property. Sunny wanted to show her husband some of the various spots that held special meaning.

"This was where my dad and grandpa used to play horseshoes," she pointed out. "I can remember hearing that clank as the shoes hit the post well into the evening. Grandma would question whether they could even see, and Grandpa said they didn't have to see, just hear. Then she would tell him he wasn't any good at that either." She smiled at the memory. "They were so well suited for each other. He called her his ornery little darlin' and she called him her mule-headed sweetheart. I loved to watch them together."

"I take it they died before you left home?"

"Yeah. Everything seemed different without them." She sighed. "It's taken a lot of honesty to realize there were good times here as well as bad. I used to hate it so much, but now I see I just had a lot of hate in me to begin with."

"Or maybe a lot of ambition. Wanting something more than what you have doesn't have to be a bad thing. Sometimes it drives us in a direction the Lord had for us all along. Mom told me that."

"I just wasn't a very nice person back then. I hurt a lot of people, but I know I can't live in regret. I want something more for us—for Lucy—and for whoever else might come along."

He pulled her into his arms. "I've been thinking about something, and I'd like your opinion."

Sunny recognized an intensity to his expression that she'd not seen in a long time. "What is it?"

"You know how I mentioned we could move and start over elsewhere?"

"Yes. I like the idea . . . except for not living near your mom. It was nice to have family around."

"Well, what about Colorado Springs?"

Sunny cocked her head to one side. "What are you saying?"

"I've been thinking that Colorado Springs might be a good place to start over. Your sister will be there. It would be nice for Lucy to know her aunt. I'd like to know her better myself. Plus it seems that you two could really lean on each other and help each other in the years to come. Then there's your aunt and uncle. I think it would be nice for them to get to know the rest of your family, don't you?"

"But what about your mother and your practice?"

"I have a feeling Mom might find Colorado Springs refreshing. If not to move there full time, then maybe to have a summer place. Of course, there's this farm as well. It could be fun to fix things up and spend some time here."

"Well . . . I must say this is a big surprise. I'd never thought about it before. I wonder how Kathy would feel about it. She might feel that I was once again imposing on her moment in the sun. When I ran away from home it was the day of her engagement to Kyle twelve years ago."

"Sunny . . . why *did* you leave?" The light was fading, but Sunny could see him studying her, as if trying to read the answer on her face.

"I left because I could. I wanted to exercise my rights as a young adult, and I ended up pulling off the covers and everything else with me as I went."

"What?" His expression betrayed his confusion.

Sunny laughed. "When we were little girls our mom would let us make forts with blankets over the kitchen table and other things. We would sometimes line up several chairs and bring in a coffee table from the living room and have this grand fort in the kitchen. We used blankets to cover the furniture, then crawled underneath and played for hours. When we went from one little room to another, we had to be careful of the various blankets. The only thing holding them in place was whatever we'd put atop them on the table. Usually it was a pair of Dad's work boots, some of Mom's heavy pans, and stacks of old magazines or books. If we weren't careful, we could pull down the covers and bring everything with them. Sometimes we got bonked on the head pretty good."

Brian pulled her closer and smiled. "Still, it sounds like a lot of fun. I never had that kind of thing."

"As a rich child, your parents could buy you a proper playhouse. Of course, that's not to say we didn't have great times. I was remembering just this afternoon that we used to play out in the barn stacking up bales of hay and making tunnels."

"I'd like to visit that barn again." He kissed her lightly. "It might be fun to tunnel in the hay with you." A coy smile spread across his face. "Maybe we could sleep out there tonight."

"Sleep there if you want," Sunny said, feigning disgust, "but not me. There are rats and snakes that like to tunnel out there too."

He trailed kisses down from Sunny's cheek to her earlobe. "I'd protect you."

She sighed and leaned into his embrace. "I know you would." She tightened her hold on him. "I know you will."

➻ ➻ ➻

Kathy had just finished balancing her checkbook when the phone rang. Startled, she got up from where she'd been sitting on the floor and finally answered it on the fifth ring.

"I thought perhaps you'd already left," Aunt Glynnis began. "I wasn't sure if you were spending the night in Hays."

"No, though I had thought about it. I mean, all the

furniture is gone. We saved back a couple of sleeping bags, but that's about it."

"Oh goodness, that's not going to allow you a very comfortable sleep. You'll be exhausted by the time you drive here."

"I think I'll be fine. It's only four or five hours. How are you doing?"

Glynnis told about her recovery from the fall. Her back was much better and the trouble it had created with her hips was nearly gone. Her garden was in great shape thanks to a neighbor girl who wanted to earn extra money that summer.

"I just sit and watch her pull weeds and deadhead my flowers. I'm telling you, this is definitely the way to garden when you're my age."

Kathy laughed, despite knowing full well that sitting while someone else puttered in her garden was probably driving her aunt nuts.

"So Sunny hasn't changed her mind about coming here too, has she?"

Kathy wanted to choose her words carefully so she wouldn't ruin the surprise of having Brian join them. "No. She's very excited."

"That's good. I have both guest rooms ready. It will be so nice to have someone visiting again. Have you heard from Kyle?"

"No, not since he sent me a postcard. He sent it global priority. Seemed like an awful lot of money just to ensure his postcard got here before he beat it home."

"Well, that's true love."

"It would be nice if true love would allow for an international phone call," Kathy teased.

"Maybe it will. You know, your uncle said Kyle is being groomed to take over one of the departments. He'll be a vice-president . . . one of several, but nevertheless it's an important position."

"Wow. I had no idea."

"Personally, I think it's done him a world of good to have had these years to build his career. Of course, he's pined over you every step of the way. If I hadn't fed him a steady diet of photographs and information, he probably would have stormed your doors."

"Photographs? You gave him pictures?"

"Indeed I did. Remember all the times we visited and I forced you to pose for photos?"

"Or snapped them at every opportunity when I looked a wreck. Oh, please tell me you didn't." Kathy suddenly felt very embarrassed imagining Kyle looking at those pictures.

"They were charming. I assure you, he loved them."

Kathy thought of the long years between them. Did Kyle look much different now? She could honestly say that she still looked very similar to her college days, but did he?

"So what's he like now . . . what does he look like?"

Glynnis laughed. "Like a man in love. Oh, Kathy, I'm glad you're finally going to give him a chance. He's crazy about you—always has been."

"And I've . . . I've never stopped loving him," Kathy admitted. "And one of the things I've loved most about him was the fierce loyalty he had for those he cared about."

"You'd best not let him slip away twice." She fell silent for a moment. "Goodness, I'd best get things wrapped up. You know your uncle likes to get up at the crack of dawn. Sometimes even before dawn cracks. I should get to bed. I'll be looking for you tomorrow afternoon."

"Well, don't fret if we don't show up until five or so. I don't know how long it will take at the title company, and then I promised we'd have a nice hot sit-down breakfast."

"You'll still be here before five. I'm certain of that. Besides, you'll want to avoid rush-hour traffic. The interstate can be such a mess at that hour. Why don't you call me when you hit town? That way we can be looking for you."

"That sounds wise," Kathy agreed. "I love you, Aunt Glynnis."

"I love you, sweetie. It's going to be so good to have you in town. I can hardly wait."

Kathy closed her eyes and drew a deep breath. "Neither can I."

Kathy hung up the phone and stared around the empty kitchen. For a moment images of the past swam before her eyes. She could almost hear her mother humming as she worked to can applesauce.

"Hope you're gonna save some of those apples for pie," her father would always say.

Smiling at the memory, Kathy began to wander from room to room. She paused at the den. Nothing remained of Dad's sick room. Fresh paint was on the walls and she'd managed to give the wood floors a nice going-over the day before the auction. Everything looked as if it just begged a family to come in and fill it with love. Maybe they would all share it. Maybe Sunny's mother-in-law would want to keep the place for family gatherings.

With a sigh, Kathy made her way to the front porch and walked around to the side. She'd already packed the hammock in the trailer that she'd rented in Hays. She'd never pulled anything behind her car before, but she needed the extra space in order to take everything she'd saved out of the sale.

The night air felt less heavy than it had earlier. A nice southerly breeze kept the bugs to a minimum and offered relief from the heat as well. She leaned against the porch rail only able to see as much as the backyard light would afford.

She thought about her sister and wondered if they would stay in touch. There was so much about Sunny she still wanted to know—needed to understand. Kathy felt that in order to truly put the past behind them, they needed to have a future to focus on together. But Sunny would also need to focus on her family now. And that was a good thing too.

"It all changes tomorrow," Kathy murmured. "Like Sylvia said, nothing will ever be the same." The thought was bittersweet. On one hand was the land of her childhood—a place that offered comfort and mostly pleasant memories. On the other hand was an unknown world that hinted of even greater things.

"I'm afraid, Lord. I don't mean to be, but I am. It's hard to go and start over. I've never known anything but this life." The verse in Isaiah immediately came to mind.

Forget the former things; do not dwell on the past. See, I am doing a new thing! Now it springs up; do you not perceive it? I am making a way in the desert and streams in the wasteland.

"'Now it springs up,'" Kathy said, and a smile spread across her face. The reference to springs and her destination of Colorado Springs did not go unnoticed.

"I do perceive it, Lord. You are making me a way—doing a new thing. But even more important . . . you're going with me."

TWENTY-SEVEN

KATHY TOOK THE CHECK handed her by the title official and noted it was more than she'd expected. She looked at the young man who'd handled the paper work. "I thought this would be smaller."

He laughed. "Usually folks complain because they get less than they expected."

"I'm not complaining, just amazed."

"Well, as I was told a couple of days ago, your father had a small life insurance policy through the bank. That money went to pay off the loan first, and then you received the balance from the sale."

"He never told me he had life insurance. He must have forgotten."

"Could be," the man said. "He purchased it twenty-some years ago. When we were processing the loan papers, his name was flagged as having a life insurance policy with us as well."

"It's a wonderful surprise." Kathy looked at the check again and shook her head. "I'm truly blessed."

She left the office and went into the parking lot, where Sunny and Brian were waiting for her.

"How'd it go?" Sunny asked. She held a look of concern as if maybe the entire event was too much for Kathy to cope with.

"It went really well. I got more out of the sale than I expected. It seems Dad had a life insurance policy I didn't

know about. So this check is much bigger than I had anticipated."

"Wow, that is a nice surprise."

Brian put his arm around Sunny. "I'm glad you'll have
what you need, but you know we're family now. You don't
need to ever go without. Sunny can tell you—we're quite
comfortable."

Kathy laughed. "Apparently so am I. In fact, breakfast is
on me."

They made their way to one of the chain restaurants that
specialized in breakfast. After placing their orders, Brian
cleared his throat and offered a blessing on the food.

"There's something we'd like to ask you," Brian said
immediately after he finished praying.

Kathy looked at Sunny. She seemed entirely youthful
and pretty today. So much of the careworn look was gone.
It was amazing what setting your heart back into the right
place could do. "Well, go for it," Kathy said with a shrug.
"I've got nothing to hide."

"Oh, it's not that kind of a question," Sunny interjected.
"But it is one that we'd like an honest opinion on."

"Okay, but now you're starting to worry me."

Brian laughed. "It's not that kind of question either.
Look, it's this simple: we'd like to know what you'd think
about having us in Colorado Springs."

"To live?" Kathy had never expected this conversation.

"Yes." Brian continued while Sunny nursed her cup of
coffee. "Sunny and I need to make a fresh start as well. I
suggested to Sunny that we could start over anywhere. Colorado Springs came to mind because it would allow Lucy to
grow up knowing her aunt Kathy. It would also let the three

of us become a real family—four if you count Kyle. I . . . well . . . I never had a brother . . . or sister."

He choked up a bit and turned to Sunny. Kathy was touched by his emotion. "I think it would be incredible," she said, hoping she sounded reassuring. "Like I told Sunny, our relationship, our road on the path of forgiveness, is a journey. It's going to take time to rebuild our trust and friendship."

"Just like with Brian and me," Sunny admitted. "When Brian mentioned moving to be near you, I wanted to jump and shout. I know you understand, because you want to start over again with Kyle. As much as you want that with him, I want that for us."

"Then it sounds like Colorado Springs is the place to start," Kathy said. "How soon would you come?"

"Well, we'd need to wrap things up in California," Brian said. "I'd have to finish up with some patients. I put off several surgeries to come here, but it won't take long. I started taking fewer and fewer patients after what I did to Sunny." He frowned. "I really wasn't much good to anyone."

Sunny squeezed his hand. "We also would need to sell the house and convince his mom to consider moving too. At least for a summer place. She's such a neat lady, Kathy. I think you'd enjoy getting to know her."

"She'd mother you both, I'm sure," Brian said, his expression lightening.

"Do you think she'd uproot herself after such a long time in California?"

Brian picked up his juice. "I think she'd find it imposs-ible to be so far from her granddaughter."

"And any other grandchildren God might give her,"

Sunny said with a grin. "Besides, she's owns a farm in Kansas. She might as well see what she's bought."

Kathy saw the exchange between Sunny and her husband. It was obvious that things were going well. Observing the easy restoration of their marriage, Kathy found her old frustrations with Sunny and their relationship resurface.

God help me, she thought.

"Trust me," a voice seemed to whisper to her heart.

Kathy knew it had to be God's reminder to her. *Yes, I do trust you, Lord. I trust you to make a new thing—a way in the desert—streams in the wasteland.*

❧ ❧ ❧

Several hours later, Kathy found her way through Colorado Springs to her aunt and uncle's mountain home. The house was a newer two-story creation that looked as though it had been especially created just for the owners.

Kathy studied the stucco and stone façade. Huge arched windows went from ground to the roof on the front of the house. No doubt they had a spectacular view of the city.

"It's quite the place," Sunny said as she came up behind her sister.

"Yes. I had no idea."

"How long have they lived here?" Brian asked.

"Only about five years. I knew they had built a new house—their retirement dream house. But I didn't know much else. I guess I was all caught up in Dad's situation."

"Kathy! Sunny!" Aunt Glynnis called as she came from the front door. "Oh, you made it safely. I'm so glad."

They all embraced and Glynnis fussed over each niece before noticing the man who stood to one side. "And who's this?"

Sunny took hold of her aunt's hand. "This is my husband, Brian. Brian, this is Aunt Glynnis—my father's sister."

"I'm pleased to meet you," Brian said, extending his hand.

Glynnis took his hand but looked at Sunny with great wonder. "He's come to take me home," Sunny offered.

A huge smile spread across their aunt's face. "That is good news." She turned to Brian. "I'm so glad to meet you. What a wonderful surprise. We must have a very long talk."

"We can stay at a hotel if you'd rather," Sunny said.

Glynnis shook her head. "Nonsense. You can see for yourself that this house is plenty big. Come on. Uncle Will has no idea of what's happening. He'll want to meet your husband and hear all about your reconciliation."

"There's more," Sunny said with a hint of laughter. "We're making plans to move here. We'll need some advice as to where we might look at real estate."

The surprised look on their aunt's face quickly faded to joy. "Oh, I can't imagine better news. Of course we'll advise you. Come on. I can't wait to tell Will." She still held Brian's hand and pulled him toward the door.

They stepped inside the house to a beautiful marble-floored foyer. The room opened up to the second floor, giving a feeling of expanded space. The warm butternut color on the walls and the beautiful way her aunt had furnished the room instantly made Kathy feel welcome.

328

"Uncle Will!" Sunny declared. "I have someone for you to meet."

The introductions were made quickly and Glynnis told them of a barbeque supper that Will had been preparing for them. "That was why I wanted you to call when you hit town. Then Will knew when to start the fire." Glynnis gave her husband a wink. "Plus I had another reason. Another surprise." She walked to Kathy and took hold of her hand. "Come with me. Will, you take Sunny and Brian out to the deck and get them something cold to drink."

She left the others to go a different direction, while she pulled Kathy down the hall to where the house opened into a huge great room. Kathy's gaze immediately went to the cathedral ceilings, then came back to settle on the face of the only man she'd ever loved.

"Kyle."

He grinned at her, looking much as he had when they'd gotten engaged. He had aged a little, but it had only served to make him more handsome.

"I'll leave you two to catch up. Supper won't be for a little while," Glynnis said, giving Kathy a smile. "I'll let you know when it's ready."

Kathy couldn't believe Kyle was actually here. She put her hand to her head and sighed. Why hadn't Glynnis warned her so she could look her best?

Kyle seemed to understand. He came forward and shook his head. "You look so beautiful."

"I wish I'd known you'd be here. I thought you were still in England."

"I got back a couple of days ago. I thought it would be fun to surprise you." He reached out to touch her cheek.

"I've missed you so much. I feel like it's been a lifetime since we were together."

Kathy couldn't speak. Tears came to her eyes. "I told you not to wait."

"And I said I'd wait, even if it took forever. But I'm sure glad it didn't."

"I'm so sorry. I was so wrong. I should never have done that to you . . . to us." The words just spilled out, and Kathy wondered if this was how Sunny felt when she'd first showed up at the farm.

"I forgive you," Kyle whispered. "I forgave you even then."

Kathy wrapped her arms around Kyle's neck and hugged him close. She felt his arms embrace her and pull her closer. "I don't deserve you."

He chuckled. "No, you deserve much better, but you're stuck with me."

She laughed amidst her tears and pulled back to gaze into his eyes. "And you're stuck with me. I hope you know what you're doing."

He grinned. "If I don't, I mean to have fun figuring it out." He kissed her long and hard. Twelve years of pent-up passion left them both breathless as they broke apart.

Kathy closed her eyes for just a moment. She felt Kyle put something on her finger and opened her eyes to find her old engagement ring.

"I don't want to waste another minute. Will you marry me? Will you marry me right away?"

Kathy began to cry once more. "Of course I will. You know I will."

He pulled her into his arms again and whispered softly

against her ear. "I love you, Kathy. I always will."

"I love you, Kyle. Now and always."

Kathy then knew a peace that had eluded her for so many years. The bitterness and frustration of the last twelve years dissolved in Kyle's arms. She had come home to the one place she'd always belonged. She couldn't help but smile as a thought came to her mind.

The prodigal had returned. Let the celebration begin.

More Moving Contemporary Fiction From Tracie Peterson

After her husband's betrayal, Jana McGuire is left with only one choice: to humbly seek refuge with a mother she barely knows yet longs to understand and connect with. But Eleanor has firmly shut the door on the past. As the heartache of Jana's situation heightens, her need for her mother compels her to seek out the truth of that past. But will Jana's search bring back a pain that was better left alone?

What She Left for Me

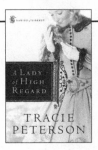

BE SURE TO CHECK OUT TRACIE'S EXCITING HISTORICAL FICTION TOO!

Mia Stanley has a knack for matchmaking—and for trouble. When her job at *Godey's Lady's Book* opens her eyes to the plight of the seamen's wives, she uncovers a scheme that puts her life in danger. But her heart is on the line as well. Have her determined matchmaking ways driven away the one man she loves?

LADIES OF LIBERTY
A Lady of High Regard

With an early winter approaching, the paths of four people intersect, taking them on a journey with dramatic twists and turns until more is at stake than just their lives. As these four struggle for survival in American's final frontier, all hope seems lost. In a land so cold and dangerous, how can faith and love survive?

ALASKAN QUEST
Summer of the Midnight Sun, Under the Northern Lights, Whispers of Winter

From her own Big Sky home, Tracie Peterson paints a one-of-a-kind portrait of 1860s Montana and the strong, spirited men and women who dared to call it home. The rich, rugged landscape of the prairie frontier presents a dangerous beauty that only the boldest can tame. Join Peterson in the Montana Territory with all the history, drama, and faith you come to expect from her books.

HEIRS OF MONTANA
Land of My Heart, The Coming Storm, To Dream Anew, The Hope Within